D0049455

A Hamptons
Christmas

Also by James Brady

The Marines of Autumn
The Coldest War
Fashion Show
Nielsen's Children
Paris One
The Press Lord
Superchic
Designs
Holy Wars
Further Lane
Gin Lane
The House That Ate the Hamptons

JAMES BRADY

A Hamptons Christmas

Thomas Dunne Books
St. Martin's Press
New York

THOMAS DUNNE BOOKS.
An imprint of St. Martin's Press.

A HAMPTONS CHRISTMAS. Copyright © 2000 by James Brady. All rights reserved.
Printed in the United States of America. No part of this book may be used or
reproduced in any manner whatsoever without written permission except in the
case of brief quotations embodied in critical articles or reviews. For information,
address St. Martin's Press, 175 Fifth Avenue, New York, N.Y. 10010.

www.stmartins.com

Book design by Clair Moritz

Library of Congress Cataloging-in-Publication Data

Brady, James.
    A Hamptons Christmas / James Brady.—1st ed.
       p. cm.
    ISBN 0-312-26604-9
      1. Hamptons (N.Y.)—Fiction. I. Title.
    PS3552.R243 H35 2000
    813'.54–dc21   00-031737

First Edition: November 2000

10 9 8 7 6 5 4 3 2 1

For my grandchildren, Sarah, Joe, and Nick

With an exceedingly deferential bow to Mr. Charles Dickens, who some years ago in London, wrote a little story memorializing and celebrating the very same glorious and jolly season.

A Hamptons Christmas

Chapter One

. . . the deadest piece of ironmongery in the trade.

Marley was dead, to begin with. There is no doubt whatever about that. The register of his burial was signed by the clergyman, the clerk, the undertaker, and the chief mourner, heiress, and executor. She signed it. And Sis Marley's name was good upon anything she chose to put her hand to. Old Marley was dead as a doornail. Mind! I don't mean to say that I know, of my own knowledge, what there is particularly dead about a doornail. I might have been inclined, myself, to regard a coffin nail as the deadest piece of ironmongery in the trade. But the wisdom of our ancestors is in the simile. You will therefore permit me to repeat, emphatically, that Marley was dead as a doornail.

This must be distinctly understood or nothing wonderful can come of the story I am going to relate.

A story which began here in East Hampton last December, the fortnight before Christmas, at 2:50 P.M. (just nine minutes late, which, for the Long Island Railroad, is precisely on schedule), when at our sleepy, single-track railroad station, a solitary passenger stepped off the noon train from Manhattan.

The traveler was a convent schoolgirl from Switzerland, unexpected, alone, and unmet, but for the usual local cab idling at the curb and hoping for a fare. The child, perhaps nine or ten, no more, was small and slender, toting a few well-thumbed books, a glossy but carefully annotated year-old December issue of an American magazine, a Louis Vuitton duffle and matching backpack. She also clutched in one mittened hand—and from time to time consulted—a crudely drawn map which she now handed to the cab driver, before climbing into the back of his vehicle. The girl's destination was a big old shingled house and tailored gardens on Lily Pond Lane, just off the Atlantic Ocean behind some hedges and an ivied, redbrick wall. I happened to know that house and who lived there. And would, within a few hours, become acquainted with our young visitor from abroad who, for private reasons of her own, and without the knowledge of its famous owner, had chosen the shingled house on Lily Pond Lane to celebrate her Christmas.

Chapter Two

As Cotton and Increase Mather might've said,
the man was "a hissing and a byword."

Maybe you already know the Hamptons out of season, with the "summer people" gone. I'm not saying it's a better place in winter, just that it's interesting in different ways. Those who keep their houses open year-round, either locals who have no other homes or fortunate folk whose work can be done from here, or who no longer need to work, are, in the main, very cool people indeed. They maintain a low profile, not bothering about image or needing to make an impression, which may be the *most* impressive thing about the people who winter out here: They are so secure they don't have to impress anyone. And that's what, for many of us, makes this the best "season" of all.

East Hampton, where my family's lived for generations (the Beechers and the Stowes, both), starts getting into its out-of-season mode right after Thanksgiving. Which is when each year Buell-Meserve, the Gin Lane magnate, ships the potted palms south to his Palm Beach compound adjacent to the Breakers, where they will sit until he ships them back north in April. Buell-Meserve's palms seem to be a sort of signal, like the lowering of a flag, and by late November the private jets are no longer flying in, and the big, sleek yachts have pulled out of the local marinas and gone

3

south to wherever it is big yachts go in winter. In the waterfront bars and restaurants, at the boatyards and the docks, you no longer encounter the yachtsmen's tough, smart-as-paint professional crews and craggy, squinty-eyed seafarer skippers, or the silver-haired, mahogany-tanned boatowners with their younger women.

This is not to suggest a flight of cash or of beauty or, heaven forfend, celebrity! from East Hampton. Simply that the village's pace slows and its frenzy calms. An example of what I mean: down that little alley past the side porch of Ralph Lauren's shop, The Blue Parrot restaurant ("Killer Mexican!" cuisine) has staged its absolutely final Surfer Dude party of the season, with bikinied waitresses taking turns lying on the bar so Kelly the barmaid or Bruce the bartender can pour tequila into their belly buttons, to be lapped up (neat, no limes, no salt) by the regulars.

Winter people in East Hampton are slightly superior to such in-season capers. And a good thing, too, you might echo.

And unless we have a nor'easter, even the weather can be pretty good. Well into December you see bikers swift as Anquetil, bent over the handlebars, smoothly shifting gears and whisking silently along under the boughed canopies of our narrow country lanes, past the courts where well-groomed people in tennis whites are *pock! pock! pocking!* yellow balls around the red clay, and glimpse the occasional foursome out there playing an unhurried eighteen at the Maidstone Club. There's usually a spirited season-ending football game between East Hampton and Southampton Highs. And the Montauk Rugby Club fields a powerful team every weekend through the winter, thick-legged young men with bloody rags around their heads, playing hard rugger at Herrick Field, behind what until recently was the A & P, but is now called Waldbaum's and is only marginally less tacky.

All those trendy new boutiques that opened in May, fully stocked with merchandise and hope, are shuttered, gone bust most of them. The Wally Findlay Galleries have cut to a skeleton staff (Cartier is closed for the year), and the Irish kids who work summers as maids and barmen and caddies are all back at Trinity College, Dublin. And making mischief there, too, you can be sure.

4

Migratory ducks in their thousands squawk and call as they whistle overhead, scooting in low and navigating south, leaving the place to far-too-many Canada geese and to our resident swans that winter here and don't migrate further than from one Hamptons pond to the next. Without any summer people, you can park on Main Street and get a seat in the movie house. There's no need to reserve a table (except perhaps on Saturday night) for dinner at Jerry Della Femina's or Peconic Coast, or queue up for hot, fresh doughnuts in the morning at Dreesen's on Newtown Lane. And Schmidt's the grocer (which used to be The Chicken House) doesn't run out of the *New York Times* halfway through Sunday morning (in midsummer, the cause of more than the occasional fistfight over a Style section).

And if we're lucky and get a hard freeze early, the shallow, algae-green town pond turns overnight into a Brueghel painting (Brueghel the Elder, I believe but can't be certain), with kids playing hockey, tweedy old gentlemen in long wool scarves skating with their hands elegantly behind their backs, little girls twirling, boys loudly chasing, and long-legged honeys gliding smoothly along, short-skirted and all rosy. A few miles to the west there's iceboating on the polished, glistening first-ice of Mecox Bay, where the fearless get up terrifying, madcap races. In some years we have one of those Atlantic-effect blizzards that comes booming up the coast and drops a couple of feet of snow out here on the east end of Long Island before it moves on to Nantucket and the Vineyard and ends up whacking Cape Cod. That's when our precious four-wheel drive vehicles cease being mere grownup toys and status symbols and earn their price, and cross-country skiers materialize on Huntting Lane, and toboggans on the Maidstone fairways, and distinguished, elderly gents are not at all embarrassed to be seen down on their knees building snowmen for the grandchildren, while in New York and Hartford and New Haven, they may be settling for flurries or a gray inch of slush. And there's our annual Santa Claus Parade Saturday morning along Main Street which, for corniness and good cheer, even Mr. Rowland H. Macy might approve and envy.

5

Then, around Memorial Day, summer returns and another "Hamptons Season" begins. And from then through Labor Day, forget it. You've read Liz Smith and Page Six and the other columns, and *New York* magazine, so you know all about that and don't have to be told.

This story isn't about the "season," but about Christmas, and specifically a Hamptons Christmas, even though, among our sensible winter people, there are some who slough off Christmas as bunkum, Hallmark Card sentimentality, strictly for kids or oldsters reliving their youth. Not me, of course; I'm not like that about Christmas.

Never will be!

I realized, of course, how and why it all began two thousand years ago, a long way off in Bethlehem, and how it was then popularized in various places and a dozen styles: in Prague by Good King Wenceslas, in Victorian England by Scrooge and his Three —Ghosts, in the Black Forest by "Stille Nacht," and in Flanders fields by British Tommies and German soldiers calling brief halt to the killing and singing carols to each other from the trenches, and by a defeated Jimmy Stewart jumping from that smalltown bridge, and by a letter in the New York paper (was it the *Evening Sun?*) which began, "Yes, Virginia, there is a Santa Claus . . ."

I'd seen Christmas in plenty of places, starting in Paris where I was born and largely raised. And in Harvard Square and Boston Common as a student and while covering wars in odd corners and once in Moscow where they didn't have Santa Claus at all but Grandfather Frost. And once aboard *QE2* between Southampton and New York with a smiling, broad-faced, flaxen-tressed, blue-eyed girl who shortly afterward would break my heart by marrying someone else (and richer).

Now *there* was a Christmas!

Yet I never realized just how fully Christmas is meant not merely for children and old men, but for damned near all of us. Not until last December, when so much happened along Further Lane, did that realization truly get hold of me; Further Lane, where my father the Admiral has his big place and I have the gatehouse, and to which Her Ladyship, Alix Dunraven, flew in on the morning BA flight from Heathrow to spend the hols with us.

Even though I wasn't at all sure a sophisticated Londoner like Alix, being a Sloane Ranger, stabled in blue-blood Belgravia and all, a name perennially dropped by Nigel Dempster in the *Daily Mail*, would be charmed by our out-of-season Hamptons. Mightn't she be bored dotty, considering the high drama and derring-do of our adventures over recent East Hampton summers? But feeling as I did about Lady Alix, as nuts about her as I was, I thought the game surely worth the candle.

And I was very excited, almost childlike, in the realization that of all the times we'd been together, the days and nights and loving sunrises, I'd never, not even once, waked on a Christmas morning with Alix in my arms, with Her Ladyship drowsy there beside me, the best gift of all.

But then it turned out no one in East Hampton last winter was to be even marginally bored. All because Martha Stewart chose to keep Christmas, not at the gracious shingled house on Lily Pond Lane, but at her home in Connecticut. Which meant that a little girl with Louis Vuitton luggage, a platinum card, a return seat to Europe on the Concorde, and visions of a fairytale Christmas filling her head, got off the train at East Hampton station on a chill December day, only to find there was no one there awaiting her, "no room in the inn." Which swiftly caught up my father, Lady Alix, the Methodist pastor, Reverend Parker, Jesse Maine of the Shinnecock Indian Nation, the Bonackers, and all of us, in the strange child's concerns, and in plots, intrigues, and conspiracies of every manner and sort. As well as in related events at the historic Old Churchyard in the East Hampton village of Springs, where for two centuries they've buried our gallant Baymen, at least until the mischief recently done there by the estate of the late Mr. Jacob Marley.

De mortuis nil nisi bonum, we are taught. "Speak nothing but good of the dead." Yet only a year or two after his death, people were not only speaking ill of Marley, there were those who in-sisted "Mean Jake" deserved to be denounced from the pulpit.

Condemned in sermons as "a hissing and a byword," much as was done hundreds of years earlier by colonial preachers Increase Mather and his brother Cotton. Nor would many in today's East Hampton—and I include our local priests and ministers and other clerics, charitable, even saintly, men all—deny that's precisely what Jacob Marley seemed to have become with his cranky, selfish, mean-spirited last will and testament:

A "hissing and a byword," damn him! "A hissing and a byword."

But had we been fair to Mean Jake? Or had the Village been too quick to draw up indictments and issue judgments? Surely, as Mark Twain once said of the devil, Marley, too, might have a case. Not much of a case, granted, but a case nonetheless.

Chapter Three

It's my fault, the Mexican problem?
I killed "Viva Zapata," por favor?

My name is Beecher Stowe, linear descendant *not* of Cotton and Increase Mather, but of another early American family of preachers, among them the Reverend Henry Ward Beecher and hot-blooded (and lecherous) Lyman Beecher, who made their mark here a century and a half ago, some generations after the Mather brothers had their run up in nearby (and every bit as sanctimonious) Massachusetts Colony. And, as I've earlier established, I yield to no one, and that includes Bob Cratchit and the missus, as a sucker for Christmas. This despite the fact that we professional journalists are expected to be hard, skeptical, unemotional, cool cookies and nobody's pushover. But we know all about stereotypes, don't we?

Let me admit my Christmas weaknesses up front: I love snow, the Three Wise Men, eggnog, Lord & Taylor's windows, shepherds in the hills guarding their flocks, Salvation Army kettles on Fifth Avenue, reruns of *Holiday Inn*, the evergreens lighted along Park Avenue, "Adeste Fidelis" in Latin, crayoned letters to Santa, red noses, envelopes pressed into the hands of Manhattan doormen, how the windows steam up on cold evenings at P. J. Clarke's, pretty girls throwing snowballs, Saks Fifth Avenue, the original *Miracle*

9

on 34th Street with Maureen O'Hara and John Payne, red wool scarves, Wall Street bonuses, midnight mass (even, or maybe especially, for non-Catholics), Brooks Brothers' main floor at 346 Madison, the yule log on television, "Silent Night," the tree at Rockefeller Center, mittens, and a nostalgic Christmas Eve martini or several at the bar of the 21 Club with a couple of CBS ad salesmen I've known since our college days on the *Harvard Crimson*.

Then just why was I, a few weeks before Christmas of last year, in that least Yule of neighborhoods, Beverly Hills, California 90210?

Blame Walter Anderson, the editor of *Parade* magazine, who'd sent me out. He wanted an interview done, and when the editor wanted something, you tended to make serious efforts. No matter the season, regardless of Christmas.

My assignment was writing a cover story about a temperamental diva (echoes of Streisand, Madonna, and several others, but I prudently won't say more) at her lavish estate atop one of the more elegantly pricey canyons, and I'd just about concluded the damned woman had it all: talent, wealth, fame, beauty, adulation, good health, and a robust sexuality, all of it luxuriously gift-wrapped in this glorious hilltop house with its extraordinary views of snowy peaks to the east and great Pacific rollers to the west. But when I said so, telling her how remarkably fortunate she was, the wretched woman burst into sobbing confession, startling me into handing her my own linen handkerchief, tugged impulsively from a trouser pocket and taken gratefully, as she owned up, amid the sobs, to being frustrated and lonely. How she missed New York, the downtown club scene, her second husband ("So he cheated on me; no one's a saint"), Page Six in the *Post*, Mayor Giuliani, the Broadway stage, Elaine's, the Knicks, Chinese takeout, the pool room of the Four Seasons, and Bergdorf Goodman. In no especial order.

"Have everything? Have everything?" she demanded, pulling herself together and giving her nose a final, vigorous wipe with my hankie, "Sure, I got everything. Last Tuesday I go out for the morning papers and right there curled up on the front step next to *Daily Variety* and the *Hollywood Reporter*, a goddamned rattler! This does not happen to me on Central Park West, I assure you. You go out your own front door to pick up the trades and rattlesnakes get you? A six-car garage, yeah, and in every corner a tarantula. Hairy-legged bastards, the size of your hand, you think that's fun? In the pool, lizards. For all I know, Gila monsters, swimming laps. Black widow spiders? Don't tell me about black widow spiders. You can't keep a cat up here. The coyotes eat them. You hear their little bones being crunched in the night. Your heart goes out. Mountain lions. Not five miles from here, a mountain lion killed a jogger. The maids heard about it; didn't show up for three days. Think of the dust; just imagine. I used to jog myself. No more. If I cross the front lawn these days I sing show tunes very loud and wave my arms about, trying to look large, which is supposed to give mountain lions pause. On my own front lawn I'm afraid. Then there's the pool boy, resents Anglos and pees in my hot tub. It's my fault, *por favor*, the Mexican problem? I killed "Viva Zapata"? Yet here's this son of a bitch pissing. I don't dare fire him; he'll come back and vandalize.

"The day the mudslide season ends, the brushfire season begins. The day the brushfire season ends . . . and don't get me started on earthquakes. This is the good life?"

There was more, and when I'd closed my notebook and driven off in the rented little Chrysler ragtop, I thought to myself I'd seen, if only briefly, the woman herself and not the carefully polished, honed and crafted superstar PR (via Pat Kingsley at PMK) image I'd come here expecting. But isn't that what makes a good magazine piece? The unexpected?

As I drove down the winding canyon road, slowed by shopping traffic along Rodeo Drive and its vanity fair of shops, en route to my hotel and then the flight back to New York, I remarked the incongruity of elaborate Christmas decorations and Salvation Army Santa Clauses (all ringing their bells in Spanish) set against the royal palms and classic open cars and bare shoulders of suntanned women in the baking late afternoon heat of a southern California December.

I couldn't wait to get back home, back East. Where Christmas really happens. Not out here. Not with palm trees and Mexican Santas and rattlesnakes curled up on your copy of *Variety* and Gila monsters in the pool. Of course at that point, I had no idea this was going to be one Christmas back East that wasn't going to be quite Currier & Ives, but instead might have been choreographed by Bob Fosse and directed by Francis Ford Coppola. With Dennis Hopper the second unit director. I signed my bill at the Beverly Wilshire, overtipped everyone and happily got out of there, off to catch the red-eye for New York.

Chapter Four

Among Santa Claus's "elves" were all those Spielberg children . . .

Forty-eight hours later, I was back in East Hampton, where a gray sky and temperatures in the forties provided symmetry, made the decorations and the date seem precisely right. Christmas in the Hamptons? That's how some of us define home. You know, sort of the way Digby, John, and Beau Geste thought of their Aunt Patricia's warm and fuzzy Brandon Abbas, before bolting off to join the Legion and being seconded to the tender mercies of Colour Sergeant Lejaune and the siege of Fort Zinderneuf.

Anderson had given me a month off after the diva assignment. I was to winnow down a collection of my magazine pieces for hardcover publication, and East Hampton seemed the perfect place to do it. While at the same time, visiting my father the Admiral and waiting for Her Ladyship to arrive. Alix had, somewhat reluctantly, bought into my argument that the Hamptons are even better without "the summer people" and, if we were ever to make our relationship more than deliciously episodic, she'd better get to know the place, *hors de saison.*

Or so I'd attempted to convince her.

The Admiral was a concern, entirely different, his wounds acting up. At his age, you don't heal as quickly. I don't know why he keeps taking on these risky assignments from Bill Cohen at the Pentagon. There are plenty of young officers eager to make their bones: the crazier Marines, paras from Fort Benning, Navy Seals, a few of the flyboys, Top Guns only need apply. But that's the Admiral; that's my Old Man. I don't think that flag officers, at seventy, ought to be slipping in and out of North Korea by rubber boat, meeting with agents provocateurs, jousting in the Hindu Kush with Osama bin Laden and similar sportsmen, and getting shot at. To say nothing of having fingers cut off, with or without anesthetic, by the Dreaded Taliban, at their strongholds in Central Asia.

Although when I got to the house on Further Lane, and his decidedly protective housekeeper, Inga, stepped back long enough to let me hug the Old Man and all that, he looked reasonably fit and grinned tolerantly at my concern, getting off a pretty good Jake Barnes line about how he'd gotten wounded.

". . . and flying on a joke front like the Italian . . ."

Inga got about the making of dinner in the industrial-strength country kitchen that graced the house and was clearly her domain, while, in deference to my father's damaged fingers, I mixed the martinis (Absolut on the rocks with olives, no vermouth) and opened a pretty good Opus One to go with the rare rack of lamb. Over coffee I told the Old Man about Hollywood, and he filled me in on the Defense Department and his brief, not terribly productive few hours in North Korea, why Syria was so dicey, and what the Pentagon brass really thought was happening in Montenegro and Chechnya. Then I cut us a couple of Cohibas and we went into his den to smoke.

"D'you see this out in California?" he asked, passing over a newspaper clipping. The headline spoke for itself: "HAMPTONS BURIAL/ THE PLOTS TO DIE FOR/ ARE FULLY BOOKED/ LAWSUIT THROWN OUT."

"Oh, no," I said. "Not Marley again?"

Another legal decision had gone against the majority of local people and in favor of one of the wealthier East Hampton

14

grandees, the late Jacob Marley, whose estate was again being sued. At stake? The remaining hundred or so grave plots in an historic old local cemetery which had been bought up by Mr. Marley's estate so that his, and his family's, bodies might enjoy eternity undisturbed by lesser corpses. And so that no competing headstone might disturb the dead Marley's water view. It was by now a familiar story, but one this recent litigation had revived as news. Hamptons families, original Bonackers, many of them here a century or more before the first Marley, were steamed that their dead had to be buried somewhere up-Island and not conveniently near hearth and home. The paper that published the story wasn't our weekly *East Hampton Star*, either; it was the *New York Times*. I tossed the clipping down without finishing, shaking my head.

"Yes, sir. Marley again," said my father. "The *Times* put the story on page one. Below the fold but definitely on page one. Marley, even dead, is still news."

The story about Marley and the graves hadn't run in the national edition of the *Times* out on the Coast, so I'd missed it. The Admiral liked it when he'd caught something in the paper and I hadn't, being that I was the professional journalist and he just a career sailor out of Annapolis.

"So that's the end of it. The Marleys keep the Old Churchyard."

"Not quite," my father said. "The trustees could still change their minds about selling the graves. Sale isn't final until the last day of the year. But it looks like the ruling will stand, which is what has local Baymen so sore. Feelings around here are running high. Do you know they even stole Jake's body right out of the crypt? Kept it on ice for a day or so in the fish-cannery reefer out near Devon Yacht Club before putting it back?"

Then we dropped the subject. I was still on California time, so I drank a bit to make up for it and slept well. Very well. Our house is four hundred yards from the ocean, and the sound of Atlantic surf is as good a soporific as we have. Maybe that anyone has without needing a prescription.

15

That was Friday night.

And on my first Saturday back, as if to welcome home the prodigal son, East Hampton staged its annual ragtag, irresistibly small-townish Santa Claus parade, which, with its sheer amateur quality, rather set the tone of an old-fashioned American village Christmas:

The East Hampton high school band, a guy on a one-wheel bike not riding it very well, Hugh King togged out in a stovepipe hat as the town crier of a century ago, the Brownies in uniform, other little kids as elves, leashed dogs being walked by the Rotarians in the line of march, and just to balance out the pet category, there was Pat Lillis from Springs, who rescues stray cats and finds them homes and is the only woman I ever heard of who successfully domesticates feral cats. Next came the antique-tractor society, fire engines from this and neighboring towns with their sirens wailing, an inept juggler, the mayor waving from an open car, three old gaffers from the American Legion as a color guard, a man on stilts, a couple of yellow trucks from Whitmore Tree Nurseries, the Presbyterian choral society, a big haulseiner rowboat on wheels towed behind a pickup, the Village emergency ambulance, a papier-mâché whale, Santa on a flatbed truck, and free balloons being handed out to children on the sidewalk, some of whom burst into tears as soon as their balloons exploded or flew off unattended. As I say, very small-town stuff, even with Alec Baldwin and Kim Basinger there on the sidewalk among the crowd and even if the "elves" included some of the numerous Spielberg kids!

The Santa Claus parade and Jake Marley's posthumous takeover of the Old Churchyard were big local news. But there were other stories. For one, Reds Hucko was still missing.

Reds was a local fisherman war hero-cum-town drunk. As a Marine in Vietnam he'd slaughtered VC by the hundreds (they said he drank to atone; others held that Reds drank because he liked the stuff). He had been working on draggers out of Montauk, and over Thanksgiving weekend he fell overboard in a half gale and was presumed dead. But you know how the currents are around here, especially late in the year with winter coming. And so the body hadn't yet turned up. Which was a shame because Reds was a popular fellow (also because he owed a little money and the insurance couldn't be paid out until the body washed up), and local folk were anxious to give him a proper planting.

Jerry Seinfeld chose the dead of winter to offer $35 million to Billy Joel for his oceanfront place on Further Lane. There was talk that Hillary (yes! that Hillary) was shaking her begging bowl again and might include East Hampton on a fund-raiser. The mere possibility of which set members of the Maidstone Club to oaths and swearing not heard on Club property since FDR ran for a third term. Bunny Halsey, scion of one of the earliest Southampton families, was divorcing his fourth wife. An historic barn in Amagansett burned down. Thibaut de Saint Phalle had visited his place on Middle Lane from his place in Naples, Florida, a rare thing in winter. There was a continuing stink along Further Lane about developers being allowed to sell off five-million-dollar lots of the Rock Foundation Nature Preserve. And a right whale was seen cruising off Main Beach, not two hundred yards from shore.

Sag Harbor's Michael Thomas had read a brilliantly persuasive and richly footnoted paper to the Tuesday Forum at the Maidstone Club that had everyone talking, and for an expanded version of which, *Vanity Fair* and Tina Brown's latest magazine were both said to be vigorously bidding. Mr. Thomas's thesis? That the fatal lapses which led a savvy, cagey Nixon to disgrace and resignation derived from the fact that his three best friends were Bebe Rebozo, Elmer Bopst, and Robert Abplanalp. Wrote Mr. Thomas, "No man is entirely normal whose three best friends are named Bebe, Bopst, and Abplanalp. Nixon, clearly, was a whack-job."

Down the beach at Montauk, an exotic novelty one might have expected in southern California but not here: the establishment of an actual government-in-exile set up in the second-best suite at Gurney's Inn (off-season rates applied). Professor Wamba-dia-Wamba, noted Congolese opposition leader and founder of the

People's Popular Front (the FPP), was in residence under tight security. There were concerns about assassination attempts and rumors an actual shot had been fired, but as an East Hampton cop explained following a cursory investigation, "These things happen out of season." The FPP's agenda, the professor explained to a reporter from Reuters, was one of nonalignment, universal suffrage, and deep-breathing exercises. The Hamptons had never had a government-in-exile before, and, except for the reported shooting, Wamba was locally quite a popular figure.

Less dramatically, Julian Schnabel, the famous artist who smashed dinner plates and then cleverly glued them up in attractive collages, was preparing a new gallery showing of his work; Uma Thurman had been seen jogging prettily behind her baby's sleek perambulator with its outsized racing wheels; the wine critics were all talking up this latest vintage from the Channing Daughters' Vineyard in Bridgehampton; Tom and Daisy Buchanan had closed their big place on Gin Lane and gone South, but Demaine the oil man was in residence on Georgica Pond and was giving a white-tie dinner for sixty at his home in the week between Christmas and New Year's. Prince Charles's paramour ("mistress!" the more literal insisted), Camilla Parker Bowles, visited friends in Shinnecock Hills. Sybil Burton, who used to be married to Richard before Miss Taylor happened along, was staging a new revue at the Long Wharf theater in Sag Harbor. The sale of Tommy Mottola's house was final (eight million plus, it was said). George Plimpton was working on a new book, an oral history of his entire graduating class at Harvard. Tony Duke scored an extraordinary late-season hole-in-one at the Maidstone and cheerfully stood a round of drinks. The new Kmart opened in Bridgehampton just in time for Christmas. In Springs, Madame Rand assured friends that architect Howard Roark was over his flu and taking nourishment. The North Haven Bridge was again closed amid fears of structural collapse. A Hamptons Coach driver went missing with the cab and the money. And local Indians gathered at the Thunder Bird Coffee Shop to protest development along St. Andrews Road, which they claimed infringed on ancient Shinnecock land, culture, and heritage.

When troopers arrested five Shinnecocks, a tribal spokesman issued a stirring and eloquent objection. "This," he said, "is literally the last buffalo."

People who don't know the Hamptons imagine it's dull out here in winter. Not hardly.

Chapter Five

*Outside, a light snow fell,
the first of the season . . .*

That afternoon, after a day at my computer editing the book, I drove into the village to stroll down the alley past Ralph Lauren's boutique for a Pacifico beer at the Blue Parrot Tex-Mex joint (*California*-Mex, they insisted). It was staying open only through the Christmas holidays and then the boys—Lee, the majority owner, and Roland, the right-hand man—would be off surfing. This year, to Bali.

Even out of season, a few of the regulars were already on station, occupying barstools, munching tortilla chips, and knocking back the cerveza and the margaritas, chatting with Kelly the barmaid who was so young she still had braces on her teeth (everyone chatted with Kelly the barmaid; it was required). I got a stool and a Pacifico with a chunk of lime jammed into the bottle and checked out Kelly's braces.

"They okay?"

"Fine," Kelly said. "Another few months."

Then she nodded toward a table against the wall near a gaudy bullfight poster promising Miura bulls (no shaved horns on those babies!) and several world-famous matadors no one ever heard of. Under the poster, at the little table, was someone who had caught

Kelly's eye and was not at all a regular. Only person in the bar who was younger than the barmaid.

She was a skinny little girl in shades (the sort they sell at an airport gift shop to travelers who want to look sophisticated), sitting alone at a good table ("good" tables at the Blue Parrot were in the eye of the beholder), paging through an LIRR timetable while noshing on quesadillas and sipping a Schweppes tonic water in a wide-brimmed, stemmed dry martini glass (her request, according to Kelly, being so much "neater" than an ordinary water tumbler). She was wearing a schoolgirl's kilted skirt, a classic, shapeless Shetland sweater, knee socks, and Gucci loafers. Her matching Vuitton luggage consisted of a roomy but decidedly chic backpack, a mid-sized duffle, and a tote. Her parka (anorak, really, if like me you prefer the European term) was by Bogner (she would later inform us there was considerable brand-name loyalty at her school, where one of the late Willi Bogner's grandchildren was enrolled). Kelly the barmaid brought me another Pacifico and some fresh tortillas and filled me in, superficially, on the kid. As the cerveza went down, I entertained myself by trying to read off the titles of a stack of paperbacks she'd arranged on the table for meal-time browsing: *The Sun Also Rises*, Salinger's *Franny and Zooey*, *Gatsby*, and *Hans Brinker, or the Silver Skates* by Mary Mapes Dodge. Next to them, a slim IBM laptop and a beat-up old Christmas issue of *Martha Stewart Living* magazine, set close at hand for easy reference.

As I watched, the little girl lit a Gitanes and puffed smoke at the railroad timetable she was studying. You weren't supposed to smoke in the restaurant, but no one complained. Hell, even in season the Parrot is pretty casual about rules. I scanned the rest of the room, taking note of who was around and who not—you know, was Gwyneth Paltrow in town? Brad Pitt? Senator D'Amato? Bill Murray practically made the joint his HQ during the October film festival.

Mellish was at the bar with a margarita in his oversized paw. He had a place in Hampton Bays and was the smartest man I knew but was forever getting screwed. You know the sort. Whatever he did went wrong. I said hi and moved my stool next to his.

"Easy for you to be cheerful," he said. "You're not putting an addition on your house."

"Well, I guess. Who's your architect?"

"That's where you delude yourself, Stowe. You buy a software package for seventy-five bucks and short-circuit all that."

"I'm sure," I agreed, knowing nothing in the Hamptons gets people so aroused as real estate. Better than Viagra. I called for another cerveza.

"Except they insist on a new survey before you start."

"Well . . ." I said, somewhat out of my depth, "what does a survey cost?"

Mellish slammed a big hand on the bar. "There's the heart of the matter. There are two local surveyors, a WASP and a guinea. Do you prefer to be cheated by the Establishment? Or by the Mafia?"

"I'm not sure that—"

"No one's sure, Stowe. That's where they have you. I got the WASP. Seven hundred fifty dollars was the fee he quoted . . ."

"Sounds about right."

"But when I told him I was scrapping that little wooden deck out back and asked him to omit it from the survey, he grew difficult. 'Can't do that, Mr. Mellish. If it's there, by law I have to include it.' . . . Christ almighty! I was *demolishing* the damned deck to build a new bedroom on the footprints."

"And?"

Mellish just shook his great head.

"To get a permit, you need a contractor. He gave me a September completion date. And hasn't yet begun! 'My digging machine broke.' Then two of his best men were in jail, Shinnecock Indians for rioting at the CATV station about rock versus rap music."

See what I mean about the Hamptons out of season? I turned to chat about Bali with Lee the owner, who's big and handsome and known as Surf God.

Other people drifted in now, and Surf God was distracted, so I went over to the little girl. Reporters are like that, curious.

I told her my name and asked how old she was. "Twelve," she said, "practically a teenager."

She was pretty small, and I'm not much good at ascribing motivation or guessing age. She was a skinny little kid with a Dutch Boy haircut, huge gray eyes, a freckled snip of a nose, and straight teeth, but, to me, she sure didn't resemble a teenager, and I must have looked skeptical. "Well, I'll be eleven soon," she conceded, finally admitting to ten. I was still betting nine. She offered me a Gitanes before providing an entertaining song & dance about grandparents mysteriously absent from their East Hampton estate. When I informed her the last train back to Manhattan had left and the first one next morning would be at six, she inquired as to which were "the better hotels" in town.

"The Maidstone Arms," I recommended cheerfully, since we have very few hotels good or bad, and the Arms served an excellent Sunday brunch, "None better."

"In the *Guide Michelin?*"

"I'm sure."

She jotted a note with an impressive gold Mont Blanc.

"Shouldn't you call your parents to tell them of your change in plans?"

Not possible, she said. They'd been injured in a recent suspension bridge collapse in the Peruvian Andes. I wasn't buying much of that and had begun wondering, was I doing the right thing and ought I instead just call the police?

She asked me what work I did, and I was soon telling her stories about being a correspondent as other Blue Parrot regulars began to join us. Mellish was especially good, cursing and swearing at a great rate about contractors and surveyors. The kid seemed to like that and told us her name, Susannah le Blanc, and said that since she was being educated in Switzerland, a country with three official languages, she was blessed with "the gift of tongues."

"Oh?"

"*Bien sûr, monsieur le journaliste,*" she assured me. "I'm understood in most major tongues and several of the lesser."

23

"Wow!" said Kelly the barmaid, who only spoke English but had now joined the small knot of idlers and the curious around the kid's table.

"Absolutely, fraulein, *danke*." To me, "*Avec plaisir, mon capitaine, yawohl!*" To a delighted Mellish, "*Ciao, mon vieux*." To Lee the owner, "*Che bella cosa*, old top!" And to other drinkers and employees, "*Du bist ein fine fellow, mon vieux. . . . Mein gott! Mon dieu! . . . Tout va bien, mein kamaraden. . . . Quel dommage*, dear chap. . . . But, and I ask this politely, *por favor*, can you cut the mustard, *monsieur le patron*?" And so on, much of all this punctuated with an enthusiastic, "*Olé!*" or "*Hoch! Hoch! Hoch!*" from time to time.

Not even Mellish attempted to provide counsel or advice, one of those rare occasions he was outtalked!

And when Susannah started to yawn, thanked us all for our time, and opened a purse to pay her bill, I saw impressively neat wads of francs (both Swiss and French), pounds sterling, deutsche marks, lire, dollars (all purchased at the *bureau de change* at Charles de Gaulle airport, thanks to her unlimited credit card, it turned out). And when paying her tab in dollars, she left precisely the appropriate fifteen percent tip.

A young child with an old head.

I still had no idea who Susannah really was or why she was here, but I found myself worrying. Could a ten-year-old already be this knowing and world-weary? Outside, a light snow fell, the first of the season, and, for the first time, I caught her offguard and vulnerable as she stared sleepily through the window. I realized her poise was, at least in large part, a pose. Were there really grandparents she'd expected to welcome her? Could she actually have been here before? And was remembering, and hoping to revisit, happier times? Or was it simply that she was a child a long way from home and over her head among strangers? And was, well, sort of scared.

I called the Maidstone Arms, confirmed that they had available rooms, and helped the kid and her luggage out to my car and drove her to the hotel. But when she thanked me for my courtesy and I asked if I could be of additional service, she shook her head briskly.

"*Pas du tout* and not at all, *monsieur le journaliste. Vous êtes très gentil.* And also quite considerate, *danke.*"

"Well, I just . . ."

"*Basta, signor.* I shall be quite well, *merci bien.*"

I carried the bags in, got a very firm handshake (for an instant there, I thought she was going to tip me), and then left. The snow had stopped, leaving only a brief coating on the lawns and trees that would be gone by morning but which, in the meantime, looked very nice.

I hoped Susannah le Blanc had enjoyed our very first flurry and would recall our simple, little village with pleasure when she left us on what I assumed would be the morning train back to New York.

Chapter Six

Bit of trouble scrambling about in small boats in the Yellow Sea . . .

Over breakfast with my father, I told him of the strange child at The Parrot, and his housekeeper, Inga, more sensible than either of us, angrily broke in. How could I send a small girl to a hotel? Was I mentally defective? How could the Admiral's only son behave so cloddishly?

"Well, I . . ."

Thoroughly chastised by both Inga and, subsequently, the Admiral (on such matters he wasn't too proud to take his lead from her), and expecting severe critiques from Her Ladyship whenever she arrived (with Alix, ETAs were poetically vague: when she arrived, she was there. You expected nothing more), I phoned the Maidstone Arms.

"Sorry, nobody registered named le Blanc," I was informed.

"Nonsense! I delivered her there myself. A young girl from Switzerland. She may have already left but she checked in last evening."

"Oh, you got the name wrong. I know the kid. That's Miss Wanderley Luxemburgo, of the Canary Islands."

When Inga (included as chaperone for propriety's sake) and I got Susannah thoroughly checked out of the hotel and into the car, I said, "Who's this Wanderley whatever-she-is?"

"It's a man, actually. Coach of the Brazilian national soccer team. Isn't it a glorious name? Especially for a Brazilian. You'd expect those fellows to be called Ronaldo. Or Joaquin, wouldn't you?"

"But why not register under your own —?"

"I use pseudonyms quite frequently. Throws people off your trail."

This is *not* your usual, everyday generic kid, I thought. *This* is an original. Alix is going to love her.

Whatever the hell her name is.

Yesterday's flurries had been a tease, and the day was fine, with sun and temperatures climbing into the fifties. At Further Lane the Admiral, nervy and unaccountably so, stood anxiously on the gravel as we drove up. He wasn't accustomed to children in the house. And from my disjointed account didn't know what to expect from this one. I made the introductions, not at all sure I had the genuine name yet.

"She uses pseudonyms," I told my father in an aside. "Says it throws people off the trail."

"It does, y'know," Admiral Stowe agreed. With all his years in naval intelligence, he was a great one for tradecraft.

But when they shook hands, he winced.

"Oh, dear," Susannah said. *"Je regrette bien, Herr Grosse-admiral."*

"Nothing serious," he said. "Bit of trouble last month scrambling about in small boats in the Yellow Sea. I'm missing a few digits and aren't as nimble as I might be."

"Mon pauvre amiral," she said solemnly. "One of our nuns at school has only one foot. A tram ran over the other just outside the Kronenhalle restaurant in Zurich, the establishment owned by Frau Zumsteg, the silk king's late mother. She gets around quite well."

The "late mother of the silk king" or the injured nun? I wanted to ask, but didn't.

As we went into the house, Inga leading the way, my father asked, "What order of nuns are those?"

"Madames of the Sacred Tower, old top. They're very *quelque chose*. Prefer French to Latin. Don't pay all that much heed to the Pope. Respectful to the Vatican in their dealings, but nothing more. Maintain a cool though cordial distance. Quite fond of reminding you they're Brides of Christ. They don't accept poor girls. As nuns, I mean. Nor as students, either. You've got to have 'a little set aside,' as they say. Rather like a dowry."

"I'd been told nuns took vows of poverty."

"Oh, hardly that. Mother Superior subscribes to *Barron's* and the *Financial Times*. On-line, as well, to Charles Schwab. She's forever lecturing us girls on investments, price/earnings ratios, on appreciating 'the value of a safe nine percent.'"

"I see," the Admiral said, not being all that fond of the Roman Catholic Church and suspicious of the papacy, and happy to see his anticlerical biases so nicely confirmed. And by a functioning Catholic straight from a convent school at that.

"What's the place called?" he asked.

"Couvent de la Tour Sacrée. Which means—"

My father interrupted her. "Convent of the Sacred Tower. We all speak French here, my dear. My late wife was French, Beecher was born in Paris, *bien élevé* and so on. And why is this tower of yours so sacred?"

"They say it's named for a historic old stone tower that stood on the spot back in the Dark Ages. A famous hermit of enormous piety was chained for thirty years to a wall in its dungeons for having insulted the emperor."

"I don't believe Switzerland had an emperor," my father objected.

"No, of the Holy Roman Empire. His name was Charlemagne. Difficult sort."

"And what could a mere hermit do to insult Charlemagne?"

"He prayed and sang hymns in the streets and didn't change his underwear. Ever. All of which offended decent authority. And, in turn, the emperor himself. That's how the social order worked in those days. Or so we're told by the Madames. Who are quite firm on such matters."

I didn't think hymn singing or soiled underwear were precisely hanging offenses, but still. My father looked thoughtful, wondering if we were being gulled, as Susannah went on.

"But we girls believe the tower's either a phallic symbol or is named for the Tower of Babel, what with all the lingos spoken by the student body. 'Polyglot,' that's the word, isn't it?"

"I'm quite sure," my father said, discomfited by the child's casual use of "phallic symbol," and not sure how to proceed. Until, somewhat weakly, he said, "But everyone's a Bride of Christ?"

That got her talking about life at the convent. "Mondays we have *primes*. French for the first day of the week. We all wear white gloves and Mother Superior hands out holy cards and badges to wear all week, to the best girls. I very rarely get either a holy card or a badge. I think it's that I curse and they're forever catching me smoking. Or because they resent my father; his being a riverboat gambler and all."

She paused. "Though on the occasional good week, I've been awarded a *pas mal* card, which means I seem to be trying." Then, rapt in thought, she went on to analyze further her difficulties with the Brides of Christ.

"Or it could be the poker games. I find girls from the Third World to be especially vulnerable. They can handle draw poker but fall to pieces when we play stud, five card or seven. Daughters of maharajahs and sultans. They have the most generous allowances, much of it in cash, and absolutely no card sense. Ready for the plucking, those girls. *Mon dieu!* I almost feel guilty about it sometimes. Because of race relations being as sensitive as they are. Still, you can't imagine how hapless the Third World is at poker. You can bluff them with a simple pair."

"I'm sure," I attempted to reassure the girl, if vaguely. "We all have our regrets. Young as you are, next term will be better, you can count on it."

There was, Susannah reported, ignoring my patronizing assurances, considerable stir this past term at the convent, which had nothing to do with holy cards or illicit poker sessions with the dusky progeny of the fabled East. All of which had my father kneading his wounded hands in considerable agitation.

No, this crisis was fashion-based. The Madames of the Sacred Tower were pondering a fundamental, even revolutionary change in the design of their religious habit. A heated debate raged, with nuns divided and bitterly so, into cliques. The Old Guard wanted to retain the status quo; the silent majority favored the Maison Dior; the New Wave rebels and the younger nuns preferred Emanuel Ungaro.

I thought Alix would side with that bunch, being a good customer at Ungaro.

The Admiral found this preoccupation with fashion incompatible for nuns bound by vows to be Brides of Christ. And questioned Susannah closely.

"Isn't there a priest or monsignor of some sort to keep these dreadful women under control? How can they be spending church funds in the Paris couture when the poor are—?"

"We do have a chaplain who drops by to hear confessions."

"Thank God for that. I hope he takes a stern line with the Mother Superior."

"He's very devout, Père Henri, a beatification in progress," Susannah said assuringly. "But since he is so young, Mother Superior bullies him dreadfully. We girls even have a pet name for him."

My father looked distracted. Pet names for priests? The Episcopal Church wouldn't tolerate such nonsense.

"Yes, *Henri Dansant*. Dancing Harry, as it were. Grand at sermons and leading a rousing hymn. But a bit light in the loafers, if you get my drift."

Everything bad my father wanted to believe of the Roman Catholic Church was coming true. As he shook his head in condemnation, reflecting on the historical inevitability of the Protestant Reformation, young Susannah realized she might have gone a bit too far and had better speak up, and quickly, for the convent.

"But fierce social activists at the same time," she insisted. "Last term the nuns had the entire convent whipped into a frenzy about the 'fallen women of Luzon.'"

"Oh?"

"Yes, we all contributed to a fund to rescue young Filipinas from the streets of Manila. Even the Brazilian girls pitched in, and you know how they are. Hate to spend money on something other than bikini waxing. We tithed from our allowances to buy back young girls, some as young as seven or eight, from establishments of ill fame, which is what the Madames of the Sacred Tower call whore-houses."

"Inga, why don't you show Miss Susannah her room," the Ad-miral said hurriedly, glancing showily at his watch as if to justify haste. For a career navy man, he had his reticences.

And so it was, almost before we knew it, that Susannah had been installed, without our yet knowing precisely who or what she was, in a spare bedroom of my father's snug old house on the dunes overlooking the great, gray Atlantic. It wasn't Ron Perelman's place, the Creeks, or the deMenil mansion, or Martha Stewart's house, but it wasn't bad either.

Chapter Seven

A randy old fellow, always trying to peek at girls in the ladies' ...

It was about then, without our yet fully realizing it, that the house lights suddenly dimmed. The Playbills were passed out and the better seats filled. The orchestra swung into the overture and the curtain slowly rose as, on our modest Further Lane set, the play began. All because Susannah le Blanc was now onstage.

"Clearly she can't stay here," the Admiral announced sternly over breakfast the next morning. "You'd best call this convent place and have them contact her parents."

"I?"

I can't recall ever having spoken to a nun in my entire life, and dealing in an adversarial manner with the Brides of Christ held little appeal for me.

"You fetched her home from the railroad station," my father pointed out inaccurately.

It was the Blue Parrot where I found her. But never mind. You didn't win arguments with the Admiral by splitting hairs.

When Susannah came down, not actually smoking a cigarette in deference to her hosts, but slightly reeking of a covert puff, my father did a cowardly thing, putting the blame on me. He'd gone into North Korea by night in a rubber boat and stood up to fiendish tortures by the Dreaded Taliban. But this kid intimidated him.

"Beecher insists we contact your parents. Through the convent, if not directly."

I insisted? I? I gave him a look. Before I could say a word, Susannah had sprung to her own cause.

"But, my dear Admiral, you can't. You just can't. I'd so looked forward to Christmas in the Hamptons. Martha Stewart's accounts in her magazine are irresistible. I've never been so thrilled. And moved, as well. Not even Good King Wenceslas, on the feast of Stephen, felt more enthusiastically about Christmas than Martha Stewart."

"I thought you had grandparents here," I protested, sensing the Admiral's smirk at my naïveté.

"That was just a tall tale, Beecher. We'd barely met and I was still sizing you up. Never show your hand early in the game. Even the Brides of Christ preach that."

"And Martha Stewart? Do you know her?" Could we believe anything this kid said?

"Only through her TV show and magazine. But I suspected that if a young girl arrived on her doorstep just before Christmas, there was no way she wouldn't be asked in, served cookies and hot chocolate, and shown about. The Christmas issue of her magazine surely is an accurate reflection of the warm, loving nature of the woman herself."

"I'm sure," the Admiral muttered, sarcastically I thought.

"But when I got there, instead of a light in the window and the Yule log on the fire, carolers in the snow, a smiling and aproned Martha flinging open doors and ushering me into a snug kitchen smelling of bakery, roasted chestnuts, and stuffed turkey, the house was shuttered and dark in the December gloom. The cab driver told me she has another house in Connecticut and was probably spending Christmas there. So I returned to the Village to puzzle out my next step. Which was where Beecher found me."

The Admiral listened but held firm.

"Child, someone your age can't just go off. Think of your own dear mother bringing you into this world, the morning sickness, no cocktails or cigarettes, all that painful labor, and then the nursing and nurturing."

"Sorry, Admiral, I was bottle-fed. Mummy was terribly liberated, having skated in the Icecapades. And I know the other way is better, but she had reservations. Concerns about having perky breasts. My father was very particular about his wife's having perky—"

"Well, we needn't go into all that," the Admiral said hurriedly. "The point is, once we notify them, you're more than welcome here until they can come and get you. But . . ."

She was spunky. "*Gruss Gott!*" she said, slapping her forehead, "You must think I'm a runaway."

"No, we don't. It's simply that . . ."

I love to see my father disconcerted like this; it happens so rarely.

"*Au contraire, mon amiral*, that's precisely what you think. But I'm not. Look, here's my return ticket to Paris on the Concorde. My Eurorail ticket to Geneva, first class. Both dated, January 3 and January 4. Classes resume at La Tour January 5. I shall be there, back with the nuns, in whatever habit they happen to be wearing. And on time, I assure you. And as for"—this with a cutting glance at me—"your turncoat son."

Ooof, that was a shot. Even my father felt constrained to stand up for me.

"That's a bit stiff, Susannah, and not at all called for. We're simply trying to act properly in this matter. Your best interests are our sole concern. And to call Beecher a 'turncoat'—"

"My dear sir, he has, as the French put it, *tourne sa veste.*" Then, to me, "Can you deny your betrayal of a trusting child, *señor?*"

Furious, I spoke for myself. "Did you or did you not tell me your parents had just fallen from a Peruvian bridge in the Andes?"

"A celebrated journalist *that* gullible? I may have floated a colorful story or two. But like so many children my age, I happen to be a victim, the pitiful flotsam of a broken marriage. My parents, alas, are divorced. And *not* amicably." She raised a dainty chambray hankie to her upturned nose.

The Admiral gave me a withering look for badgering the poor girl. Inga saved me.

"Car coming."

It was at this critical juncture, with a young girl's immediate fate undecided, that Her Ladyship Alix Dunraven arrived from London. And, as was customary, her lean, insouciant, but essentially joyous presence sent a fresh breeze through the old house and up and down Further Lane, invigorating us all, even my old dad, who pretended to disapprove of her but, like me, was putty in her hands. And why not, with Alix greeting him with kisses and small, laudatory gush:

"But how splendid you look, Admiral. Absolutely fit, with a high color and clear eye. Shades of Drake, Frobisher, and Hawkins! There's not a sea dog to match you even marginally these days in the entire Royal Navy. No wonder your chaps rule the seas."

My father grinned, still boyish at seventy and clearly smitten. Though not precisely *as* smitten as I, nor anything like as randy. As good as Alix looked right now.

Her car was something, too, once we got a close look at it.

Air kisses exchanged, introductions made, refreshments served, I was hardly surprised that Her Ladyship and Susannah were nattering on like old chums, heads together and conspiring, kindred and mischievous spirits.

In all fairness to her, Alix's briefing had been pretty fragmentary.

"But how dreadful," she told the child, "I've trekked across some of those Peruvian bridges myself, the chasm far below, with its snow-melted streams rushing icy toward the sea. Your parents clinging desperately to each other. Sheer terror."

"Far, far below," Susannah confirmed, "jagged rock and a rushing stream."

"Her parents are divorced. Not amicably," I said.

"Oh, dear," Alix said, "before or after the bridge went? It means everything in the law courts, y'know, and to the estate, if the parents were still married when they . . . well, plummeted from that horrid bridge."

"Oh, they're alive," Susannah said, pulling out a Gitanes. "Injured but alive. Saved by fierce Incan tribesmen using forest poultices and native remedies of all sorts."

Susannah seemed to be taking charge. Especially with Alix reflexively holding out to her a gold Dunhill's lighter.

I attempted to reestablish a factual tone. "No one fell off a bridge. In the Andes or anywhere else. It's just 'a colorful story she floated.' Susannah attends a Swiss convent school," I said somewhat desperately.

"Convent school, my. Just imagine," Alix said with enthusiasm.

"Where the nuns are changing habits," Susannah said brightly. "The old dowdies favor Dior; the younger, trendier sisters are all for Ungaro. As are most of the girls."

"But of course you are. Ungaro's the only one," Alix declared. "That innocent yet knowing spirit inherent in his work. Don't you agree, Admiral?"

There was a brief impasse when my father suggested Alix ought to stay in the big house rather than with me in my gate house.

"Lest our young visitor be scandalized," he suggested in hushed tones. Since his wife, my long-dead mother, had been a Paris cover girl, and in more recent years, his and Inga's relationship clearly went beyond that of master and servant, this seemed to me disingenuous.

It was Alix who began to winkle out of the girl just who she really was and whence she came.

"First of all, this 'le Blanc' business. That's made up as well, isn't it?"

Susannah answered quite directly for a change.

"A *nom de guerre*. But not my idea, I assure you. My parents didn't want me put down under my actual name. Kidnappers, y'know. Prey on the children of the rich. The Red Brigades. The Black Hand. The Lindbergh baby all over again. So I'm a little nobody labeled 'le Blanc.' A blank page. Even my passport bears the pseudonym. Though just how that was arranged with U.S. authorities, I haven't the foggiest."

"There *are* ways," the Admiral said murkily, knowing something about bribery and blackmail in the intelligence trade.

"And not to belabor the point," Susannah went on, "but I've already been kidnapped twice."

"Actually kidnapped?" I demanded, suspicious by now of the kid's every other statement.

"Yes, but it was during the custody stage of the divorce, and one parent was stealing me away from the other. And vice versa. The courts didn't take it all that seriously."

"Oh."

Leave it to Alix to bring up obscure political-science lectures at Oxford, the sacred right of sanctuary, of political asylum.

"But those hardly obtain in this case," I protested. "A marital custody dispute in which—"

"Don't be so literal, Beecher. Deal in large issues, not the picky detail. Consider the Barons at Runnymede with Prince John. The Magna Carta. English common law and all that. Those chaps didn't nitpick, not a bit of it!"

"We're not in England, Alix. We're in New York State, where different laws—"

She didn't let me finish.

"If you'd read at all deeply in law at Princeton—"

"Harvard!"

". . . you'd know that much of your American Constitution is clearly founded on its British antecedents. Chaucer and his *Tales*. *Beowulf. Piers Plowman.* I could go on."

"Plus, of course, the Napoleonic Code," my father put in, even at the risk of pedantry, unwilling to be entirely bypassed in the debate.

"*And,* as your father the Admiral rightly points out, the Napoleonic Code," she said, anxious to please, and then quickly tossing in, "as well as Malory's *Morte d'Arthur.*"

"Please, please, please let me stay," Susannah wheedled, returning the argument to her predicament. And persuasively, at that.

She swiftly explained that since each parent believed her safely to be with the other, and the school was closed down, no one was alarmed or concerned. "Nor should they be. Classes resume January 5 in Switzerland. I have my return tickets and would dearly love to stay until then here in the Hamptons, experiencing a true American Christmas." One that by her vivid description would be by Norman Rockwell out of Martha Stewart.

"Dammit, child!" the Admiral thundered at flank speed and in tones traditionally reserved for the chewing out of midshipmen, "a girl your age can't simply move in with total strangers, including two grown men, as if we were running a bed-and-breakfast. Just not done. Nor should it be. Quite improper. An offence to the village mores. We're Episcopalians, I'll have you know. Not at all accustomed to having underage females running about."

As he broke off momentarily, perhaps having run out of steam, I offered a proposal.

"Father, you suggested I phone the convent. Why don't we do that right now and see if anyone's raised the alarm?"

A bit reluctant and uneasy, Susannah gave me the telephone number and I rang through directly.

A man picked up. "Yes, Igor," I said. "This is Beecher Stowe in East Hampton. May I have the Mother Superior?"

"Igor's the caretaker," Susannah informed us in an aside. "And not to be trusted."

"Oh, all right. Thank you." I asked a few more questions as Susannah continued to fill out the caretaker's résumé for us.

"A randy old fellow, Igor. Always trying to peek at the upper-form girls in the ladies'.."

When I hung up, both Alix and the Admiral said, "Well?"

"Nobody home. Closed for the holidays. The sisters out of town visiting shrines or out taking brisk walks, I suppose . . ."

"*Mens sano in corpore sano,*" Alix put in piously.

". . . which still doesn't justify the child's staying here."

"*Grand seigneur, s'il vous plaît . . .*" Susannah addressed the Admiral, quite collected and calm, as she played her trump card.

"I won't be talked 'round," he protested stubbornly.

"Of course not. But I'd thought all this through in advance, *mein herr.* And if it turned out that Martha Stewart was abroad . . . or had gotten married, or for some other legitimate reason was unable to offer me her hospitality, I did have a fallback position, y'know."

That halted my father in midcourse.

"Oh, you do, do you?"

"Yes, suppose I told you my godfather has a house in the Hamptons?"

I guess my mouth fell open and my father's certainly did. Alix was the first of us to recover.

"But that's capital! What a splendid development," Alix enthused.

"If true," I murmured.

"I knew you'd think so, Your Ladyship," Susannah said, ignoring me. "I haven't seen him since I was a mere infant, but he's a wonderful man. My parents asked him to sponsor me at baptism. They were associated in business at one time, he and my father. A patrician and philanthropist, world-famed for good works. He has a big old shingled house out here. I can just barely remember its wide verandas and shaded porches with swinging gliders, fruit orchards with a big pond beyond. There were golden carp swimming about, as I recall. Very fat, very golden. I was only two or three, but I can still see the carp."

Does she just make this stuff up? I wondered.

"That sounds like half the houses in town. What's his name?" the Admiral growled skeptically. "We probably know the fellow."

"*Ce n'est pas possible, messieurs/dames.* To reveal that would surely tip you to my own identity. Within the hour my parents would be flying in aboard chartered jets in considerable alarm. To say nothing of kidnappers."

"Natural thing for parents to do," remarked my father.

Susannah shook her head.

"*Por favor, maestro . . .*" she said, snuffing out her cigarette in the ashtray and looking innocent.

"Don't wheedle, child."

". . . and that would not only locate me precisely for the kidnappers but be the end of my holiday, *ma petite aventure.* Over before it ever really began. *Zero à gauche.*" She looked around at us, her big eyes gone liquid, focusing on each face in turn. "You've made me so happy here. Not knowing me but taking me in. The generosity of spirit, the warmth and good humor. It's unlike anything I've ever—"

"Oh, damn!" my father swore. He resented being burdened with guilt not truly deserved.

Despite myself, I was enjoying this depiction of the Admiral as a saintly old Father Flanagan of *Boys' Town*, but I limited my remarks to a final, pressing question. "If le Blanc is a pseudonym, what about Susannah? Is that your actual given name?"

"No, I lifted it from Shirley Temple, 'Susannah of the Mounties.' It was one of my favorite flicks when I was small, and I've used it ever since in tight places. *Che bella cosa, che bella ragazza.*"

Alix, who by now was firmly allied with the kid, snuffled into a tissue.

"Oh, Beecher, think of a little girl watching Shirley Temple and wanting to be her. You can't just coldly turn her out into the storm."

There was a brilliant sun and no storm, and I gave her a look. "You're a pair, you two," I murmured. Both she and Susannah looked exceedingly innocent. But not overplaying their hand, neither rubbed it in or said a word.

Chapter Eight

"Just what is keelhauling? And does it hurt?"

I hadn't seen Alix since summer, and so no matter how intriguing was young Susannah's story, you can imagine I was pretty eager to be alone with Her Ladyship. To talk. And so on. If you know what I mean.

"Come on," I said. "We'll get your bags in from the car."

In deference to the lateness of the season and winter coming, instead of her accustomed rental of an open sportscar, she had a dramatically husky Humvee in camouflage paint with rallye headlights mounted and a ski rack, lacking only a machine gun and siren. It looked like that command car George C. Scott rode across Tunisia in the opening reels of *Patton*.

"Are you competing in the Iditarod?" I inquired.

"It is impressive," she conceded with pleasure. "Does everything but desalinate water. And I got it on tick."

"Oh, no, Alix." She was notorious for getting otherwise cynical corporations to lend her things.

"Well, Beecher, I did suggest, without actually lying, that I was the motoring correspondent for the *Times* of London. One of Mr. Murdoch's star byline writers. They practically forced me to take the car on a fortnight's trial. The chap at the Hummer shop provided all

41

variety of manuals. I still don't know where half the controls are or what they do. And I've yet to find a cigarette lighter," she said. "Even has a global-positioning device as an option, and it certainly does draw the eye. All the way out on your Long Island Motorway."

"Expressway."

"Chaps in huge lorries kept peering down at me, waving and blowing their klaxons and staring at my legs. Jolly good sports, those fellows. Not at all surly, like the lorry drivers one encounters in Britain."

"That's your legs, darling, not the Hummer."

"You are sweet, Beecher. Do kiss me properly, won't you."

I did.

"Mmmm," she said, sort of leaning against me and moving slowly in that appealing way she has, "can we go to bed or are you expected to lunch or something?"

I looked at my watch. Only eleven.

"Let's go to bed."

"Oh, yes," she said.

About an hour later we were sitting up in my bed propped against down pillows, getting our breath and smoking my cigarettes. "Did I tell you I'd quit again?" she said.

"Am I to feel guilty about getting you back on them?"

"That, and other things. You should feel enormously guilty, Beecher, especially for a chap descended from all those famous preachers." But she didn't sound terribly stern and lifted her head to kiss me again while one hand . . .

"I realize it's naughty of me, but I do love your body."

Hers wasn't too shabby, either, I thought. She was still wearing my nipple ring, the one Ralph Destino at Cartier helped me pick out a year or so back. I stroked it gently with my forefinger. "You ought to have another of these."

"One is perfect. I'm not frantic about symmetry."

"I know."

"Except," she continued, "that I do like being kissed all over and not simply on one side. Or t'other."

Being an amiable fellow, I kissed her in any number of places, lingering a bit here and there.

"Ohhhh," she said softly. And then when I kept up, a bit noisier.

"Yes, darling," I said, knowing she liked encouragement.

Alix Dunraven and I had been in love, on and off, for just over three years. It was more "on" than "off" on my part, I guess it's fair to say. And I realize there's something absurd about nipple rings. A silly fad. And one your bluestockings and truly liberated women find ridiculous. But it was the only ring I'd ever given her, the closest we'd yet come to a ring of another sort, and so it meant a good deal. To both of us, I hoped.

She occasionally strayed, got engaged to chaps without actually meaning to, and when caught (an item in Nigel Dempster's column in the *Daily Mail*, or still worse, an engagement notice in the *Times*—soon to be rescinded—might alert me), she was always sweetly repentant. Problems rarely came up when we were together; but give Alix time, opportunity, and three thousand miles of ocean between us, and situations tended to arise. It was one of the reasons I wanted her here with me having Christmas on Further Lane. Her Christmas two years ago had been a young viscount and skiing off-piste at Gstaad. Last year, the German race-car driver and midnight swims on Tahiti. Nothing serious, of course. As she herself put it: "An innocent little flirt, darling. You know how I get in the moonlight. Or on islands."

"Of course," I said, recognizing that England itself was an island, but not arguing the point, knowing she admired cool.

That evening, to make up for skipping lunch, I took everyone to dinner at the Maidstone Club, a quiet night with the rooms near empty. After cocktails in the library and before we'd ordered at the table, the Admiral again brought up the subject of Susannah's godfather and just which of the neighbors he might be. But he was no longer probing as aggressively or demanding answers. A cocktail or two invariably relaxed my father, and he enjoyed a good martini, no denying that. But credit the kid as well; she played him like a violin, sort of how Alix manipulated me, and it occurred to me that instead of resuming the argument, Susannah was subtly recruiting the Old Gentleman to her side.

Although he does take a stiff line ethically, and you might expect a man of his age and reputation to be stuffy and veto unconventional behavior, my father is by nature and training a born conspirator. As such, he was soon falling in enthusiastically with various of the child's schemes, especially when Susannah expressed great interest and admiration in how, even missing fingers, he could do card tricks, perform simple feats of magic, and manipulate gadgets. "Quite amazing, *mon cher amiral*, and very well played," she solemnly informed our country's former Chief of Naval Intelligence, as he entertained us by tugging this or that small puzzle or gadget from his pockets during cocktails.

"Granted, granted," the Admiral conceded gruffly. He enjoyed showing off, always had.

Later, over chilled Dom Pérignon and steamed lobster, he revisited the subject. "But if we fall in with your program, just how do we explain you away to the neighbors, the shopkeepers, the authorities? Or even here at the club? A small girl doesn't just descend on East Hampton from her Swiss convent school the fortnight before Christmas, alone and unchaperoned, tossing about *noms de guerre* and declining to share, even with her hosts, the identity of a mysterious local godfather and benefactor. Quite possible we Stowes ourselves might be suspected of having abducted you when all we've done is provide hospitality. Ever think of that, young lady? . . . You demand a great deal of us but don't give very much on your part. Shouldn't trust cut both ways? Eh?"

"At your service, *mein herr*. But I have an idea. At least, I think I do."

Susannah shared the Admiral's fondness for costume and disguise, and instead of addressing his pointed question about trust, she now deftly moved the conversation back to his field of expertise, suggesting that, given a few props, wigs, false mustaches, and spectacles, and following his expert coaching, she might pass herself off as any number of characters: a dwarf, an aged crone, a retired governess, or a victim of some mysterious shrinking disease

44

caused, perhaps, by recent nuclear fallout from Indian and Pakistani atomic tests. I noted that with her short hair and slim, tomboyish manner, and togged out in jeans and sweater, Susannah might play a boy.

Alix absolutely opposed that idea. "Cross-dressing at too young an age can damage one's sense of identity and self-esteem. Later on, with the personality formed, it's quite all right. Might she instead be passed off as my firstborn?" Alix asked vaguely.

"You're just slightly too young. And aren't married," I pointed out.

Alix knew my tendency to stuffiness and gave me a look, as if to say, Have you never heard of single parenting? So I attempted to look pensive, studying the situation.

"I know!" Alix said, "Susannah can be my ward. Wards are all the rage these days. In Belgravia, the better families all have one."

So young Susannah le Blanc got her way. She'd be Lady Alix's "ward" for the moment. For how long? Well, we hadn't really settled that, had we? And there was the matter of yet another *nom de guerre*. If her passport were in the name Susannah le Blanc, and if there truly were enemies out there, potential kidnappers, we'd better call her something else.

"Could I be called Jane?" she inquired.

Why Jane?

"Jane Eyre," of course. "I had thought, in haughty moments, of wanting to be Estella, who was Miss Havisham's ward in *Great Expectations*, and called Pip, 'boy,' and made him cry. I enjoy stories where girls make boys cry."

"I liked her, too," said Alix.

"You liked Cathy in *Wuthering Heights*," I said.

"No, in *Wuthering Heights*, I identified with Heathcliff."

Talk about cross-dressing and identity.

The Admiral looked thoughtful at all this transgender chat and said he preferred something French—Gabrielle? I proposed Anastasia, but Jane carried the day. Though there was one dicey moment over dinner when an elderly member, somewhat deaf, was told by Alix, "Jane is from good Shropshire stock; they make by far the best wards, y'know. Very much in demand," and the old man said, "The child herself just told me she's from London," only to have "Jane" salvage the moment: "No, *pas du tout, monsieur*. London was our pied-à-terre, you see. Shropshire is the true bone and sinew of the line."

The "ward," possessed of one of those "ears" that swiftly commandeers an accent and picks up on another's speech cadence or verbal tic, making it her own, was starting to sound like a younger edition of Her Ladyship.

"Might I taste your Dom, Alix? I love the bubbles."

"Well, just a sip."

"No, you *cannot* taste Her Ladyship's champagne!" I said firmly. Alix kissed me lightly on the cheek.

"Forgive me, Admiral Stowe, for these displays of affection in your club. But I do love Beecher when he draws decisive lines in the sand, don't you?"

"Yes, ma'am, I confess I do."

So between the two of them, Alix and the girl had captivated my stern, dignified, and even intimidating old father. By the time we were back at the house with its roaring fire and a warming brandy, and Inga serving coffee and petits fours, they had him discussing various of Captain Marryat's sea stories for boys (on which Alix was practically brought up, along with John Buchan and Sherlock Holmes), and had him promising one day to sing the old sea chanteys (learned half a century ago at Annapolis). As well as answering queries: "Just what is keelhauling? And does it hurt?" Before long the Admiral was threatening in his own house to dance the hornpipe, which no jolly tar had danced for a hundred years or more!

Though I think that might have been the brandy speaking.

Only once that night did Susannah/Jane give him pause, with his old-world courtliness and Episcopalian reserve, when the topic of wish fulfillment and ambition arose.

"We all, when we're younger, have our soaring, long-term ambitions. Sometimes they work out, usually not," the Admiral remarked. "Have you thought yours through yet, Susannah?"

46

Short-term only, she said: "I can't wait to be an adolescent so I can wear a bra and have improper thoughts."

"*What?*" the old gentleman thundered.

"Yes, I know it's wicked. But the nuns are forever going on about improper thoughts, warning us off, so they make the whole business sound delicious. The upper-form girls are said to be having them all the time."

Alix wasn't much help.

"Odd, I felt that way myself at your age, though far too shy to bring it up in mixed company. But we girls certainly exchanged confidences. As, for example . . ."

My father gave Her Ladyship a look and called upon Inga to put the child to bed.

Chapter Nine

When Jackson Pollock crashed and burned, they planted him there...

The Admiral took me aside next morning. Something about needing to have the main house roofed in spring and did I want my cottage reshingled at the same time.

"Amazing about that child's father," he said when we were out of earshot and gazing skyward, as if entranced, at roofs. "To make a corner in soybeans on the mercantile exchange and then just drop it all to go off to the Himalayas."

"What Himalayas?" I demanded.

"Nepal. The monastery at Kathmandu. Studying to be a monk."

"A monk?" I realized I was sounding sappy, but this was all news to me.

"Yes, a Zen adept hoping for admission to full monkhood and busily turning prayer wheels. She gets the odd postcard from her dad but little more. The merchant bankers at Rousselot Frères pay for her schooling and send an allowance. The father's apparently put the whole bundle in trust and taken vows of poverty."

"Mmm," I said. I hate to spoil anyone's good story or to disillusion my old man. But Susannah had confided in me her father was a geologist wintering (it was summer down there) at McMurdo Sound in Antarctica, taking salinity readings from ice cores in a study of global warming. This was when she wasn't blaming his being a riverboat gambler for her failure to be awarded holy cards by the nuns. Or recalling that, although he used to send her gaudy postcards from distant climes, these days he kept her abreast of his commercial dealings with mailed clips from *Fortune, Business Week,* and *Forbes.*

"I am proud of him, y'know," she'd assured me. Too proud, apparently, to keep her stories straight.

It occurred to me I was spending entirely too much of what the trendy (and the child psychologists) call "quality time" thinking about this appealing, but probably spoiled and surely confused, runaway child, when the woman I loved and was plotting to marry was here under my roof for the first time in half a year.

So rather than choose between them I took Alix and Susannah to Main and School Streets in Bridgehampton for thick shakes at the Candy Kitchen. I'd been an only child and knew nothing about how youngsters these days wanted to be entertained, but reckoned you couldn't go too far wrong with ice cream.

"Did you know her mother dances with the Kirov Ballet?" Alix asked when Susannah had excused herself to go to the ladies' room.

"She told me she was at the Institut Pasteur in Paris, advancing Madame Curie's research into molecular structures and the half-life of certain isotopes."

Alix's brow knit. Though prettily. "She can hardly do both, can she?"

"I don't believe so."

We ordered the thick shakes. But before I could tug out my wallet, the kid slid her credit card at the waitress.

"My treat, *messieurs/dames,*" she said firmly. "The ice cream in Geneva is grand, too, especially the chocolate. But everyone says American ice cream is the best. Why is that?" Susannah asked.

"Jane," she corrected me when I used her name.

"Yes, Jane. It's the buttercream content," I said, not having the slightest idea but suspecting that sounded pretty good.

Bob White, who used to tend bar next door at Bobby Van's,

came in, and we reminisced about the place, which was where Willie Morris drank. Willie's dog, Pete, was popularly accepted as the "mayor of Bridgehampton," since he spent so much time on Main Street, sleeping in front of Van's while his master drank. Capote drank there as well. And Jim Jones, who wrote *From Here to Eternity*. And George Plimpton. Jones was dead now, as was Willie, and of course Truman, who was forever losing his license in Bridgehampton for driving under the influence. So instead of serving drinks to drunks, Bob White was now selling cars to the sober. These days he is one of the star salesmen at Buzz Chew Chevrolet. In fact, he sold me my last two Chevy Blazers. And good, reliable cars they turned out to be.

I introduced Bob to Her Ladyship and to Susannah, whom I identified vaguely as ". . . and of course Lady Alix's ward, Jane, as you know."

The kid promptly stuck out a hand and shook Bob's, identifying herself as, "Jane Pendragon, *a sus órdenes, signor.*"

Where the hell did she get that, the Pendragon part, I mean?

"Sure, I guess," Bob said, probably wondering why this kid thought he was Italian, or was it Spanish? He ordered a coffee and slipped into the booth with us, being right at home. After a few remarks about the weather and Christmas shopping, Bob asked, "Did you hear the latest about the Old Churchyard then?"

"Only that another lawsuit was thrown out."

Like most of us in East Hampton, I knew how Jacob Marley's estate bought up all the gravesites. On a small, parochial scale, there hadn't been anything like it since the Louisiana Purchase. It was the kind of yarn you might long ago have argued about half-drunk at Bobby Van's with Capote and Willie and maybe Irwin Shaw if he were in town and drinking. The kind of story that belonged in *nouvelle vague* movies by Renoir or Truffaut, with film noir subtitles.

But I'd been back in town only a few days, Alix hadn't been here since last summer, and young Jane (Susannah) was a convent schoolgirl from Switzerland. So none of us was really up to speed on cemetery happenings. Bob White filled us in.

"They stole Mean Jake's bones again. Got into the mausoleum."

"So that's twice now!"

"Three times," Bob corrected me.

"That is rum," added Alix, not at all sure who Mean Jake was or why anyone kept stealing his bones. "Is this a sort of Dr. Frankenstein affair?" she asked. "Trafficking in body parts?"

"Frankenstein and Dracula," said her dutiful ward, Jane. "Those are the chaps. I dearly love those stories."

Since my father had briefed me already with that clip from the *Times*, I picked up the thread, explaining about the Old Churchyard. "There are forty-five cemeteries in East Hampton but only this one's controversial."

"Why's that?" asked Alix. Jane/Susannah was listening carefully but not saying much. Maybe she was measuring Bob White, who again took up the story.

"Because of a rich guy people called Mean Jake, now dead," Bob began. "They set up the churchyard early in the 1800s, about two centuries back, mainly for local blue-collar people, Baymen and other fishermen and farmers mostly, and the nonconformists. There never was a church there on the property, but still they called it the Old Churchyard, because that sounded nice, holier even. Then when Jackson Pollock crashed and burned, they planted him there, which was quite okay since he lived right down the road and was considered local for all his fame. Except that after they buried ol' Jackson, the place got trendy. Frank O'Hara and A. J. Liebling were buried there, Elaine de Kooning, Jean Stafford. A big advertising noise on Madison Avenue, guy named Ad Reinhardt, even told a joke about it just before he croaked, 'The place is so famous people are dying to get in there.' "

"Ha!" said Jane brightly, "that's pretty good." Kids like it when they get the punch line right away.

Bob gave her a grin, pleased that she appreciated his yarn. Then he resumed. "That was thirty or forty years ago. And when Ad died, sure enough, they planted him there."

I didn't rush Bob. Let the story come out. He'd tell it better than I could.

"So when Mean Jake died they brought a marble mausoleum into the Old Churchyard and moved him in. No problem. He lived half the year in Palm Beach, but he had a big house here and people knew him. Didn't mean they liked him. But he wasn't an outsider. The trouble came when they read Jake's will. And named his only kin, his sister, executor as well as sole heir.

"There were one hundred and ten plots vacant in the churchyard when Jake died, which made it one hundred and nine, and by God! didn't Sis take out her checkbook and write a check to the cemetery trustees for the whole damned one hundred and nine? Said that was what Jake wanted her to do, writing it into his will, so he wouldn't be bothered for all eternity by having anyone 'round him that he couldn't stand. Or put up ornate monuments that blocked his view of the bay." To his few intimates, and with irritating frequency to Sis, Mean Jake had made his wishes apparent with a brisk, if crotchety, candor. Bob White filled us in on Jake's dislikes, ticking them off in a gruff voice supposed to be the dead man's:

"Jerry Della Femina, that sourpuss Paul Simon, Helen Rattray (she edited the local weekly paper), Ron Perelman of Revlon, Macklowe the real-estate man, and Peter Maas (who once wrote a piece about him in *New York* magazine). Do I need them planted next to me over the centuries?"

No! And these were all, for better or for worse, Jake's neighbors. And on whom, he was turning a dead back.

According to Bob White, Mean Jake was concerned that East Hampton's Old Churchyard was becoming a tourist attraction. "Like that place in Paris."

"You mean the Cimetière Père Lachaise?" I said.

"Oh, I adore Père Lachaise!" Alix enthused. "Where Colette and Proust sleep alongside Baron Haussmann, Oscar Wilde, Sarah Bernhardt, Lalique, and Proust's lover, Reynaldo. Did you know, Jane, Sarah Bernhardt had only one leg?"

"Like our Sister Euphemia?"

"I dare say," Alix agreed, not knowing yet about the sister and the tramcar, but forging ahead with more on Bernhardt.

"Only one leg, but did it give 'the divine Sarah' pause? Not a bit of it. Had scads of lovers, well into her sixties."

I got back into it then, knowing how explicit Her Ladyship could be. "But today Père Lachaise is where they bury rock stars and actors, with groupies trampling the other plots, weeping and lighting candles, all the while littering the grounds with scrolls of bad poetry."

Bob White nodded knowingly. "Yeah, that's the kind of stuff drove Jake nuts."

As we talked, you could almost hear Alix's mind working.

"Mmm," she said now, "just think. Now that he's a neighbor of yours and the Admiral's, Beecher, you might have Puff Daddy in there one day as well."

"Wow!" said Jane. "Does *he* live here too, Puff Daddy?"

"Cut a certain figure last summer when I was visiting," Alix responded. "He and that lovely Miss Lopez he squires about."

"Beecher?"

"Yes, Jane."

"If Puff Daddy ever dies and they bury him out here, will you let me know? I'd love to pay my respects on school break."

This was some kid, or maybe it was typical at her age, thrilled by both a Martha Stewart Christmas and a rapper's grave.

"Police called in to find Jake?" I asked Bob.

"You know Bonackers, they're being pretty hush-hush about it. And Sis doesn't want any more bad publicity. The other two times they stole Jake's bones, they brought 'em back. Besides, a couple of the Bonac Boys are on the force."

The Bonac Boys were locals, contemporary equivalent of the Sons of Liberty up in New England just before the American Revolution, patriotic fellows who tarred and feathered Tories or anyone else who objected to their bullying tactics. A Bayman named Peanuts Murphy was their leader.

Mean Jake's will cut his sister some slack. She could parcel out the plots at her discretion, admitting people she thought brother Jake would have tolerated. "I'd go through eternity anytime with Tony Duke," her brother had allowed. Okay, too, was Gordon

Vorpahl, the genius mechanic who used to tune Jake's cars and who died in the pits at an auto race.

Maybe the Admiral would qualify. I resolved to ask Sis one day. If she was in a good mood, that is. Jake wasn't the only "mean" one in the family.

When I went to get the car, I just barely heard Susannah's (Jane's!) question:

"Alix, do you happen to know the family name of the gentleman whose bones they keep stealing? Mean Jake, I mean."

"Haven't the foggiest. Why, did you know someone like that?"

"Oh, no. Just curious."

Chapter Ten

He drank hard and drove fast. And died trying not to hit a deer...

My father had known Jacob Marley; I hadn't. But I knew about him. You couldn't live in East Hampton and not know about Jake.

Maybe wherever you lived in America, you knew.

Marley's father had been in the Cabinet, Eisenhower's, because of his wealth and connections. And when he found bureaucracy a stifling bore, he resigned and began giving away his money. The money came from real estate and construction. He put up some of the first shopping centers in America, and the rich man became even richer. And so he shared the wealth: museums, universities, research hospitals, beach erosion, cancer, regional theater, libraries, his alma mater, worthy causes, you know the sort of thing. Marley senior died before he'd spent all the money, and from there on, Marley's daughter, Sis, and his son, Jake, assumed the burden. She took her half and put it in municipal bonds and treasury notes; Jake used his to make more and gave still more away to the right causes. There was still plenty to go around; this was back in the fifties, before inflation, before prices went up.

Here in East Hampton people, some of them, came to think of Jacob junior as the meanest man in the world (meaning, he wasn't a soft touch and turned away spongers). To the country and the world, he was seen as an enlightened philanthropist who gave away plenty. Such people paid him homage, thought of him (with his second-generation money) as a patrician.

Marley was also a warrior who had enemies, both locally and around the States. He was contemptuous of most of them, gave grudging respect to a few even as he battled them. "It's my money and it's my land, my property," and in the end when he died, "my graveyard." That was his style. The classic face-off here in East Hampton was between the glacial patrician and the local riffraff, the trailer-park white trash. Or that's how it's been seen. Only his sister and a few others knew the injured heart at the core of the man, old and vengeful, who bought the churchyard for reasons maybe no one fully understood.

It wasn't always like that. Sure, he was tough; he hadn't always been bitter. Jake fell in love and married spectacularly. After two years and one son, she ran off with a cultivated adventurer. The son was raised by nannies and good prep schools. Jake doted on his boy. But one year out of Princeton young Marley also ran off with an adventurer. This one, female and not all that cultivated. She gave him a fun year or two. And left. Couldn't be bothered, I gather. Jake must have wondered if his line was cursed.

Jake's son made an effort, give him that. But he also drank hard and drove fast, and he was killed on Route 114 in North Haven, near the ferry slip, trying to avoid a deer and hitting a fieldstone wall instead.

Oddly, he was sober that time. And died saving a damned deer. On North Haven that November they voted to have a hundred local deer shot because they were pests and there were too many of them, and Jake's kid died trying not to kill one.

Jacob Marley was never really the same after that. Oh, he functioned. But he lost focus, permitted a young protégé to take on more and more of the work at the office, and began leaving small and eventually large decisions to the young man, whose name was Dick Driver. Marley was a great construction man. Driver wasn't much of a builder but an instinctive genius at dealing. The company called Marley Inc. became Marley & Associates. When Driver married a European glamour-puss named Nicole, Marley attended the wedding, sent lavish gifts. People who knew Jake said he'd begun thinking of Dick not merely as a protégé but a surrogate son. The firm became Marley & Driver. Then Marley/Driver & Partners. When the Drivers' child, a daughter, was born, Marley sent a corny card and an almost as laughable stock certificate for a few thousand shares in a promising new outfit called Microsoft. His own company was now Driver & Marley Associates. Then . . . well, you get the picture. There were tensions building, but despite them, each year, on her birthday, Dick and Nicole's daughter received a birthday card and stock. Not the kid's fault her father was manipulative and a user. Jake had plenty of the folding; money was never a problem. Control was. Jake just didn't have the muscle anymore. Driver turned out to have a gift. He made deals and the company grew even bigger, richer, more powerful. Never mind about construction; Dick could always hire architects and men who knew structural steel and reinforced concrete, contractors who understood the building codes. He encouraged Marley to indulge himself a little. Winters in Palm Beach. No need to come in to the office. Leave it to Dick. Play a little golf. Leave it to Mr. Driver. No, Mr. Marley hasn't retired; he's just not here very much. Mr. Marley? Not here, sir. He's abroad, traveling, ill, on vacation. But Mr. Driver's here; he makes those decisions. . . .

Mr. Driver makes *all* the decisions.

Dick Driver was the final straw in turning Marley antisocial. The roots of Jake's bitterness lay elsewhere and earlier. But Dick helped. Oh, yes, how he helped.

Alix, being English and of a family with a long genealogical tree, wanted to see the Old Churchyard, so I took her up Three Mile Harbor Road next morning for a quick gaze. Too cold to hang about. The Admiral was teaching Susannah/Jane speed chess. Fifteen seconds between moves. She seemed content enough, and I don't believe in pushing cemeteries when it comes to little kids. We took Alix's hummer and she drove.

I'd not seen the place for years, not since I was a schoolboy and cemeteries were places where you played and hid on dark nights, scaring hell out of passersby and, incidentally, yourself. I remember it in summer, all abloom, the grass greener than anywhere else, function of the fertilizing effects of moldering bodies, we all supposed. Now, in winter, pretty nice still. There wasn't a locked gate or anything, only a faded white board fence in need of fresh paint, and I led the way in, reading off the stones the old East Hampton names: Bennett, Talmage, Lester, King, Miller, Vorpahl, Osborne, Schellinger, Mulford, Gardiner, Price, Duryea, Gerard. And the dates, most of them in the 1800s, a few even earlier.

From here, you could smell the sea. Three Mile Harbor just to the west, Accabonac Harbor, and beyond that, Gardiners Bay and the ocean, just to the east. Maybe it was forty degrees, but there was wind and the damp was in it. You know that feeling. "Cold?" I asked, looking over at Alix, snuggled deep into a fur coat of some sort. Ocelot? I wondered but didn't ask. She shook her head.

"No. Well, a bit. Just the wind, actually. As I told your friend Mr. White about Père Lachaise, I like graveyards. The one up at Scarborough in Yorkshire is wonderful. Ever so many Brontes. Going there and walking between the stones, looking at the names, the dates, it's like carrying a small, leather-bound book of your favorite poems, and reading them aloud when you're all alone and not at all self-conscious, because no one's listening."

I slung an arm around her furred shoulder and hugged her close.

"That, too, is nice, Beecher. Both the Brontes *and* you."

"You can share me with the Brontes anytime."

She kissed me lightly. But very well. Then, brightly, "Do show me where Mr. Marley is, the chap whose bones they're always stealing. Do they just leave an empty hole or what?"

I remembered it was a mausoleum but had no idea where they'd sited it, nor was there any sort of rational layout that I knew of. But the Old Churchyard isn't very big, and there were only three or four aboveground structures, so we found Mean Jake without much trouble.

"Carrara marble," Alix said with some assurance, "you can always tell good Carrara. It's the bluish gray tint, y'know. Leonardo insisted on it, they say. No matter how distant the Tuscan quarry."

"Oh?" I'm not much on tombstones or marble. Though if it were good enough for Leonardo . . . But I recognize fresh hardware when I see it.

"Jake must be back. They wouldn't have put on a new deadbolt and lock if he weren't."

"I wouldn't think so," she agreed removing a sheepskin-lined glove to run a hand lightly over the lettering. Then, "I always like the stone to be a bit softened by age. You know, the way a good saddle doesn't feel precisely right until it's been ridden a bit."

Not being a rider I limited myself to, "I'm sure." And then, both of us feeling the chill, we got out of there and made our way back to the Hummer.

"Will there be snow?" Alix asked, regarding the gray sky.

"Not according to the Weather Channel, not yet. But sooner or later, sure. We always get snow out here."

"Oh, good. I do love snow."

Snow, the Brontes, graveyards, and me. To say nothing of Carrara marble. Alix had her enthusiasms. I looked over, enjoying and admiring her profile as she drove. God, she had a lovely face. Sensing my look, she half turned her head and smiled.

"Almost no one else takes me to graveyards the way you do, Beecher. I do love you for it."

"Almost" no one? "Almost"? Now what the hell did that mean?

59

Chapter Eleven

"That's the honey wagon. John K. Ott's cesspool service . . ."

Back in Manhattan, the summer people and subscribers to *New York* magazine are sure there's naught going on out here in the Hamptons in winter. Or, being contrarian, they imagine it's all very picturesque, precious even, the "nobs" roughing it in the cold.

And they're both wrong. They don't know about bodies being stolen out of churchyards or about the Bronte sisters or strange kids like Susannah le Blanc using pseudonyms or about Willie Morris's dog, Pete, or my old man playing speed chess and doing card tricks even without all his fingers. In our winters, much like the Season itself, people are born and die, they fall in love, go to the hospital, contest wills, are arrested for DWI, play the lottery, catch the flu, and get into fights at Wolfie's Tavern. Kids attend school. Even go to college in Southampton. And now and then there's a shooting in Montauk. The railroad issues a new timetable. Last winter two locals were busted for jacklighting deer behind the high school. In the damned parking lot! And local teens beat up a nice old gay man at Two Mile Hollow Beach just because he got excited and asked them home with him. Or a couple of Central Americans, who mow lawns in season, get into a knife fight over . . . well, *dinero* or a *muchacha*. Or up in Springs a deer loses a collision on Old Stone Highway, and three local fellows come out of the woods almost on signal to sling the carcass into a pickup. If there's no work and you're too proud to go on the welfare, or just wary of putting your name down on any sort of rolls, a properly dressed-out deer, roadkill or no, provides pretty good venison for a time. Or a hardworking young guy OD's on drugs and everyone agrees it's an aneurysm to spare the family. Or a fisherman named Reds Hucko falls off a dragger.

December in the Hamptons. Well, maybe it wasn't quite Pigalle with Toulouse-Lautrec and Jane Avril. But it wasn't Harold Ross's famous "Dubuque," either. So that next morning we took our visitor from Switzerland, whatever alias she was now using, for a little tour of the town.

With my father at the wheel of his old Packard touring car, intent on showing Susannah (or Jane) the Christmas decorations and other village sights, we turned into Main Street from Huntting Lane, passing a shiny white truck idling by the curb. Women, emerging from the Ladies Village Improvement Society, hurried by, stepping up their pace, their heads haughtily tilted leeward of the shiny white truck.

"Wow! What's that stink, Admiral?" Susannah inquired. You had to like that about her, a girl who spoke her mind clear and plain, no mincing about.

The old gentleman half turned to check. It was a chill, bright early-winter day, and you could see for miles. Painted colors stood out crisply against the polished white. Couldn't mistake the lettering.

"That's the honey wagon. John K. Ott's cesspool service. See their slogan on the back, 'There goes the poop-pee.'"

"Oh."

"You do know about cesspools, don't you?" he asked.

"*Bien sûr, cher amiral.*" Pause. "*Merde. Caca. Sheit.* But what do they do with it in the Hamptons?"

My father cleared his throat.

"I'm not quite sure how it's disposed of. Or where. But you can bank on John Ott. Provides an essential service in a courteous, professional manner. Reliable and discreet in such matters. It's solid, serious men like John Ott emptying cesspools, that make a town work, count on that, girl."

"Oh, look at what's on at the cinema. The new Liam Neeson film," Alix intervened, knowing about all she wanted to about Mr. Ott and the cesspools. "They say it's splendid."

"I've seen it," Susannah responded. "The nuns insist on the first-run releases."

"Jolly good!"

We pulled up in front of Village Hardware and crossed the lane to Dreesen's, the grocery store. Even out on the sidewalk you got the sweet smell of baking doughnuts, cleaning the stench of Ott's honey wagon from memory. Rudy, who owned the place, was at his accustomed station behind the meat counter in a white butcher's coat and apron, cutting lamb chops, while Raymond and Jimmy parceled out doughnuts, and idlers paged through the morning papers with no intention of wasting good money by actually buying them, half watching the stock futures over CNBC on the tube. My father rubbed his hands briskly. He liked Dreesen's, the loafers and the small-town bustle both, what we had in place of the village pump. And rubbing his hands stimulated circulation in those scarred and shortened fingers. Like the rest of us, he licked at his fingers as we shuffled along in line, lest the best of the doughnuts go to waste.

As we waited to pay, the Admiral explained just who Alix and her ward were. Only trouble, he introduced the kid to some people as Susannah, to others as Jane. Did the Pentagon know their senior spy was beginning to get names confused? Hardly a son's business to turn in his old man, I concluded.

Rudy, the owner, was all smiles. He never got anyone's name quite right and saw nothing amiss.

And now as we resumed our stroll, along came Jesse Maine, chief of the Shinnecock tribe, window-shopping.

"On my way to pick up a few things from Ralph Lauren. One of them genuine northwest-woods logger's shirts they got, all flannel and such," Jesse explained to my father, "like them pioneer days of yore we all claim to miss. If we Shinnecocks ever gonna be recognized as a genuine nation by the feds, we got a responsibility to start dressing the part. Ralph Lauren's flannel shirts, that's a dandy starter kit."

The Admiral nodded his agreement, but by now Jesse was in full flight:

It seemed, he explained, that the Shinnecocks had recently come into something of a financial windfall. Punitive taxes had hiked the price of a pack of cigarettes to nearly five dollars, while here on the tribal reservation in Southampton, the Indians were permitted by law to sell an entire carton, tax-free, for about twenty.

"It's a wonderful thing, democracy," said Jesse. "God bless America and all here assembled."

"Amen," murmured Susannah/Jane out of sheer good manners and convent teaching.

"And Sir Walter Raleigh, too," Jesse added, "the fella got white folks first hooked on Lucky Strikes and don't you ever forget it, kiddo."

"I shant," the child promised, though she'd not yet even been introduced. But Jesse didn't pause.

"A year ago we would have settled for Eddie Bauer flannel shirts. Maybe the Gap. Look at us now, patronizing Ralph Lauren." He shook his head in wonderment.

"You just consider that Senator Ben Nighthorse Campbell of the Northern Cheyenne down there in Washington sashaying about, casting vetoes, and going on *Meet the Press*, with society hairdressers competing to comb out his ponytail. That's what we Shinnecocks need, a genuine Native American look. Trouble is, most of us Shinnecocks is half to three-quarters African-American, and with hair like mine, it's hell doing ponytails." Then, having justified his window-shopping, he addressed me. "I heard you was back in town, Beecher. And Your Ladyship, too? Well, I'll be damned. This is a pleasure."

We all shook hands, with Jesse staring down from his great height at Susannah/Jane, as if to ask, "And just who might you be giving out 'amens'?" I made the introductions, giving Jesse his full due as far as titles and honorifics were concerned.

"I never met a Native American war chief before," the girl informed Chief Maine solemnly.

"Few do, Miss," said Jesse, "we are a reserved and careful bunch."

"But in history we studied the French and Indian Wars. The nuns are very big on wars in the middle form."

"Does them credit," Alix put in. "Were our chaps in that one?"

I assured her they were. "It was the French and Indians versus the Brits."

Jesse had his say, as well.

"I have read up on that war myself, Miss. But don't know many Frenchmen personally. Only Pascal the pastry chef at that joint in Water Mill."

"Miss le Blanc attends school in Switzerland," I explained absentmindedly.

"Pendragon," she corrected me in a hushed whisper that Jesse ignored.

"That's a place I never been. Not being all that much for scaling nor falling off Alps."

"There are flat places, too, Chief. And unlike what many believe, not all that much snow. In Geneva, for instance, there are palm trees growing along the lakeside."

Jesse shook his head. It wasn't that he doubted the child; simply that a war chief and tribal sachem withheld judgment until he had time to ponder the matter. Then, noncommittal but wanting to be genial, he assured Susannah: "You can check with Her Ladyship, miss, but what we lack in the Hamptons in palm trees and Alps, we make up for in grand times. Our Christmas out here is pretty special. Even the summer people trek enormous distances just to see it." He shook his head at memories of Christmas Past.

"I am so looking forward to it," Jane/Susannah assured him. "Christmas, that is. I've saved Martha Stewart's Christmas issue from last year as a sort of guidebook."

"My, my," Jesse said, "just think of it."

"Come along," said the Admiral as Jesse made his farewells and ducked inside Ralph Lauren's store to price the flannel shirts, "I believe that's Wyseman Clagett coming along, and I don't like that man."

Alix leaned down to alert our youthful guest.

"If Mr. Clagett does approach, avert your gaze. Try not to look directly into his face."

"Oh?"

"He has a monstrous tic that gives him the appearance of attempting to eat his own ear."

"I would dearly love to see it," Susannah said mildly. "We have nothing like that in Switzerland that I know of. Goiter among the peasants. But no tics of Mr. Clagett's sort."

Clagett had turned into one of the shops and was safely out of sight.

"Gone in to frighten the shopgirls, I suppose," my father remarked sourly.

That afternoon Alix and I were finally alone back at the gate house drinking tea, something I hadn't done since last she was in East Hampton. The tea wasn't very good, but that Alix bothered to brew it made it all right. More than right.

"Jane's quite something, Beecher," Alix informed me. "We chatted a bit last night at bedtime. She told me she prays every night, on her knees, that her parents will get back together somehow."

"I had the impression she felt herself well rid of them."

"No, she loves her mother and father; it's their current lovers she can't abide. Her mother has a chap called the 'Impaler.' And her father, I take it, has a serial relationship with any number of interchangeable young cover girls that Susannah dismisses as a group. Calls them Gidget. Wasn't that a cinema series, *Gidget Buys a Bikini*? That sort of thing."

"I believe so. But she still doesn't hint who the parents are?"

"No. Just goes on and on about how she wouldn't mind if her pa were involved with someone serious, intellectually weighty. A Brooke Shields, for example. And not these strumpets."

"She calls them 'strumpets'?"

"Well, no, that's my term, actually. Susannah refers to them as chippies."

Chapter Twelve

Corny cards, silly notes. "You shall have great expectations . . ."

It was my father who innocently (not trying to be clever or con the girl, not a bit of it) finally got out of Susannah just who she was. A thin morning rain was falling, but the huge, walk-in fireplace in his den threw out a dry, toasting warmth and soft light. I was having a second coffee while she and the Admiral played speed chess (fifteen seconds between moves), when Susannah, who was actually holding her own, asked apropos of very little:

"At the ice-cream shop Bob White told us the most extraordinary story, *mon cher amiral*, all about a gentleman called Mean Jake. And how enemies keep stealing his corpse. Right out of the grave-yard."

"True," said the Admiral. "Every word of it. Odd story, though. I agree with you on that."

"And did you know him? Mean Jake, I mean?"

"Surely did. Everyone knew Jacob Marley."

"Oh."

That was all. Just "oh."

But men who run Naval Intelligence are trained in the nuances

66

of a simple "oh." The Admiral sensed a shift in body language, in tone of voice, even as his young opponent was pulling off a rather sophisticated rook to king's pawn.

"Damn!" he said, annoyed to be caught by the move even as he admired it.

"Thank you," she said, flattered by the admiration and not at all nettled by his annoyance.

"Quite." He continued to watch her without seeming to do so. Then she spoke, very quietly, articulating the words carefully. Because they were important.

"My godfather's name, the one I wouldn't tell you; it was Jacob Marley. I suppose that's he, Mean Jake, I mean. Whose old bones keep getting stolen."

My father inhaled, his eyes on her face.

"I'm sorry, child. I had no . . ."

What can you say? The Admiral threw me a glance as if to say, "help me out, Beecher, for God's sake." He had murdered the Cold War enemies of his country and had fought several hot wars in addition. But he'd never had a daughter and was terrified by the idea of a child's sobs.

I got up and went to her, touching her shoulder, half-pat, half-stroke of, I dunno, support? Understanding? She nodded and reached up to pat my hand in response, then said quietly, no tears, no sobs, to both of us or neither of us, "I suppose I knew he was dead. The cards for my birthday stopped coming two years ago. I continued to get statements from Mr. Rousselot at the bank. But nothing from Mr. Marley. No corny card or little note. No more stock certificates." She paused. "I miss those silly cards, those little notes. Especially a scribbled line that always came at the end, 'You shall have great expectations.' The first few times I didn't know what that meant and then a girl at the convent told me that was what the convict told Pip, when they met in the graveyard in *Great Expectations*, which inspired me to read the book and learn about Estella and Miss Havisham."

So she missed Marley's corny birthday cards, his scribbled notes, his Dickensian assurance of "great expecations." No regrets over the stock certificates that stopped coming.

"And no one told you?" I said. "Not even your parents?"

She looked up at me.

"They'd be the last ones to keep me up-to-date on Jacob Marley. My father is Dick Driver, who took Mr. Marley's company away from him."

She pushed back then from the chess table and went to the window, with her back to the room and to us, looking out at what was left of the rain and at the morning sun struggling to get through. Finally, having pulled together conflicting memories— Marley's generosity to her, his antagonism toward her father, the sudden shock of learning he really was dead—she faced us and said: "They didn't speak. My father and Mr. Marley. Business differences of some sort. Terrible things happened. A big fight. Like breaking up Ma Bell as the government did years ago."

"They teach that in convent school? To ten-year-olds?" the Admiral asked, rather beside himself.

"Not really teach. More like every so often during *primes* Mother Superior regrets aloud various investments made or not made by the convent. She bet wrong on the Baby Bells versus AT&T."

"Oh, I see."

She went on about the Marley-Driver feud. "They didn't speak of him in my house. It was about the same time my mother and father were starting to divorce. So the two of them didn't speak at all. I was at the convent by then and was shy about asking there about Mr. Marley. After a year without having been told, I just assumed he was dead. I knew he loved me in his own way and wouldn't just stop writing. Not unless something terrible had happened."

"Poor kid," I said, thinking about being shunted off to the convent and her parents getting divorced and her godfather's dying all lumped together, and now without warning to find out people were stealing his body. Kids didn't need that, did they? But Susannah wasn't feeling sorry for herself, not at all. Just moving on.

"I still don't like it, Beecher, that they steal Mr. Marley's bones. No one dead should have his bones stolen, I don't believe."

The Admiral answered. "Of course they shouldn't. It's why sailors get buried at sea, the proper way. No vandals or graverobbers in the ocean, I can tell you. In any event, don't concern yourself, child. Ghoulish though it is, it's stupid local feuds at work. Don't mean anything by it. And, besides, no one can touch Jake anymore. Not really. Not the Bonac Boys. Not . . ."

". . . not my father."

"No, not your father. Just a shame Bob White had to tell the story in your hearing. Not that he realized there was a connection. None of us did, of course. Not until now. But it wasn't something you should have had to hear."

Alix came in then.

"Rain's over. Just look at that sky."

I gave her a high sign.

"You wanted to take Susannah shopping, didn't you?"

"Jane," Susannah corrected me.

"Silly Beecher," Alix offered, "can't keep the *noms de guerre* straight. Good thing his old dad's the spy and not Beecher."

"A spy? Are you, sir? Really?"

"Well, of a sort," the Admiral said. "Years back, when we and the Russians . . ."

"Tell me, do tell me, *kleine herr grossadmiral.*"

"Yes, yes, of course I will. Soon as you and Her Ladyship buy out the stores and come home."

Chapter Thirteen

Had I been prettier, my father would have spent more time with me...

If you read the newspapers at all, you knew about *Driver v. Driver*, the only divorce/custody case anyone ever heard of that ended up being adjudicated in the World Court at The Hague. That's how complex it was and how corrosive it became. It involved a variety of jurisdictions; for sheer bitterness it echoed *Kramer v. Kramer*; for bitchy infighting (and number of mentions in Page Six of the *New York Post*) it promised to challenge *Duff v. Perelman*; and for longevity, it threatened to be as enduring as *Jarndyce v. Jarndyce* in *Bleak House*, which went on for so long no one on either side could remember what the case was all about. Not even the lawyers or the Court of Chancery itself!

Prenups were part of the problem, of course, as was the wedding site, aboard a privately chartered yacht of Panamanian registry, owned by a Société Anonyme in Monaco, temporarily leased to a Baltic syndicate, which was sailing in international waters (the ship, not the Baltic syndicate). The ceremony had been performed by the ship's captain (himself a stateless person for reasons too complicated to spell out here), now missing and presumed dead in a subsequent Indian Ocean typhoon. Until the unfortunate captain's body was found, no finding of his competence or lack of same could be made. Whose was the jurisdiction? The sides couldn't even settle on a hemisphere, never mind a country, state, or Canadian province.

Nicole was a Mittel European with dual citizenship, Dick an American incorporated in the Bahamas. Those questions had had to be answered before a court and a judge could be assigned. Getting at Colonel Qaddafi and the Libyan terrorists was simpler. Long before the case moved on to The Hague, a lower court had denied both parents custody, deciding instead in favor of the prominent Wall Street merchant bankers Rousselot Frères as guardian pro tem, with the bankers in turn selecting the Couvent de la Tour Sacrée in Geneva to act in loco parentis. But only during term — not in school holidays or vacations. When the kid wasn't attending classes, guardianship reverted to the bankers. Trouble was, Little Miss Driver occasionally went missing.

What had the court especially cross was that Dick and Nicole seemed to take turns in having the girl kidnapped. Their own child. First by private detectives retained by her father, the second time by private detectives retained by the mother. Each parent was innocent, of course, denying culpability; they were acting out of love, simply intent on rescuing the child from fates worse than . . . well, you get the picture.

Now, several years later, child custody and child support remained the real sticking point. As with little Gloria Vanderbilt generations before, money was at the bottom of it, both cash and a mysterious trove (no one knew precisely how many shares there were!) of Microsoft stock certificates presently in the care of her guardian Rousselot Frères chairman Henry Rousselot. But those certificates were the property of a little girl who might or might not — depending on rumors and on that day's stock market — be one of the wealthier people in town. Was that possible? Or had her godfather's largesse been limited to a thoughtful few hundred thousand shares? Mr. Rousselot knew and wasn't saying. Nor was "the child." The child, of course, being "our" Susannah. Our "Jane." "I'm a plain girl," she said, neither apologetic or self-conscious, just a simple statement of fact. "And my mother being a great beauty, she's slightly embarrassed by me. And had I been prettier, I'm sure my father would have spent more time with me. He likes having pretty young girls around."

"But you're very . . ." I began. She ignored my politesse.

"I don't believe either of them actually wants me, Beecher," she assured me. "It's just that neither of them can stand the idea of the other winning anything, including me." All this with an extraordinary placidity and little, if any, hint of feeling sorry for herself. Then why would Dick and Nicole battle so tenaciously to retain or at least share custody? Could it be as Jane suggested, sheer bitchery? Was it those substantial custody payments that bothered him and drew her? Or was there a motivation we didn't yet understand? Real money, for example? Where would a ten-year-old child get serious money, unless it was those shares Jake Marley used to send on birthdays?

The Drivers were such dreadful people, one could only guess.

Nicole had her own concerns (beyond suing and being countersued by Dick), which very decidedly included her current beau. A child, well, kids got in the way, didn't they? But yet . . . Nicole was finding Count Vlad a somewhat expensive toy, and the child support all by itself was a major chip in the legal poker game she and her former husband were playing. The divorce had been granted (in but one court, there were multiple challenges elsewhere), but the final amount of child support (several million a year, in dollars) was still being haggled over (the World Court was not known for haste). Of course the money, whatever the figure, was earmarked for Susannah. But there was always a wink and a nod of understanding that the parent granted custody decides precisely how support payments are to be spent.

So far, quite normal in a messy divorce. Though, with Susannah Driver, there was the additional matter of that Microsoft stock.

Now that the secret of her actual name and parentage was out, Susannah was surprisingly eager to fill us in on just about everything. Which she did that night after dinner to a rapt audience of the Admiral, Her Ladyship, Inga the housekeeper, and me. Rather enjoying the role of pivotal figure, the child spun her tale. How accurate it was (given her penchant for the deft lie), or how complete, we had no way yet of knowing. But you had to admit it was a yarn worth listening to:

Her actual given name was . . . no, not Susannah. Nor Jane. It was Emma. Emma Driver.

"Yuckie, isn't it?" she asked rhetorically, before doing a bit of stage-setting, then diving straight back into her account, a narrative right out of Chaucer — "The Convent Girl's Tale."

I can assure you we were all listening as Emma began by telling us she was indeed ten years old ("virtually in my teens!"). The gorgeous Nicole, at seventeen an Olympic figure skater, now in her thirties, lived mostly in Europe, sleeping with and largely supporting Count Vladimir, a handsome, dashing, but dubiously titled playboy from Bucharest. The construction mogul Dick (no, he was not a riverboat gambler or a monk slaving over the prayer wheels) had a string of centerfolds. He was a ruthless real-estate developer (his speciality: the eviction of widows and orphans) with a vast ego (Ibsen's *Master Builder* might well have been about *him*, Dick modestly suggests; although he didn't know the story but loved the title!) and ambitions to match (in 1996 he attempted to lease Vancouver; more recently he'd bid on Governor's Island for a theme park and casino. Dick also suspected any day now someone will float his name as a future presidential candidate (never mind third parties, a *second* party was sniffing around, he hints).

Nicole had a career as well. She wrote (well, a ghost did the actual writing) treacly books on child rearing which, despite their transparent piety and hokum, had been enormously successful. Or were until the divorce got into the newspapers and gullible readers learned Nicole's own, and only, child, Emma Driver, aka Susannah le Blanc, had been from the age of five bundled in and out of a succession of boarding schools (the books rather quickly stopped selling!), finally settling more or less permanently at the Swiss Couvent de la Tour Sacrée and rarely seeing either self-absorbed parent except in court or when being kidnapped. (The lawyers insisted that "placed in protective custody" was the more appropriate term.)

One parent, Nicole, needed money; the other parent, Dick, needed to burnish a playboy's image. And their child seemed the key to both. To escape the reality of her predicament, Emma began to live largely in a world of books (Dickens, Hemingway, J. D. Salinger) and old films (Shirley Temple and horror movies were special favorites), and had become a convincing and very practiced liar. When asked about her parents (especially why they almost never bothered to visit her), she would concoct Walter Mitty-esque identities for each of them.

Despite their chill disinterest (if the kid couldn't be *used*, then what possible *use* was she?), Emma was proud of her parents. They truly were beautiful people, both of them, and she wasn't. So she kept scrapbooks. Two cover stories in *People*, one in *Newsweek* (more about her father than about Nicole), and numerous *National Enquirer* coverlines. Some girls at the convent had no press clippings at all about their parents.

Perhaps her most winning invention was the identity of her mother's lard-headed, if sexy, latest—the count, whom Emma explained was a linear descendant of Vlad the Impaler, the literary inspiration for the original *Count Dracula* and known familiarly to her and her mother (though not in his hearing) as the Impaler. When a schoolmate would ask, "What's an 'impaler'?" Emma would plunge without hesitation into detailed, deliciously gory descriptions. But a little knowledge is a dangerous thing. Especially inside the head of a precocious child.

Emma was drawn into an even more pernicious habit than card playing, lying, or smoking Gitanes: the careful reading of American magazines to remind her of what home was like. And to remind her that she was still a Yank. In the boarding school's library, she came across a dog-eared copy of *Martha Stewart Living: The Christmas Edition*, which had an enormous impact on the impressionable child, and as the Christmas holidays were approaching and the other girls packing to go home until the New Year, Emma evolved a romantic, if not very practical, scheme, starting with a convincing and quite plausible E-mail message to each parent suggesting she would be spending Christmas with the other.

And a third E-mail to Rousselot explaining she would be visiting with a classmate's family in Tuscany. By court order, Dick and Nicole were observing a sullen truce, and neither felt free to raise a voice in protest. And in an instance of slovenly staff work, nobody at Rousselot Frères bothered to check with the "host family" in Tuscany. Once Emma's falsehood was established, she set off for East Hampton, where childish memory recalled a happier time when her parents were still together and she herself was innocently happy. And where she intended to present herself at the front door of . . . ta dah! Martha Stewart herself!

But there was another, naïve though fiendishly clever agenda at work here. As with all children whose parents have split, she hoped that Nicole and Dick would one day get back together. No matter that the Impaler had moved in with Nicole or that Dick was sporting with his tootsies. For kids, the world presents endless opportunities and infinite wonders. And Emma came up with a scheme: If her parents thought that she had vanished over the Christmas holidays — not kidnapped yet again by their respective private eyes but by unknown third parties preying on the offspring of the rich — and that she might be in actual peril, wouldn't they make every effort to track her down? And, as both parents galloped to the rescue, arriving dramatically in the Hamptons amid falling snow and holiday cheer, they would forcibly come together once again as a family?

So off she went, leaving behind a few cleverly planted clues (plus a few false leads) so that her parents could pick up the scent, just not too quickly. The clues, her bread crumbs, were easily traced credit-card charges and E-mail messages. And being mischievous (and undeniably a bit spoiled) Emma did what kids do in such situations: She played off one parent against the other, sending Nicole and Dick highly imaginative and provocative E-mails: "Just imagine where Daddy's taking me tomorrow — to a taping of the Letterman show! Then dinner at Le Cirque 2000." And, "Mommy and I lunched at the Paris Ritz in the Espadon Grill (where, as you know, Princess Di ate her last meal!) and we went shopping on the Faubourg St. Honoré. She bought me an Hermès scarf and the most delicious party dress at Lanvin Jeunes Filles!"

Armed with her very own platinum card, Emma entrained for Paris, where she boarded the Concorde to New York, a crude map of the Hamptons (and directions to Martha's house) having been provided by a schoolmate. One transatlantic crossing and Long Island RR train ride later, she got off at East Hampton, hailed a cab to Lily Pond Lane and Martha Stewart's house, only to find it shuttered and dark in the chill gloom of late afternoon.

But the kid was nothing if not resilient (not quite Tatum O'Neal in *Paper Moon*, but close), and so she ordered the cabbie to take her back into East Hampton village. Amid the first few snowflakes of early winter, she went to a movie and, while mulling her next move, alone in a strange place, took shelter and a meal at the Blue Parrot, which is where I, Beecher Stowe, encountered our little heroine.

"Well, Emma . . ." the Admiral began when she finished.

"Isn't that an awful name? Emma?"

My face may have given me away, but Alix was smoother. "Not at all. Emma's a smashing name. Can you imagine going through life as Alix? Jane Austen did an entire book about an Emma, as I recall. Or was it Fielding? I like Emma, enormously, don't you, Beecher? Admiral?"

My father and I stumbled over each other issuing insincere assurances. But Alix carried the ball.

"Let me say this, Su—I mean, Emma. Your name is gorgeous. Byronic. Perhaps more than Byronic. Keatsian. I'd say Shakespearean if it weren't so much more modern. Not twentieth century, precisely. Much more late nineteenth, which is far more interesting. Yes, Emma, decidedly Victorian, better still, neo-Victorian, don't you agree?"

Emma Driver rolled her eyes at all this polite rubbish and raised one eyebrow. But she was tolerant, didn't really put all of us in our place as she had every right to do, restricting herself to a single remark before, blessedly, changing the abhorrent subject:

"As a name, Emma stinks. But, *tant pis*! Thanks for being nice about it. *Et maintenant, mes amis*, can we get on with matters at hand, such as a hand of poker, Admiral, old top? A fifty-cent limit, deuces and one-eyed jacks wild?"

Chapter Fourteen

Burning churches, shooting priests,
raping nuns at a great rate . . .

Tom Knowles called. My boyhood pal was now a detective lieutenant on the Suffolk County force.

"Beecher, there's a foreign woman with sinister overtones staying
at the American Hotel in Sag Harbor and asking pointed questions."

"A novelist," I suggested. "Got to be a novelist. They don't rent
rooms to anyone who isn't writing a novel. Ted Conklin has a
rule."

Mr. Conklin is a great snob who owns the place and in summer
won't permit Bermuda shorts in the restaurant or bar. And there
was a local understanding he would not at any time rent rooms to
people who weren't authentic artists or authors. "Novelists are
best," he'd tell you. Ted had only twelve rooms, eight of them
permanently occupied by people writing the Great American
Novel. It was that sort of place, with an atmosphere of that caliber.
Or, if the guests were painters, they were cubists. The occasional
neo-impressionist. Ted believed in the artistic traditions of the
place and maintained standards. As a result, it was a grand place
to eat, to drink, or even to stay (*if* you were an artist).

"Sure, I know," Tom said. "But this dame is looking for a small girl."

"How small?"

"Beecher, don't fence. I don't know what you're up to on Further Lane, but I hear talk of a kid being seen around, staying with you and the Admiral and Her Ladyship. No skin off my nose at homicide. So I'm not prying, just giving you a friendly heads-up."

I told him I appreciated it, and I did. And gave him a conventional out as to Emma. "You mean, Alix's ward."

"Whatever," the detective said. He saw through me like pane glass. Always could. So I turned the conversation back to the mysterious lodger in the American Hotel.

"What sort of woman? And what sinister overtones?"

"That's the odd thing. Mid-thirties, maybe forty tops. Tall and with bearing, carries herself well. Reasonably attractive in a severe sort of way. European, I'd wager. She identified herself as a nun." He paused, then added, "Possibly one of Mother Teresa's flock."

Nuns at the American Hotel? Had Ted Conklin wigged out? He might have bent a rule for Mother Teresa herself. But not for "one of the flock." I thanked Tom and got hold of Emma.

"Well," I said, regret and resignation both in my voice, neither of them feigned, "the game's up, kid. Didn't take them a week but they've tracked you down."

Alix and I swiftly convened a council of war in the Admiral's library. Joining us, as he had in earlier adventures, was Chief Maine of the Shinnecocks, famed as a local poacher and a man you wanted on your side in tight places. Besides, he was there at my father's house already, replacing dowels in a staircase banister for contractor Dale Uhll, with whom Jesse frequently worked.

"Mmm," Emma said, not at all panicked but coolly assessing the situation. "I wonder who sent her."

"Your school, of course," said the Admiral. "Took them a few days to act but, by God, they've done it. Mother Teresa's global networks, I suppose. Got to admire their efficiency even if it is rough on you."

"A shame," Alix said. "We'd been so looking forward to taking

78

Emma to the covered-dish supper at Nick and Toni's for hospice care. And the iceboating Beecher promised. But now you'll be back with your mum and pa, I suppose. Or at the convent."

I started to explain the covered-dish supper was at the Presbyterian Church, not at Nick & Toni's, but Emma got there first.

"Don't leap so quickly to conclusions, Lady Alix. This may be a transparent ruse."

"You mean this nun isn't from your school?" I said. "You don't run into that many nuns in the Hamptons, whatever the season. How can you be sure?"

"First of all, *our* nuns had nothing whatever to do with Mother Teresa. Hardly the sort to go about begging alms. Mother Superior wouldn't have it. And besides, Mother Teresa's dead . . ."

"Oh, damn!" said Alix, "how stupid of me. Of course she is. It was in the *Times*. They had a very decent obituary."

". . . and our convent is closed for the Christmas hols. Except for Igor the caretaker that you spoke with, Beecher, and Sister Euphemia, the one who lost her foot to the tram in Zurich, the nuns are all in Paris meeting with couturiers, fingering swatches, getting quotes, and negotiating volume discounts on new habits. Check with Dior or Ungaro if you doubt me. You won't catch a single Bride of Christ wintering in the Hamptons when she can be sipping a kir in the cafés of the Boulevard St. Germain and chatting up the Paris couturiers."

My father, of course, having been for so long chief of Naval Intelligence, and with reliable operatives everywhere (an international city such as Geneva might boast of several!), was the one man in the Hamptons in a position to check. Within seconds over the E-mail he was on to someone in Geneva called Marcel.

"Concierge at the second-best hotel in all Switzerland, ranked by the *Guide Michelin* just behind the Baur-au-Lac in Zurich," my father provided us an aside, "knows bloody everyone. Been on our payroll for years. Used to freelance for the KGB as well. Nice sense of the absurd, which, considering he worked for both sides in the Cold War, was a prerequisite. And you could trust the man. The KGB did as well. Gentlemen's agreement of sorts. Fine chap, stout fellow. When you bought Marcel, he stayed bought. You like a reliable man like that."

It took Marcel about fifteen minutes.

"Here's his reply: 'The caretaker assures me the school is padlocked until January 4 or 5. Local shopkeepers confirm Igor's account. Their subscription to the *International Herald Tribune* and scheduled deliveries of Evian water both suspended for a fortnight. Only a crippled old dame who drinks is still on site.' "

"There, you see," Emma broke in, "I forgot to mention Sister Euphemia takes a cocktail. Says it deadens the ache in her missing foot."

The Admiral continued to read Marcel's report: "The rest of the nuns are shopping in Paris or skiing at Megeve."

"That's odd," Emma remarked, wrinkling her brow.

"Yes, I agree," said the Admiral. "The very idea, nuns skiing."

"That isn't what I meant, *gran maestro*. It's the part about Megeve. They customarily ski at Alpe d'Huez, where they get a very nice clerical discount on the lift tickets. Mother Superior always demands a good discount."

So there we had it. The nuns were all off skiing or in Paris dickering with Dior. Who, then, was this woman at the American Hotel? And what explanation could there be other than that she was tracking Emma Driver?

"A nun suddenly arrives looking for a little girl in the Hamptons in winter," I protested. "It beggars the imagination that there could be more than one missing child or one nun who—"

"*Cher ami* Beecher," Emma said, "do not upset yourself. I simply suggest this woman may be an outright fraud. The Convent of the Tour Sacrée is very handsomely endowed. No Mother Teresa begging bowls or hanging about with the Untouchables and similar castes, I assure you. This may not be a Bride of Christ at all, but an imposter hired by mercenaries to track me down. Don't forget my own parents have had me kidnapped previously. It could be that one of them is at it again. Or perhaps this time it's someone else, a mercenary, in it for pecuniary reasons."

80

"Kidnappers, Beecher!" Alix put in hurriedly. "Recall John Buchan's *Three Hostages*, three young people spirited away by that clever fiend Dominick Medina, leaving Sir Richard Hannay and Sandy Arbuthnot to rescue the victims."

"But a nun . . . ?" I challenged her.

"Recall that Medina, until he was unmasked, had been a confidant of the king and one of the most admired men in parliament. A published poet as well."

"Quite true," my father added. "And Emma did speak of kidnap threats in first explaining her parents' use of pseudonyms. The child certainly gives you fair warning. Doesn't spring surprises on you."

Jesse Maine shook his head. "It sets my blood to boiling, I can tell you. You'd think we was dealing here with the damned Pequots. After all these years of uneasy peace, they're back at it. And hiding this time behind holy women dedicated to prayer and good works, out there with their rosary beads, aiding and abetting the Untouchables."

"Brides of Christ at that, let's not forget," Alix added.

"Who are the Pequots?" Emma asked. "I'm not up to speed on them."

"Mean bastards, forgive my language, miss. But if the Pequot Indians is on your trail, you got problems. They never quit. Relentless as bloodhounds. If you got Pequots, you got countless woes besides."

"Oh, dear," Alix said, recalling earlier Shinnecock difficulties with the Pequots.

"But then," said Emma, "please recall that we studied the French and Indian Wars last semester. Montcalm and Wolfe on the Plains of Abraham. Perhaps your Pequots were involved there, too, Chief?"

"Not at all surprised if they was. Probably they was at the root of it. Usually are. And working with both sides at once, Wolfe and that other fellow, Mount Comb, both. Tricky as snakes."

"It just occurred to me, then, that many of our nuns are French

81

royalists whose minds dwell largely in the seventeenth century, under the Louises. Such women, no matter how saintly, are no friends of democracy."

" 'Looies'? What looies might they be?" Jesse inquired.

"Kings of France, chief. All their kings used to be named King Louis."

"Good gawd ahmighty," Jesse said, perhaps thinking of sowing confusion among the Pequots along those lines. He looked as if he were going to ask how the French told them apart if they all had the same name. But thought better of it. Not my father, who appeared ready to explode.

"Damned women! Calling themselves Brides of Christ but scheming with royalists, and against democracy. Wasn't Mother Teresa devoted to the poor, the homeless? How can the Catholic Church encourage such people yet send poor Teresa out begging alms? And how are *we* expected to fathom them? We're Episcopalians!"

He calmed down then, his hearty assertion of Episcopalianism providing comfort.

"Did your policeman friend tell you what name the nun was using, Beecher?"

"Why, yes, Emma. Sister Infanta de Castille. Mean anything to you?"

The girl shook her head. "No, it's not a name I've ever heard at the convent. But it's clearly Spanish, and the nuns at Tour Sacrée, even the French ones, are historically partial to the Spaniards. First of all, the Inquisition. Which fell in neatly with their notion of discipline and keeping good order. Torquemada and all that. But only the more subtle tortures, not the thumbscrew." More recently, she said, *Mesdames* of the Sacred Tower had been all for Franco and the Falange.

"But Franco was a fascist, having cocktails with Hitler and Mussolini," I protested.

"Yes, but the Madames are rarely swayed by public-opinion polls. They go their own way. And don't forget, while clearly fascist, Franco's nationalists were fighting the loyalists, who were burning churches, shooting priests, and raping nuns at a great rate. Why, in Salamanca alone . . ."

I glanced over at my father, who looked more than uncomfortable. For all his bloody career in global espionage, he wasn't accustomed to having ten-year-old girls discussing the rape of nuns. And it got him going again.

"What kind of Brides of Christ *are* these?"

"Emma never heard of this woman," I pointed out. "She probably isn't a Bride of Christ at all, but a fraud."

Emma thought for a moment.

"There are affiliated convents, *s'il vous plaît, mes amis.* In St. Tropez, Bali, Monaco, St. Barth's. So Sister Infanta may yet be genuine, while unknown to me. But Beecher could be on to something: After all, I use pseudonyms; why can't the enemy?"

"Got to like this kid's thinking, Beecher," Jesse Maine announced. "Won't find Emma taking a lollipop from the dirty old man at the schoolyard."

"*Merci beaucoup,* Chief," she said. "Most gracious of you. And, having been alerted, I shan't go anywhere near the Pequot tribe."

"A wise and prudent decision," he told her.

Chapter Fifteen

Emma looked about as harmless and vulnerable as a scorpion.

We lazed about in the winter sun on the front lawn of my father's house, all of us, enjoying a frivolous morning warmth that could hardly last, when Doc Whitmore went by on Further Lane peddling hard atop his battered bicycle.

"Look at that, Jane," the Admiral ordered from the bridge, as if moving midshipmen and ensigns to action stations—and getting their names wrong. "That's Doc Whitmore, the tree surgeon. Knows bloody all about trees and hedge. His brother a few years back gave a million or three to the local college. So there's money in tree nurseries. Not that Doc bothers about it. Rides about all year on that old bike of his, whatever the weather. Got to be older than I am, at a minimum. My neighbor Dr. Barondess, who knows such things, says Doc'll bury all of us with the cardiovascular system he's got."

Emma watched the bicycle disappear with a farewell wave from Doc.

"I don't think Doctor Whitmore's wearing socks. Is that possible?"

"Famous for it. Winter, summer, never a sock. But you saw his earmuffs."

The girl thought for a bit.

"In a Swiss winter, you wear socks. Even the peasants."

Leave it to Alix to break the impasse.

"Suppose I drop by the American Hotel and chat up this Bride of Christ? You know, check to see if she's wearing proper nun shoes, that sort of thing. Obviously we can't send Susannah . . ."

". . . Jane!"

". . . I mean, Jane, Emma. Sorry."

"Not a bad idea," the Admiral agreed. "A reconnaissance on the ground. Say what you will about satellites, U-2 planes and spies-in-the-sky, nothing beats a first hand re-con. Look the fellow in the damned eye, straight on. Sniff his breath, test the cut of his jib."

The Admiral was very stern when it came to the "cut" of some-one's jib, sniffing a man's breath.

Lady Alix had the Humvee warmed up in a moment, and I climbed in next to her. "Just for backup, darling," I assured her. "The way Colin Powell went riding with General Schwarzkopf in the Gulf War."

"Of course."

The Admiral seemed relieved to be rid of us. Inga had our child guest in hand, and my father said he had calls to make. Sounded like business. And with him, "business" meant intelligence. Fine with me. Actually, I just wanted to be alone with Alix.

Everywhere you turned around in my father's house, there were calls from Suffolk County homicide and visits by Shinnecock chiefs or E-mail from Marcel the concierge and kids playing poker and in peril of being kidnapped. None of which was very helpful in managing a love affair. And it wasn't just next door in my father's place; people were forever coming into the gate house to say hello or to have a hearty little chat. I kept trying to get Her Ladyship undressed and into bed and couldn't even arrange to be alone with her without a delegation of concerned citizens on hand.

En route to the American Hotel and its resident nun, we lunched, so as to have a brief moment together, at Babette's res-taurant on Newtown Lane. Bill Clinton once stopped by the place, and they've been living off it ever since. In winter, in the Hamptons, you take lunch where you can get it.

"Can we smoke here?" she asked.

"I don't think so. But give it a try. If they accepted Clinton, why not the odd coffin nail."

"Mmm," she said thoughtfully, half to herself. "I don't have any. Should have borrowed a Gitanes from Emma."

She was inside the American Hotel less than an hour while I loafed about, whistling tunelessly and imitating your everyday innocent bystander, pretending to window-shop up and down Main Street.

"Damn!" Alix reported on emerging. "This is murky business indeed. There's been nothing like it in my reading since the Babington Plot of 1586 . . ."

"Which was?"

". . . a scheme to assassinate Queen Elizabeth and put Mary, Queen of Scots, on the English throne."

"Think of that," I said, duly impressed. "So she wasn't wearing nun shoes?"

She ignored the question. "When I realized I wasn't getting very far with her, I inquired how one went about enlisting in the Brides of Christ. Said I had a powerful mystical experience at Cap d'Antibes recently that suggested I might have a religious vocation. I'd always been a materialistic sort until now. How could I make amends? Where did I apply? Were there forms to fill out? Initiation fees? Letters of reference? Get Oxford to recommend me. Anything that would impress God. Or whoever it is that welcomes new nuns into the club. And so on."

"And?"

"She was quite snippy. And in a superior sort of French accent. Said it helped if one were a Catholic."

"Sarcastic, was she?"

"I even offered to convert if they let me take orders. That's how enthusiastic I was. Love little children. Dying to tutor young minds. All that terribly sincere bosh . . ."

"Which she wasn't buying."

"Not a farthing's worth. I felt quite deflated."

"What did you make of her? Beyond your suspicion she may not be a nun?"

"Good. She's very good. A professional of some sort. I can usually charm pensioners out of their chocolates. This one didn't give an inch. Not a millimeter. Like you, Beecher, she's a hard case."

I loved it when Alix called me "a hard case."

We were back at Further Lane about four. I had a wild notion about slipping back with Alix into my gate house for a bit of a romp before cocktails and . . .

"Mr. Beecher!"

It was my father's housekeeper, Inga.

"Yes?"

"Tea, sir."

Uh-oh.

Over tea Alix briefed us all on the American Hotel's "nun." But it was sufficient to set my father raging.

"Despite my doubts, Admiral, I'll concede a slim possibility she could be the genuine article, a Bride of Christ and all that," Alix began. "When I told her how eager I was to become a Catholic . . ."

"You didn't!" the Admiral declared.

". . . not in all sincerity, Admiral, no. A ploy of sorts."

"Well, then, that's better . . ."

"But she gave me this rosary, sprinkled me with holy water, and we prayed together. On our knees right there on the floor of the hotel room, much as Mr. Nixon and Dr. Kissinger did that night in the White House so long ago . . ."

The Admiral wasn't buying that, not without rebuttal.

"Don't believe everything you read, Lady Alix. The *Washington Post* is a decent paper and Bob Woodward a fine journalist. But he has a lively imagination when it comes to setting scenes he never witnessed. Did Nixon describe this fascinating moment, praying with Henry? Or did Dr. Kissinger speak of it later? Woodward cites no sources. Being an Oxford graduate with a skeptical mind, you must be aware of this."

I thought to myself, without siding with my dad and against Her Ladyship, that Alix did have a way of drawing on the damnedest allusions.

Without conceding the point, Alix continued as if in the same breath. ". . . and she urged me to renounce Satan. And all his works and pomps."

Even the Admiral looked impressed at that. Episcopalians like hurling defiance at the powers of darkness.

"She just might be the goods," he conceded.

Emma looked dubious. "Admiral, at the convent they're forever renouncing Satan. But then, don't all decent people anywhere? No one goes around boasting he and Satan are like that, y'know. Doesn't prove she's a nun at all. Anyone can renounce Satan . . ."

". . . and his works and pomps?" Alix asked. "Don't forget those."

My father got up to pace a bit. "I'm calling Conklin. His instincts are pretty sound. Let's see what he has to say."

When he reached the owner of the American Hotel, they spoke for perhaps ten minutes. As my father hung up, he turned back to us, his face thoughtful.

"Ted's a decent chap, a Protestant. Was skeptical at first. But he thinks your Infanta de Castille may indeed be legitimate. The LVIS, for one, has asked her to speak at their weekly lunch . . ."

"The LVIS?" Emma asked.

"Ladies Village Improvement Society. Very respectable local body. Mostly Protestants," the Admiral explained. "But there's more."

"Oh?"

"Yes. Ted Conklin says *60 Minutes* may be doing a story. Don Hewitt lives out here, and he heard about this Bride of Christ in the Hamptons. Thinks there's a big story in her. A holy woman doing good works, counseling the local Baymen, assuring them that a man lost at sea, such as this fellow Reds Hucko, may not be lost at all. That they can pray him back to life. Or at least retrieve the corpse."

"That's certainly rubbish!" I broke in. "Hucko was washed overboard Thanksgiving week in the North Atlantic. And a nun is telling East End Baymen he's still alive? That they can *pray* him back into port?"

The Admiral ignored my protest. He didn't mind criticizing Catholics; he wasn't attacking prayer. Then, he went on:

"Ted Conklin says the *60 Minutes* business has the media on its competitive toes. Tina Brown has a writer sniffing around the Montauk docks. Sister Infanta might be a story for *Talk* magazine. Or even a movie idea for the Weinstein brothers, you know, the triumph of faith in a secular age. And you know McLaughlin on Further Lane, the power behind Rush Limbaugh? He and Nick Verbitsky, who runs those Dick Clark radio stations, they're underwriting a testimonial at Jerry Della Femina's. While Steve Brill's threatening to expose all of them as opportunists, exploiting Sister."

That's all we needed, media tycoons!

My father nodded, as if reading my thoughts. "Along with all that, Beecher, the Papal Nuncio is coming up from Washington for the testimonial dinner."

The Nuncio? The Vatican's man in the States? It was impressive, but I wasn't going to get all teary; I had a Rolodex of my own.

"Whom are you calling?" my father asked.

"Peggy Siegal in Manhattan." Peggy might be the "flack from hell," but she was wired. Peggy usually knew what was going on, had her sources in Rome and a pal who covered religion for *Time*. When I sketched out the position here, she thought for a moment.

"You know the Vatican," she told me. "They're shrewd. If the Nuncio vouches for her, this woman is legit. Remember, during the war even Stalin was impressed. Asked, 'And how many battalions has the Pope?' "

"Golly," said Her Ladyship, "sounds to me as if we're a bit outgunned here. Poor Emma. The Pope himself and all those battalions on her case."

Emma Driver just sat there, sober and quiet in one of my father's leather easy chairs, listening to all this.

"I don't think she's a Bride of Christ at all," she announced. "I think she's a private eye hired to track me down."

Even my father protested.

"But if the Ladies' Village Improvement Society, as well as Peggy Siegal and the Catholic Church . . ."

"*Je m'excuse*. Don't forget, *maestro*, my parents have utilized private eyes before, 'all the better to kidnap you with, my dear,' " she recited, mimicking the wolf that ate Grandma.

"But, Emma, not togged out as a nun, holding prayer meetings . . . ?"

Deep inside the Admiral's big old leather armchair, Emma fell silent, skinny legs tucked under her schoolgirl kilt, never looking younger, smaller, or more vulnerable. I found myself feeling absolutely protective toward the poor kid, this defenseless child. But then she grinned, as if delighted to be at the center of excitement, recalling earlier kidnappings, saddened by her parents' mutual detestation and anger but otherwise enjoying the adventure: speeding cars, sinister figures lurking, disguises and midnight raids, private eyes and other hired guns.

And when she grinned at such secret memories, Emma looked about as harmless and vulnerable as a scorpion.

Chapter Sixteen

"Bill Gates? A nerdy guy in glasses. Invented the laptop or something..."

"I don't really care if the wretched woman is a genuine nun or not," the Admiral declared. "Unless someone convinces me of error, I have no intention of sending this child back to such charlatans. Child prostitutes on the streets of Manila. 'Henri Dansant,' indeed, 'light in his loafers.' Religious habits being sewn up by the Maison Dior. Nuns skiing in the Alps, negotiating discounts on their lift tickets. The ramifications of a convent school being operated along such lines are simply staggering." Then, looking Emma directly in the face, he declared adamantly, "With all due respect, young lady, you won't find Episcopalians carrying on so."

"I suppose not," conceded Emma amiably. She wasn't terribly fierce on proselytizing for Rome.

Having gotten that off his chest, the Admiral shifted gears in a very curious way:

"Emma?" he began.

"Jane, sir," she said, sensing the Admiral preferred working with aliases.

"Yes, Susannah. Do you by any chance know who Bill Gates is?"

The child answered right away, though why did it matter?

"A nerdy guy in glasses. Invented the laptop," she said. "Or a search engine or portal or something. He's awfully rich. My father speaks of him in awed tones, which he does of very few, and almost never of nerds."

"Why do you ask, father?" I couldn't resist putting in.

The Admiral gave me a mischievously jolly look, amused by my having fallen for his move, much as he enjoyed sucking an opponent into a trap at chess and crying "checkmate!"

"Simply want to know how up on current events are the middle-form girls of the Couvent de la Tour Sacrée."

I got him aside later.

"What was that Bill Gates business all about?"

"I've made some calls. I'm not quite sure what's going on. But there's a bit of a stir at Microsoft. No question of a hostile takeover or even a proxy fight, of course. Gates has firm control. It would take someone with the resources of Gates's former partner, Paul Allen, and then some, to make a serious run at Microsoft. But with these various lawsuits going on and the federal government harassing him, Mr. Gates is believed to be looking over his shoulder with more than the usual caution."

". . . at Emma?" I said, not masking incredulity.

"Don't be impudent," he advised me. "I'm not sure. Just that my sources tell me there's a bit of concern about very large blocs of Microsoft shares on the loose. Not answerable to this clique or that, or nailed down by anyone, neither the Board or an insurgent slate. Just out there, under the control of vague trust funds managed by who knows whom. Gather sufficient of those blocs of shares and sooner or later, you've got yourself a substantial position in Microsoft stock." He paused. "I don't follow the gossip columns as closely as you do, and I should, but even a cursory reading of the *Driver v. Driver* divorce hardly speaks well of her parents. Cold-blooded and selfish. You suspect it's not beyond them to cheat young Susannah . . ."

". . . Emma."

"Oh, damn! Can't the child settle on one name or another?"

"You were saying?" I asked, trying to get him back on track.

"Yes, yes. What little I know of her parents, I wouldn't put it past either of them to cheat her out of the holdings of Microsoft, all that stock Jake Marley supposedly settled on her. Not actually steal the shares but vote them one way or another, leveraging control of the child's property to their own advantage."

"Her trust funds."

"Yes, Beecher. Emma's situation is hardly unique. Millions of blue-chip shares in the names of minor children. Left to them in wills. Or signed over at birth." My father paused briefly. "You've heard of such things, haven't you? In your journalistic endeavors and inquiries?" Oh, he could be sarcastic, having never quite forgiven me for going directly from Harvard to work at the *Boston Globe* as a cub reporter, rather than becoming a banker. Or joining the CIA.

The Admiral issued no additional enlightenment until, as I wrestled with the possibilities, Her Ladyship joined us again in my father's den.

"My ward Jane wants to know if anyone's in the mood for a hand of poker?" Alix asked amiably.

The Admiral's bluntly growled "No!" was shocking in its vehemence. He must have seen Alix's stunned reaction and my face. As for me, I wondered if his hearing had suddenly gone, and as old men do, didn't realize he was yelling.

"Sorry," he said mildly, "didn't mean to shout."

"Quite all right, Admiral," Alix said, her voice cool as cucumber sandwiches at tea. "Only a suggestion, y'know."

"I know, I know . . . it's simply that I did play with her the other afternoon."

"And . . . ?"

The Admiral set his jaw.

"She cheats," he said.

Chapter Seventeen

Lefty Odets "nearly" helped break "the
Westies" and "almost" went on Letterman . . .

So the kid was a card sharp. But where were her parents, whose chill indifference had sent a child careering halfway across the hemisphere in search of a spare room at Martha Stewart's B & B, and just what mischief were they truly up to?

Her father, it so happened, was easy to trace, having just (yet again) been profiled in *People* magazine, the news peg this time Dick Diver's recent and astonishing disclosure of his plans for the afterlife.

"When my latest building (the tower on Sutton Place) is up and running, surely one of the seven wonders of the modern world, I intend to designate it my final resting place."

The plan?

"One of my few heroes is Jeremy Bentham, the legendary English don who founded and headed University College London. I expect to emulate Bentham."

The reporter shook his head. Just what was it that Bentham did, actually?

"He had himself mummified and set up in an appropriate

setting at University College and, to this day, functions as the institution's totem and principal tourist attraction."

Being still alive, and not yet embalmed, Emma's father was scarcely a hundred miles away in the penthouse suite of his Manhattan tower, fresh from a few days golfing with Prince Andrew at Lyford Cay, assiduously poring over architectural renderings of yet another future Manhattan tower intended to blot out what little remained of urban sunlight. As Dick Driver worked, a gorgeous young woman, his girlfriend *du jour* and the last Miss Lithuania but one, sauntered into the paneled study bearing a silver serving tray, the crystal goblets and ice bucket in Waterford, his Diet Dr. Pepper freshly uncapped, her split of Moet not yet uncorked, and Miss Lithuania high-cheeked and prettily barefoot in a vast terrycloth robe bearing the logo of the Paris Ritz.

"A little bite of lime, darling?" she asked.

"Without."

Dick Driver was fierce and disciplined about the small things. Diet, for one: a chunk of lime today, soufflés tomorrow. That's how such things went. If you lacked discipline, life was a slippery incline indeed. For beautiful women, Driver cut a little slack.

"How's your kid?" the girlfriend inquired. "You gonna see her for Christmas?"

"She'll be with her mother."

"That's good, Deek. Kids oughta be with their mothers. Specially for Christmas. In Lithuania we're very strong on shit like that."

Driver pursed his lips in disapproval. He wished she wouldn't curse. Even people who thought him a louse admitted Dick respected the old, established values. Consider that, out of deference to the prince and sensitive about possibly compromising royalty, he'd not taken his girlfriend to Lyford Cay for the golfing.

But when he corrected the Lithuanian, she protested.

"You like it when I talk dirty in bed, no?"

She had a point there, he conceded. Yet it was nice to know she too respected the old, traditional, bourgeois family values. So many American cover girls, thinking only of themselves, their own pleasure. At one time he'd believed Nicole shared with him those same established values, but by the time he realized his mistake, well . . .

"Let's not argue," he said, sipping at his Diet Dr. Pepper as she popped the champers, her lovely but scornful face half-smiling its superiority at a man who could buy, and sell, her. And had.

It occurred to Driver that except for answering the Lithuanian's question about Emma's whereabouts, he hadn't recently given his daughter much thought. Maybe he ought to look into it, see how Emma was making out, spending the holidays in Europe with her mother. "The bitch."

Who was skiing at St. Moritz, believing their daughter was in Manhattan dining at Le Cirque with her father. "The bastard."

But for all his espousal of traditional family values, it wasn't Dick Driver but his wife, Nicole ("former wife?"), three thousand miles east of Further Lane, who first became uneasy about their child. Was that maternal instinct? Or simply the accustomed paranoia of the self-absorbed?

To review the bidding, which had confused even my father, the master spy:

In order to sneak off to East Hampton and hang her Christmas stocking from Martha Stewart's mantelpiece, Emma Driver had concocted a scheme requiring her to lie shamelessly to everyone but Ken Starr, telling her mother she was spending the hols with daddy, telling her father, well, she was with mummy, and assuring the convent (and her merchant bankers) she was with . . . someone, the entire sham bolstered by a raft of phony E-mails dispatched into cyberspace. And abetted by the fact that neither parent really seemed to give a damn.

As transparent as all this seemed in retrospect, it had been pretty effective for young Emma Driver. Who hadn't yet been arrested, bumped off, accused of juvenile delinquency, kidnapped, or, worst of all, sent home. And who was in fact living off the fat of the land in out-of-season East Hampton.

Except that now, the week before Christmas, questions began

to be asked by a visiting nun, launching mysterious investigations from a suite in the American Hotel.

It was Nicole who began to ask herself just where and with whom her daughter might *really* be spending the Christmas hols. Not that she even missed the child; simply that she feared that, in some devious way, her husband (ex-husband?) might possibly be gaining an edge. Her daughter's dutiful E-mails about "fun with Daddy," which had been arriving from the time Emma left the convent in mid-December, were reassuring, detailed, upbeat. But true? Nicole wouldn't put anything past Dick, not even milking their mutual daughter for PR value as Christmas neared.

On Further Lane, we knew nothing of all this, of course, nor would we for several days.

In St. Moritz Nicole sprang vigorously into action. "*Aux armes!*" she cried aloud, rousing the Impaler from his midday torpor. (Count Vladimir wore ski clothes beautifully but didn't actually ski. Never had. He spent his days tanning.) Within hours they were en route in a hired Mercedes to the airport at Zurich and a flight to Paris.

But only following a brief tantrum from the count. "Why not flying from Milano?" he argued. "Same distance but Italian airport snack bars be more yummier, you know. The chocolates gooder! *mein Gott.*"

She was astute; he was stupid, but Nicole was brutally aware that she was five years older than the Transylvanian and feared losing him when her looks went. Especially considering how the book royalties had gone dry and how Dick felt about sending support checks. So she allowed her lover to make minor decisions (airport snacks and the like) and retained the big ones for herself. "Yes, Count," she said equably, "next time we'll fly via Milano. You're so clever."

He preened and wondered if he might travel to Paris in the flattering new ski clothes she'd bought for him. "I look so good, no?"

"Of course, darling. Very chic, indeed."

Their Paris stopover was brief, efficient. Dancing at Castel's, a night at the Crillon, a visit to an old flirt at the Sûreté, another to a man she knew at Interpol. And Nicole Driver was swiftly and authoritatively put in touch with the most reliable private detective agency on the Continent, whose Paris headquarters would, within the hour, assign their best, their highest-paid, their subtlest yet most ruthless operative, to what seemed on the face of it the simplest of assignments: To help a concerned mother involved in a bitter custody battle track down a small child who was supposed to be with her father in America for the holidays.

When they found the child, Nicole Driver wanted instant notification. No instructions about retrieving the kid and getting her back to a loving mother. Just where she was and with whom.

The operative assigned to the Driver case by Paris was named Mademoiselle Javert.

And as part of her briefing, Nicole had provided Mademoiselle this crucial item of information: if Emma Driver was indeed spending Christmas with her father in Manhattan, dining at Le Cirque and the Four Seasons as her E-mails suggested, why was the kid charging on her platinum card ice creams from a place called the Candy Kitchen on Long Island?

Dick Driver, goaded by Miss Lithuania, had also grown curious about his daughter's whereabouts. Like Nicole, he had his sources (she bribed people at the credit-card companies; he paid off hackers who scoured the Internet for private E-mails). Since he employed security people on a more or less permanent payroll basis, he didn't have to go through Interpol or the Sûreté. He retained as a private eye the celebrated Lefty Odets, who talked such a good game that even Driver occasionally was said to be "waiting for Lefty."

Lefty was a former cop who very nearly made the special squad (under legendary NYPD detective Joe Coffey) that broke the notorious West Side Irish gang called the Westies and put Mickey Featherstone behind bars. A man who "almost" broke the Westies was not to be trifled with. Trouble was, Lefty was "almost" a lot of things. He had Knicks tickets that were "almost" courtside. He palled around 21 and P. J. Clarke's with a broadcast exec who "nearly" became head of ABC. Lefty was "almost" on Letterman the season Dave had the bypass. And he was "almost" a regular on the *Imus in the Morning* radio show. Except that Imus preferred another ex-cop, Bo Dietl. Now here was a chance for Odets to distinguish himself on a project of personal, rather than financial or commercial, importance to Dick Driver.

His orders: Find the kid and determine whether Nicole was using their daughter to gain advantage in their never-ending legal scrum. Whether Nicole was or not, Dick might also "need" to have his daughter for PR reasons at some point over Christmas. The purloined E-mails, perused in Manhattan, pointed east. But oddly, not to Nicole and the Impaler in their European playpens, but to a closer and decidedly unseasonable East Hampton.

Neither parent seemed worried about a young, helpless child's well-being. Only that she not be used to profit the other. Talk about *schaudenfreude*!

But then again, how helpless was young Emma Driver? Wasn't there a naïve, but in ways fiendishly clever, agenda at work here on the kid's part? Reuniting her parents—at least for Christmas?

So off she went, the trail of E-mails and credit-card receipts (her latter-day equivalent of Hansel's bread crumbs and, all to the good, not eaten by birds!) could easily be picked up by even the clumsiest of private eyes. To Lefty Odets, and to a Frenchwoman named Mademoiselle Javert (now doing business as Sister Infanta de Castille), the task was laughably simple. Or so it seemed.

Chapter Eighteen

You fall in the Atlantic in winter.
You're dead within the hour . . .

Even the ocean slows in winter here at the end of Long Island. The Atlantic is still all around us, embracing the land and its people, the green lawns and the gardens sloping down toward the beach, which is still golden if no longer warm. But in the cold, the surf slows. Not calms, I don't mean that. There are still the great waves, heavy, powerful, booming. But the pause between breakers becomes appreciably longer. Not eight but twelve seconds or fifteen. Full minutes pass between the "sets" of greater, more powerful waves that come in multiples of five, or is it nine? The surfers can tell you all about them. People say it's the molecules of sea water that slow in winter, jellied by the cold. And their sluggishness communicates itself to the actual waves as the ocean congeals, turns more ponderous, less skittish and playful. Not that it becomes less dangerous; the sea is always that. Only that its chill sluggishness may lull the unwary into complacency.

Which is surely not to say that anyone out here in the Hamptons was either complacent or sluggish, not last Christmas.

There remained gift shopping to be done, and the feast itself to be planned and laid out. The Admiral had Emma cheating him at cards, I had Alix in my bed, the Baymen were still sore about the Old Churchyard, the cemetery trustees had until December 31 to hand down a final, binding decision, and Reds Hucko's corpse had not yet turned up. And if it did, the Baymen concluded glumly, he couldn't be buried anyway. All because of that damned Marley and his sister!

Nor had Sister Infanta de Castille gone sluggish or complacent.

The assignment handed her in Paris a week ago by the great detective agency had been a simple one. Track down a missing child who had left her Swiss convent school, presumably to spend Christmas with either of two divorced parents, but suspected not to have gone to either. Find the child, report back, and await instructions. The subject was not to be "rescued" or even approached; this was hardly one of those bizarre cult cases that called for deprogramming. Sister — or Mlle — Javert, as she really was, was ordered to do nothing unless Mr. Driver appeared on the scene, when she would instantly contact Nicole for orders.

Until then, do nothing. Just wait.

The problem? Mademoiselle was bored. As a true Javert, direct descendant of the famous Javert, "an Inspector of the Police," who stalked Jean Valjean in *Les Misérables* and who herself despite the five generations of Javerts that separated this particular Javert from her illustrious ancestor, shared his intensity and passion. You didn't just take a Javert off a case and tell him to stand easy. When a Javert got the scent, the bloodhound in the genes came through, as he or she ran the prey to earth, much as the original Inspector Javert had tracked poor Valjean. So when she found Emma Driver so quickly (taken in by a local family called Stowe on Further Lane), and forced inactivity loomed, Mademoiselle kept herself occupied by picking at other loose threads in the puzzle:

There'd been bad blood between Dick Driver and the late Jacob Marley? Good! The late Marley was the benefactor of young Emma? Even better! The surviving Sis Marley had stoked into flame the smouldering enmity of East Hampton's celebrated Baymen? Excellent!

Simplest thing in the world: get close to the Baymen and work her way back to the Marleys through their resentments. Being paid (and handsomely) by the day, Mademoiselle could easily have shrugged Gallic shoulders, enjoyed an American Christmas, and done nothing.

Except that a Javert never rests! What made her the best in the business was a thorough professionalism, a passion for her craft. A sleuth ought to be sleuthing. It was at this point that Mademoiselle Javert dove below the surface of her undercover role and literally became a nun, a Madame of the Sacred Tower. Mademoiselle understood, as John LeCarré reminds us, that a good agent has entertainment value. And that a great agent not only assumes a role but lives it. And who were the very best nuns? The saints! Mademoiselle Javert would not only become a nun, but a . . . saint!

Ministering to the hopeless and to those in despair. And who in East Hampton were the most hopeless, the most despairing people? Simple! The Bonac Boys in their grief over Reds Hucko and their anger at the Marleys for forbidding the dead their hallowed ground.

Sister Infanta summoned the anointed chief, Peanuts Murphy, ordering him a cup of the American Hotel's coffee and blessing herself.

"You despair too quickly," she informed Murphy, silently telling her beads, getting briskly to the point.

"What's that supposed to mean, Sister?" Peanuts asked, surly but wary at the same time. He didn't yet understand this woman.

"It means you give up your friend Hucko to the sea and lay plans for his burial, when the graveyard is forbidden to you, and as yet there's no evidence he's even dead."

"For God's sake, begging your pardon, Sister, but Reds went into the North Atlantic a hundred miles out last month. You telling me he's still treading water?"

The rosary beads slipped smoothly through her fingers as she and Peanuts parried.

"Have you prayed?"

"Sure, lots of people prayed. We got serious Catholics out here. Irish, Polacks, Guineas. They all pray. They got novenas, retreats, rosaries. During Lent, they give out ashes, they give out palm. Lots of stuff."

"But have you specifically prayed for the unfortunate Hucko?"

"Not me, but I ain't much for it. Others, sure. They're praying all the time for Reds's soul. Night and frigging day."

"See, you of little faith, you capitulate too easily, send up the white flag. I tell you, Mr. Murphy, set your priorities. Pray for the man's body first. That he survives. You have all eternity to pray for his soul. There's no rush."

"Lady, Sister, he's dead. You know religion, your rosary beads. I know the Atlantic. You fall in the ocean in winter, you die in an hour. A couple of hours. Reds fell off the *Wendy E.* three weeks ago."

Mademoiselle Javert wasn't buying. Nor was Sister Infanta de Castille.

"We shall pray together, Murphy! At the margin of the great ocean that took your friend. Each day until he returns, you and I will kneel by the water's edge and attempt to bring him back."

"Yes, ma'am. Outstanding! Right you are," Peanuts stammered, on his feet now and backing away. He would have agreed to anything, couldn't wait to get out of there.

That night over beer Peanuts briefed the Bonac Boys, six or eight of them gathered at Wolfies's Tavern.

"She's a whackjob," he said. "Wants us to kneel in the surf and say the rosary and stare at the horizon. Six Our Fathers, six Hail Marys. Hymns, as well. And watch for Reds to come wading up the goddamned beach, seaweed in his hair and returned from the deep."

"Let's have another round," someone said.

But in the end, because it couldn't hurt, and maybe might even help, a dozen or so Baymen, with a couple of girlfriends and wives and little ones along for moral support (plus three guys Reds owed money to), gathered the following morning at daybreak (just before eight A.M. at these latitudes and in this season) on the beach below the cliffs where teeters the ancient Montauk Lighthouse, to be addressed by Sister Infanta de Castille, now sporting a brand-new and roomy scarlet down parka, which kind of gave her the look of a cardinal of the church.

"You have no faith. Pray without ceasing, that's what the saints tell us. And the mystics. You don't just rattle off an Ave or a Pater Noster and retreat into despair. Think of St. Sebastian punctured by arrows. Or the Jesuit Isaac Jogues skinned alive by Iroquois. Did they despair? Or Peter, our first Pope, crucified upside down. This Reds of yours, well, who's to say he's lost. Really lost?"

There were shrugs and a few mutters, then the Frenchwoman clapped her hands.

"*Bien*, now, let's kneel, here at the margins of the sea, and pray for Reds Hucko . . ."

One of the women knelt first, following Sister Infanta's lead, and then another, and then two or three of the men. Then they all knelt, including, Sister was surprised to note, Peanuts Murphy.

Who had earlier told her of prayer, "I ain't much for it.

Chapter Nineteen

Sis drove a powerful Range Rover with the logo altered to read "Deranged Rover."

I would shortly learn of these dawn prayers (they were all the talk that night at the Blue Parrot, where Don Hewitt of CBS heard the story and started the reportorial ball rolling even more powerfully at *60 Minutes*), but not until later would I hear what else Sister Infanta was up to.

Lefty Odets's progress, or lack of same, I knew all about and quickly.

Dick Driver had given Lefty roughly the same instuctions as Mademoiselle Javert's agency got from Nicole. Find his daughter, sure, but find out what Nicole (and the Impaler) were up to and how she planned to use the kid at The Hague. Lefty, who thought he was more clever than most, decided he wouldn't just camp out watching for young Susannah (Dick gave Lefty her passport name). Easier to find two high-profile jet-setters than some skinny school-girl.

So Lefty Odets started his search for Nicole and her boyfriend by hanging out at East Hampton airport, scrutinizing the private jets coming in. And paying a local fellow a few bucks to check the railroad station. And limos, if any.

The local fellow was the Indian chief, Jesse Maine. And before

another day and a half was out, Jesse had one-third of the population of the Shinnecock Indian Reservation on Lefty's payroll,
working per diem, looking for a beautiful blonde who once skated
in the ice show and a dashing European gent named Count Vlad.
My father knew Joe Coffey pretty well from various undercover
assignments.

"Ask him if this Odets is as dumb as he seems," I prompted.

My father gave me a look.

"I can think up the questions all by myself, thank you," he said.

"Okay, okay."

When he got Coffey, they talked for a time and then the admiral
thanked him and hung up.

"He says as far as Odets goes, if confidence was brains, he'd be
a genius. Otherwise, except that he talks a good game and tries to
get himself on some radio show . . ."

I called Jesse. "It's like taking candy from babies. You ought to
be ashamed."

He was, a bit, Jesse admitted when he came by the house a bit
later. "But with Christmas just about here and the little ones sending their lists to Santy, we Native American fellows can use a few
dollars that ain't otherwise working."

In addition to taking Lefty's (or rather Mr. Driver's) money, the
Shinnecocks were leading him seriously astray. Up the Peconic
River from Riverhead in a canoe. Over to the North Fork to scru-
tinize a perfectly innocent potato farm. Out to Gosman's Dock in
Montauk to study fishing boats. Surveillance of an abandoned
house on Dune Road in Westhampton Beach. To watch deer grazing over in North Haven. Odets put hundreds of miles on his
odometer and hours on the car's cell phone. In Manhattan Dick
Driver cursed him out and told him he didn't want any more
negative reports. Until he found Nicole and what she was actally
doing with the kid, and where, Lefty should observe radio silence.
"You don't know who the hell's listening in," Dick said angrily. "If
I'm running for president, I don't need *People* magazine sniffing
around or a story on *Entertainment Tonight!*"

When Odets demanded a closer accounting of the Shinnecocks,

Jesse Maine looked grave and told Lefty that the Great Spirit worked in strange ways and that Odets would be rewarded for his patience.

"Strangers often become confused out here in the Hamptons, among our fens and bogs, Lady Alix," Jesse reminded us. "Remember that Kuwaiti fellow, the archery champ who fell among turtles in Hook Pond?"

Did she not, Alix shuddered.

"Which turtles were those, chief?" Emma asked, coming into the room.

When I failed to shut Jesse up, he was off and running. "They got snappers out there, Jane, snapping turtles go a good sixty pounds. Maybe more. Take a man's foot sure as look at him. I won't pull one into the canoe with me, not a big one. Them bastards scurry around so and bite at your damned Nikes and go for a bare ankle if they can reach one. You get distracted and start to lurching about the canoe and whacking at the turtles with your paddle, and next thing you know you're capsized, flailing about the pond or worse, bogged down."

"What's bogged down? Sounds awful."

"Oh, it is, Emma, er, Jane," Alix assured her. "Don't even think about it. You'll have nightmares."

"Do tell me, Beecher, do!" Emma protested. "Not at all fair teasing innocent children with little morsels, and then not telling all."

By now, I was on the cusp of concluding she was about as innocent as Jesse's killer turtles.

There'd been a couple of nights of hard freeze, and you began to hear talk we might have good ice for skating before Christmas. I hoped so. Even if the kid did attend school in Switzerland, skating here was something. The village had begun filling up for the holidays. Not summer-filled; you could still get a seat in the movie house and a table at Nick & Toni's or the Laundry. But the Christmas people were here and more coming in each day as the prep schools and Ivy League closed down. Is it okay to call them that, Christmas people?

The Admiral took us to dinner at Gordon's in Amagansett, and at the next table a sleek young man, in-between cell phone calls made and received, was busily trying to convince a very beautiful young woman she ought to go someplace with him that he had to go. Or *was* he attempting to convince her?

"Look, I really, really, *really* want you to go with me. But not if you're going to hate it and be miserable."

"You really want me there?" She was quite fine to look at and sounded sincere.

"You know I do. But I also want the right thing for you. And for you to be at ease and enjoy yourself."

There was a bit more of this. Until Emma, sort of sotto voce but not quite, if you know what I mean, said:

"I don't think he wants her to go at all, do you?"

"My thinking precisely," agreed Alix, her voice even less sotto and more voce.

"Let's have a look at the card then," said my father loudly, passing around menus and talking over the others in deference to the young couple at the next table.

"Swell idea," I said, falling in with his strategy. "And wait till you see the desserts . . ."

"Because," Emma picked up again, "if you really want someone to do something, you can always tell. At least I can."

"The swordfish steaks here are unusually fine, Jane," said the Admiral. "Have you ever had swordfish?"

"I'm not sure. Do they serve it with the sword on or off, *cher* Admiral?"

"Off, usually."

"And is there gravy? If I don't like a new dish but there's gravy, I can usually get it down without barfing."

"There's a good deal to be said for that theory," Her Ladyship remarked. "I'm told the secret of contemporary French cuisine, their savory sauces, derives from the siege of Paris by the Prussians in 1870. Parisians were reduced to eating dogs and rats, and the great chefs of the three-star restaurants saved the day by concocting and ladling on the most delicious and savory of sauces."

"Ugh, Alix! Eating rats? Phooey on that."

"They were parlous times, I assure you. Desperate moments, born of necessity."

Over dessert Emma asked my father, "*Grand seigneur*, considering that Mr. Marley is dead, so there's no way I can ever thank him properly for his kindnesses when I was a little kid, do you think it might be possible for me to call on his sister and thank her?"

The grand seigneur cleared his throat. "Well, you know how she is. Or perhaps you don't. But she—"

"Sometimes I think I remember her. But then, maybe there was another lady at Mr. Marley's house with the verandas that I remember. I can't be sure."

My father sought an analogy.

"You know the film *The Wizard of Oz.*"

"*Bien sûr.* One of my faves."

"Well, young Dorothy had an aunt, Auntie Em, I think was her name, very much like your own, and she—"

"Oh, I do hope she's like that, like Auntie Em, *Herr Grosseadmiral.*"

"Yes, yes. Except that I was about to say, Ms. Marley is sort of an anti–Auntie Em, if I can make the point. There are times when Sis Marley may remind one more of, well. . . ."

"Oh, you mean the Wicked Witch of the West," said Emma, making a face.

"Not quite that bad. No flying monkeys. But she has her moments."

Emma thought for a time.

"I'd still like to pay my respects, *mein herr.* And if she's in a testy moment, I can always drop a swift curtsey and back off, no?"

Alix shook her head in admiration.

"Precisely the posture I'd take, Beecher. Wouldn't you?"

"Oh, yes," I said. To curtsey on departing Sis Marley, or not to curtsey, wasn't the sort of thing you want to debate with the aristocracy.

In the morning the Admiral made the phone call, looking sour about it. "I don't get on with that woman. All very well that she's the keeper of the flame for brother Jake. But she is a piece of work."

I knew that much for myself. Sis was locally reconizable for driving, and driving fast, in a powerful Range Rover with huge oversized tires and a souped-up engine. Above the reinforced front bumper where the brand logo is located, she'd had the printing professionally altered so that it now read "Deranged Rover."

"Mind, now, I'm only doing this for you, Beecher," my father said.

"For me? Not my idea!"

"Well, you're forever bringing these waifs home."

"Waifs? Waifs plural?" He was never going to allow me to forget it.

Sis Marley, the Admiral said, sounded reluctant at best. "Perhaps after Christmas. I'm occupied until then." And hung up. He reported this to Emma, who didn't seem to feel snubbed, and said that after Christmas would be fine.

Chapter Twenty

He'll look into a man's eye and tell his age within a year.

The Maidstone is a very old club sitting atop the East Hampton dunes, with the ocean as a backdrop. It has a carefully culled membership with a long waiting list, and it is managed and operated by intelligent people. One of their more prescient decisions, long ago, was to take into consideration the frenetic hubbub of an American Christmas-shopping season. And to try to do something about it.

Slowing it down, for one.

The annual pre-Christmas dinner took place on December 22. The next evening but one, clearly, was unsuitable, being Christmas Eve. A night or two before, members were still at their chores, their office parties, their shopping and errands. The twenty-second, three nights before Christmas, seemed a sensible time to sit and draw breath, to chat, eat and drink, perhaps exchange, though not open, a few small gifts.

The Admiral traditionally took a table. A large one. Not quite large enough this year. We ended with several tables, moderately proportioned. By now half the winter population of East Hampton had joined in our plot to protect and conceal Emma Driver. The Admiral understood where his bread was buttered, I assure you.

Consider just who was there at the club that night (either members in good standing or as invited guests):

The mayor; artist Julian Schnabel; Uma Thurman with her baby (now sitting up brightly in a youth chair); Kurt Vonnegut, Jr.; painter Childe Hassam, Jr.; Rudy the grocer; Councilman Zenk from Southampton; Budd Schulberg; Netterville the sturgeon king; Calvin Klein's estranged wife, Kelly; Annacone the tennis pro; Billy Joel and his daughter, Alexa; Peter Maas; Valerie Heller; Joe's widow; young Dr. Willard the opthamologist and his pretty wife; George Plimpton with Mrs. P. and their twin girls; and the de Menils from Houston, the oil people. From a nearby table, old-timer Schuyler Quackenbush III waved at my father, saluting him, I guess, for putting together a first-rate group, which now included, having arrived a bit late, Jesse Maine in his brand-new Ralph Lauren (authentic Native American) togs. There were rumors Martha Stewart might actually come down from Connecticut to flog a servant or weld a burst pipe in the pool house, and that both Ben Bradlee and Wasserstein the Wall Streeter planned cameo appearances. Jerry Della Femina and wife, Judy Licht, hosted a table of their own, having long since come to accommodation on such matters, Jerry celebrating the Jewish holidays with Judy, she marking Christmas for him.

"Golly, Admiral," said Her Ladyship, "this is a corking group."

"May I have some, Beecher?" Emma asked when the wine steward came around to take the drinks orders.

"You certainly may not," said Alix, determined to be on the right side of the Admiral with the holidays looming.

Sister Infanta de Castille was the center of a hub of admirers at one of the better tables near the windows, overlooking the ocean. By now her working of miracles at the surf's edge had passed into local legend. Several local clergy and one fellow in ecclesiastical purple jabbering Italian (I suspected he might be the famed Papal Nuncio) were in attendance, and considerable wine was being consumed. Sister herself was doing her part.

"Are nuns supposed to drink?" my father inquired of Emma,

who'd been fobbed off with a Shirley Temple. "Don't they take vows?"

"Not of abstinence, sir, *pas du tout*. Chastity, yes, those are the serious vows. No licky face or carrying on. But a cocktail or after-dinner brandy, *pourquoi pas?*"

He made a stern Episcopalian face. "I'd have thought drink might also be on the list."

I wondered if we should approach the nun (Alix having previously made Sister's acquaintance) or if she possibly might head for us, curious to see her quarry (if that's what Emma was) up close. As the table organized itself, and nearby tables called hullo and exchanged kisses, Emma was variously introduced. Some knew her as Alix's ward Jane Pendragon, others as Susannah le Blanc, while she was simply Emma to the rest of us. I fretted over the inconsistencies, but sufficient drink had been taken on by most guests that I don't think the confusion of names was even noted.

Nor, by now, did I believe it mattered. Sister Infanta surely knew not only precisely who the Drivers' child was but which of her aliases she was using.

A tall, ruddy fellow of fifty or so stopped by to chat. "This is Ulf den Blitzen," I said, introducing him to Alix. There was some brief chat and then Ulf passed on to the next table, calling out hearty "Merry Christmases!"

"Who's he, Beecher?"

"Used to be a noted alpinist. Made all the usual eighth-degree ascents in the Himalayas, scaled the toughest Chamonix needles. Perfectly normal lifestyle until a few years ago, when he joined a cult. Signed over half his money to them. They go on outings in the Adirondacks, chant and dress up, all that male bonding nonsense. Then they climb pine trees without underwear. No one knows quite what to make of it, but I've got to admit, Ulf's never looked fitter."

"A good club wants a few eccentrics on the membership roles," my father offered, "so long as they don't frighten horses or children."

"Why would they climb pines trees without their underwear?" Emma asked. "I should think the needles prick, wouldn't you?"

"Part of the mystique, I'm sure," said Her Ladyship at her most nonchalant. "Not polite to ask."

Over the entree Emma nudged me. "I've learned a piece. 'The Gift of the Magi.' Can I recite it? It's very seasonal. Quite in keeping with the occasion."

"Yes, very famous American short story. O. Henry."

"Who's he?"

"Fellow wrote the story."

"I'm sure not. A Mr. Porter. William Sydney Porter, 1862 to 1910," Emma informed me.

"O. Henry was his pen name. You know, like you. Sailing under false colors for good reason, I suppose."

"Did he keep getting kidnapped, too?"

"No, but I think he was in jail. Though briefly."

"What for?"

My God, the kid could ask questions. I hushed her up by promising if things got dull later, she might recite over the brandy.

"Oh, Beecher, you are good!"

Jesse Maine seemed to enjoy himself. "By damn, this is a dandy club. I'd join here myself if I had the dough and thought I could get the votes."

"I can't speak to the money, but the votes might well be there, Jesse," the Admiral said. "You know half the men in this room, I'd wager."

"Trouble is, Admiral, half of them know me."

And there was, he went on to remind us, the matter of his arrest record, mostly for poaching but with a few fistfights and a DWI or two thrown in.

"What's DWI?" Emma wanted to know.

"Hush!"

A minichorus of West Point cadets came on then and sang carols, very nice in their gray uniforms, and the singing not bad either. And on the final, traditional pieces, we were all urged to join in. And did, my father especially loud and occasionally on key.

"By damn!" Jesse said again, even more enthusiastically, "this is one hell of a club you got here, Admiral."

Venison (local, you understand, part of that culling of the herd up at North Haven) with yams and cranberries was the main dish and that wasn't bad, either, especially with the wine stewards trotting out the vintages without even being summoned. Over the mince and pumpkin pies and coffee Jesse confided that he might be stepping down from one of his multiple leadership roles in the Shinnecock Indian Nation.

"We're appointing a new shaman if things work out. I got enough to do being sachem and war chief without also being medicine man, and going down to Washington and up to Albany to lobby for recognition as an official tribe. As well as getting them to ease up on minimum lengths for striped bass and the poaching laws."

"Who's this new shaman?" my father asked jocularly, "not Ulf den Blitzen, I trust."

"No, one of the Latham boys, old Hamptons family. He's almost all Shinnecock and a hell of a lad, Admiral. Claims he can see right into your soul. And to prove it, he'll look into a man's eye and tell his age within a year and his exact weight within two pounds. And he's got one of them aluminum baseball bats he keeps handy in his pickup if anyone objects to being looked in the damned eye, I swear!"

"Wow!" said Emma, "Could you bring Mr. Latham to Geneva sometime, Jesse, so he could meet Mother Superior and look all the nuns in the eye and tell their age and how much they weigh. There's nobody like that in Switzerland at all that I know about."

"I shouldn't think so, miss. These are rare gifts few has."

As the coffee was served and the dancing began, here came Sister Infanta de Castille. Had I been more alert I would have inserted myself between our young Emma and this formidable and somewhat intimidating figure. Too late.

Ignoring the rest of our table and holding out a hand, staring down with piercing eyes from her great height, the nun made immediate eye contact with the girl. "I am Sister Infanta de Castille," she announced.

"Yes, Sister," Emma replied, inclining her head slightly in a show of manners, "and I am Miss Wanderly Luxemburgo of the Canary Islands."

"Of course you are," said the nun, eyes piously lowering, and not believing it for an instant. And then, eyes flicked again upward and blazing, she was off, headed back to her own table, as Emma, totally unperturbed, spooned up a dollop of pêche melba. A pair of genuine fakes they were, those two, and mutually recognized it.

"Well," said the Admiral, "and what was *that* all about?"

"A passage at arms, father," I said, "antagonists measuring each other in advance as they wait in the lists, just before the shout goes up, 'Let the games begin!'"

"Mmm," Her Ladyship remarked, "most curious."

And it was, I thought. But then, Christmas parties at the Maidstone, what did one reasonably expect?

Alix flirted with the West Point cadets, George Plimpton's twins and Emma became acquainted (getting along swimmingly), Ulf den Blitzen told stories of grand old times up there at base camp in the Himalayas, "casting about for a glimpse, trying to get a photo of the dreaded Yeti."

"What's that, sir?" Emma inquired, a bit restive at having Ulf telling stories while she hadn't been asked to recite.

"Also known as the Abominable Snowman. A great, red-headed rascal that leaps out at one."

"Oh," said Emma. I could hear Jesse murmur under his breath, "I'll be goddamned!"

Ulf told a good yarn but was tight-lipped about the cult (and climbing pine trees without underwear). While Sister Infanta de Castille so charmed everyone that the chairman of the dinner committee (certainly *not* a Catholic himself, I assure you) got up and asked her to close the evening by giving a blessing.

So we never did get around to having a recitation of "The Gift of the Magi" by O. Henry, or Mr. Porter, but I think that may have been just as well since, as I recall, it's a pretty sad story to have recited at you on the night just before Christmas.

Especially after a few drinks.

Chapter Twenty-one

Sister Infanta is repudiated privately by the order of Mother Teresa . . .

"Reds come ashore. Reds' body washed up!"

That was how the next morning began, and a cold one it was. The thought of Reds Hucko's corpse making an appearance, so shortly after Sister Infanta de Castille and the Baymen prayed over him, was eerie. Of course East Hampton people wanted the poor fellow's body found. You don't want to think of a good man out there in the winter ocean being fed upon by cod. Even if Reds did take a drink. And owed money. But here on shore, in divided East Hampton, as long as Reds was missing at sea, the hostile confrontation between the Marley estate and the Baymen over his gravesite was on indefinite hold. And a good thing. Sis Marley was Mean Jake's sister, and you know what that meant, how mean. And the Bonac Boys were already angry and getting angrier.

The body was pitched into the bed of a pickup and sped to Southampton Hospital for an autopsy, but long before they had the cadaver on the coroner's table, Sister Infanta de Castille had called on Peanuts Murphy to console him.

"Hey, Sister, ain't your fault. Don't sweat it personally."

"Monsieur Murphy, faith, if truly genuine, endures regardless of these occasional setbacks. And indeed, the sea does give up its dead."

"Just like I always say," said Peanuts insincerely. Somehow, he did not find this sentiment all that comforting. And after declining to join the nun in further prayer, he went off to Wolfie's Tavern to organize another Bonac Boys demonstration before the locked gates of the Old Churchyard. With Reds back in town, and being carved on at Southampton Hospital, the question of his burial place couldn't much longer be deferred.

"Maybe we oughta steal Jake again," one of his cronies suggested over the beer. A nice symmetry, Jake out of the cemetery and Reds in, if they could pull it off.

"We might," said Peanuts, jaw clenched. They'd stolen Jake before, with Peanuts prominent among the Boys, and they knew how to do it. They could do it again, even with a dead bolt on the mausoleum, "sure as hell, by God!"

"Yeah, to hell with the Marleys! Maybe we'll just take his mausoleum for Hucko."

It never got to that.

"It ain't Reds!"

The good, if mystifying, news spread rapidly through East Hampton. Peanuts Murphy, who'd taken on the role of chief mourner (Reds owed Peanuts a few bucks; it was no secret), was called upon to issue clarifying statements (much in the style of White House press secretaries confronted by embarrassing gaffes and disclosures): "The sawbones who did the autopsy says the stiff got stainless-steel teeth. Probably fell off a Russki trawler. The fish been working him over for considerable time but they're sure. Reds was six-two. This fellow's a foot shorter. But the big thing is, Americans don't do steel teeth."

Not everyone was convinced. Suspicion still lay heavily on the Marleys, damn them!

"Who knows about Hucko's teeth? Anyone check his dental records, just to be sure?"

"Oh, hell, if Reds had steel teeth don't you think we'd all

remember that? I punched him myself in the face more than once at Boaters. Or here at Wolfie's. Didn't you? Didn't all of us? Reds was always begging for a shot in the mouth."

"Sure, and if Reds had steel teeth, he would of showed them around. Reds enjoyed making an impression. Always did."

"Sure, he would of had pictures taken, that bastard."

If others were disappointed Reds's body was still missing, Mademoiselle Javert was not among them. She was by now so deeply into the persona of Sister Infanta de Castille that she was attending early mass every morning and watching the *Sister Angelica* show on cable TV. To have thought Hucko dead and his body recovered one day, then the very next to be informed the corpse was a party of the third part, and with steel teeth at that, was simply too good an opportunity for Sister Infanta to let slip. So rather than regret Hucko was still missing, she prayed in the streets of Montauk, and aloud, raising Te Deums of gratitude that Reds Hucko might not yet be dead. Or at least not proven so.

One mourner was so enthused by her message he shouted, "Hucko lives! Hucko lives!"

Women of the village didn't go that far, but they and a few small children followed her about, chiming in on the prayers, less well on the Te Deums, since they knew no Latin. But Sister Infanta was certainly building a following and at least two hundred people turned out when her thanksgiving prayers were offered in all solemnity just outside the Old Churchyard. By now there were two TV crews and reporters from *Newsweek* and the *Times*. We drove up out of curiosity and because Emma wanted to see the churchyard from which Jake Marley's bones were occasionally stolen.

Sister Infanta was standing on a sturdy milk carton and addressing the troops when we got there.

"Let's be grateful and not mourn. The man can yet turn up. I'd prefer to pray on the beach, at the water's edge, closer to where Monsieur Hucko met his fate, whatever that may yet turn out to be, but it's too cold."

Admiral Stowe, going impatiently foot to foot and feeling the cold in damaged fingers, grunted assent.

"The woman may or may not be a genuine nun, but about that, she's right. Too damned cold! Finally, the pond's freezing."

"Will there be skating?" Emma asked.

"Looks good. One more night like this, I'd say." We'd need skates, of course. I had a pair, so did my father. Inga was practically a pro. Being Nicole's daughter, Emma would have the genes but still would need a pair of skates. As for Her Ladyship, Alix didn't travel light (the only person of her generation still toting a steamer trunk), and you never knew what might turn up when she unpacked.

Alix was all for a good cold spell. "I can't wait to try out my Hummer on ice and bolting through snowdrifts, sounding the klaxon and crying, 'Yoicks!' "

As the frenzy over Reds's "body" calmed and faded, young Miss Driver's introduction to Sis Marley again moved to the front burner. When the date came, the Admiral was determined to deliver the child himself.

"Wouldn't miss it. Sis Marley's not my cup of tea, never was. And can't blame Sis for being reluctant, for setting 'tentative' dates, with this bad blood between the Marleys and Dick Driver. Not that Sis will hold it against the kid. But after all, Emma *is* Dick's daughter. Still, knowing how hard-shell Sis is, and getting the chance to see her with young Emma . . ."

This genial interlude was not to last. A lengthy E-mail now arrived (in code) for the Admiral from his "man" in Geneva, the hotel concierge Marcel.

Decoding as he went, the Admiral read the message aloud:

"The nun known as Sister Infanta de Castille is repudiated by the order of nuns founded by the late Mother Teresa. They wish no unseemly publicity so will confirm this only privately or not at all. Nor can any formal links to the Couvent de la Tour Sacrée be established. All nuns there are incommunicado (one elderly sister seems to be drunk), either skiing or buying clothes in the Paris couture until January 5."

"The drunk one, that's got to be Sister Euphemia," Emma interrupted.

The Admiral continued: "Independent inquiries say 'Sister Infanta' may be in actuality a French investigator named Javert."

Well, we'd all been assuming her "nunship" was a pose, and she was probably a private eye. But this was the first time any of us had heard the name Javert.

Which got Emma started again: "Doesn't that raise your hackles more than slightly, *mon vieux* Beecher?"

"Well, I . . ."

"Javert, in *Les Miserables*," the girl announced, "was 'an inspector of the police,' and, in point of fact, the bloodhound who ran poor Jean Valjean to earth. Sister Infanta clearly derives from someplace other than the Convent de la Tour."

"Damn!" Alix responded, embarrassed that a child seemed better informed than an Oxonian with a double first. "Mightn't this simply be a coincidence of names?"

It took the Admiral to bring her back to reality. "Hardly likely, Alix. The French have a good deal of respect for lineage. A policeman named Javert will spin off children who become policemen, and they in turn have children of their own, who become policemen. Much in the way that Mafia godfathers beget Mafia sons and grandsons."

Picking up on that line of thought, Alix added, "And let's not overlook Sherlock Holmes's brilliant brother Mycroft."

I wasn't quite sure I followed either my father's logic, or Alix's, but he now resumed reading the E-mail from his agent in Geneva.

"Mademoiselle (or Madame, there's a suggestion here the woman has been or is married) Javert is widely respected by the Sûreté and especially by the Deuxième Bureau (they're the French federal cops who wiretap everyone, including foreign correspondents, as I happen to know from firsthand experience). Mlle Javert is said to be relentless in pursuit, fearless, and quite adept at disguise. Several years ago she solved, and single-handedly so, the famous case of the missing Andaman Islander and was instrumental in running to earth the jewel fence in the affair of the Beryl Coronet."

"Golly!" Alix said, having read about the Beryl Coronet in her pa's copy of the big English Sunday paper, *News of the World*, to which the Earl of Dunraven had a subscription for life. "Wasn't she also the sleuth who caught on to the Three Garridebs?"

I shook my head:

"No, that was definitely Holmes and Watson."

"Oh."

But while, thanks to the Admiral's man in Switzerland, we were now clearly able to see through "Sister Infanta's" act, she was playing exceedingly well elsewhere in the Hamptons. As I say, not only a strong following among the Baymen and the tabloid press, but in more exalted circles, namely *60 Minutes* and the Catholic Church. People really were starting to believe Reds Hucko could still come back. (And pay his debts? Anything was possible.) But for us who knew her true identity, critical questions remained:

Who was paying her? One of the parents? A third party? Was she a rival of Lefty Odets or an ally? Just what were her instructions? And was she any threat to Emma Driver, a child who had, after all, been kidnapped before?

"So what do we do now?" I asked. "Confront the woman? Or what?"

My old man replied, "Whatever we do, we may have to get Emma out of here and tucked away somewhere else."

"A safe house, *Herr Grosseadmiral*," Emma interjected with considerable anticipatory delight. "*Olé*! And cut both ears and tail! That's the ticket."

"I've an idea," said Alix. "The Shinnecock Reservation. Why doesn't Beecher ring up Chief Maine and see if they can make the arrangements?"

The Admiral shook his head. "People know how close we are to Jesse. Suppose Emma were concealed temporarily not among friends. But with apparent . . . enemies?"

I think we all, even Emma, knew what he was thinking.

Sis Marley.

Chapter Twenty-two

With Emma, not as a guest, but as a member of our family . . .

You know how the Bob Cratchit line goes: "There never was such a Christmas." Well, there hadn't been, not at our house, that I could remember.

Not even the looming menace of Mademoiselle Javert (aka Sister Infanta) could spoil things. Once the holiday was over, we might be moving Emma to "a safe house" with Sis Marley or someone else, but not yet. Here was a child who deserved to have a decent Christmas with an actual family and not, as in past years, to be ping-ponged between a self-absorbed pair of sparring litigants. Let Emma celebrate Christmas here with us first.

On the plus side, a big snowstorm was coming, Alix was here, my old man was recovered from his wounds, my new book was shaping up, and for the first time since I was a little kid, there was a child in the house at 130 Further Lane.

And maybe that was the best thing of all. The Admiral, who had his glacial moments, was so excited he wanted to go out and buy her an electric train.

"That's what you always wanted, Beecher. A Lionel train set, as I recall, with crossing gates that went up and down, and two switches. We were living in Paris and your mother and I went down to Au Train Bleu on the rue St. Honoré and bought one. Damned expensive, too. Bright red, O Gauge, I think."

"Yes, father. I remember it as if it were yesterday. Great trains. But she's a girl."

"Nonsense! All children love electric trains. Unfair to little girls to limit them to dolls and sets of dishes instead of a proper Lionel train. That's where the trouble starts between men and women, over the electric trains at Christmas and a crossing gate where the arms go up and down. The girls are always shortchanged and are smart enough to realize it, sensitive enough never to forget it. Years later, married and with children of their own perhaps, the resentments still smoulder. Many a time a couple will break out bickering and the husband shakes his head and asks, what the hell did I do *now*?

"And it could well be the missing set of electric trains."

Yes, my father does tend to beat a theory to death. I'd hate to have served under him as a mere ensign or lieutenant, junior grade, and have to keep saying, yessir, right, sir, aye aye, sir. But in the end Alix and I, with moral support from the sensible and pragmatic Inga, got the Admiral to shelve his electric trains *pro tem*.

Emma began making her presence felt a few days before Christmas. Her appalling parents had sent agents (we were by now assuming they were paying Odets and Sister Infanta) to the Hamptons to keep an eye on her, make sure the rival claimant wasn't gaining advantage, but were otherwise indifferent toward their only child. It said plenty about the kid's resilience that she was able to shrug it off. I don't mean she wasn't hurt, but she didn't limp or let it show. "I'm sure my parents'll be here at some point in the holidays, Alix," Emma kept assuring us, making excuses for Nicole and Dick, "you know how difficult it is to get airline reservations at this time of year."

She usually had a project into which she poured her energies. Good therapy, I suppose, though I don't believe ten-year-olds, even one like her, would define it as such.

She was seated on a footstool in my father's den over near the fire, with a magazine on her skinny knees—*The New Yorker* I believe—used as a drawing board, with a few sheets of borrowed stationery from the Admiral's desk and one of his fountain pens with a Naval Academy crest. "You do know about fountain pens, don't you?" he first ascertained, not wanting a fine pen to be treated as a mere ballpoint.

"*Mais oui, monsieur l'amiral,* even though at school we use number two pencils and ballpoints mostly, but the nuns are very big on fountain pens themselves and teach us to wield them efficiently."

He grunted his pleasure. "Respect for good tools, there's the difference between surgeons and butchers," he murmured. Precisely what that meant, I wasn't quite sure, being respectful of both, but Emma nodded vigorously in agreement.

"I've often felt that way myself," she said.

Her task was the compilation of a Christmas list, punctuated by questions. How Inga spelled her name, what size waist did I think my father had, did Alix like the color green? And did we think if she bought Doc Whitmore a pair of red wool socks, would he wear them to match his biking earmuffs? When Jesse Maine dropped by, she grilled him:

"On the reservation, do Shinnecocks exchange gifts?"

"I should say we do. We're civilized as anyone. These ain't Pequots you're dealing with."

"But do they prefer locally crafted gifts, of tribal significance, or is it considered okay to buy stuff in stores?"

"That do depend largely on the state of the exchequer that particular season. I've seen Christmases when I was tanning away on pelts starting in mid-November and sewing up mocassins at a great rate, just 'cause the funds was short. Other years I've went all the way upIsland to Route 110 in Huntington or to Macy's at Roosevelt Field and bought my fill, gift wrap 'n all."

She jotted a few notes. Then, more thoughtful, "Jesse, suppose there's someone you love, but you're not getting on with all that well. Does he or she go on your Christmas list? Or do you send a message by leaving them off?"

"Oh, I dunno. Depends. Christmas's supposed to be a time for making up, ain't it? For ending grudges instead of starting them?"

"But you wouldn't send gifts to the Pequots?"

"Not hardly. But that ain't the question. You're talking about folks you love but it temporarily went sour. I don't love no Pequots and never did. Nor do many of them return me the favor."

Emma got Alix aside for considerable whispering.

"Beecher, Jane and I are driving into the village. Chores and calls to make. Back shortly. Ta ta."

And when Emma (Jane) and Her Ladyship weren't plotting, the kid and Jesse were in a corner someplace laying plans. Emma was something when it came to cabals and plots, conspiracies and *coups d'etat*. Or, in Jesse's term, "in cahoots." It was this quality in Emma that drew the Admiral, himself a born conspirator and coup-ist. Cassius and Brutus on the Ides of March would have appreciated them both.

As Alix and Emma got into their coats, my father pulled me away. "Shouldn't we give the child some pocket money. Surely she's planning secretly to Christmas-shop."

"I've seen her purse, Father. She can buy and sell both of us."

"Oh," he said, sounding impressed.

A more significant issue was the behavior of her parents, neither of them making the slightest move toward arranging Christmas with their only child. And, wealthy people, not even sending along a few gifts. You might have expected wicker baskets flowing with ribbons and wrapping paper. Instead, their private eyes, the bastards!

While Sister Infanta de Castille visited the parishes, attended the sick at Southampton Hospital, spoke reverentially of Mother Teresa's torch shortly to be passed ("to one far worthier than I, you can be sure"), and huddled with reverend clergy from as far away as Manhattan, Boston, and (in the Papal Nuncio's case) Washington.

Sister Infanta's act was diverting. The Drivers', unforgiveable. After Emma was tucked in the night following her shopping trip, Alix returned downstairs to the Admiral's den, where he and I sat over scotch and a cigar.

"Yes, I will have a drink," she said, unasked. "I need one."

When I handed her a glass, she looked up and smiled. But it was a smile creased with fatigue, frustration. You don't see much of that in Her Ladyship, I can assure you.

"Oh, Beecher, that wonderful child. What *are* we to do?"

When I chewed on it, not knowing just what to say, she turned to my father.

"Admiral, your entire career has been spent solving puzzles. Can you suggest *anything*? I can't face Emma again without having done something."

My father looked as unhappy as she felt about the whole business. But he had an answer. Whether it was the appropriate answer, who could yet say?

"We can't speak for her parents, Alix. Nor force their behavior. The thing for us to do, my dear, and we shall, is to celebrate Christmas in our own way in our own house and with young Emma Driver, at least for tomorrow, not here as a guest but as one of the family, yours and ours!"

Chapter Twenty-three

There'll be some happy little Shinnecocks this Christmas.

In deference to Emma, we went to the Catholic church Christmas morning. Early mass. "I have errands, Beecher," the girl informed me. "Got to be up and doing."

The mass was okay. Nothing more. Father Desmond's sermon was fine. I liked him. Emma went up and took Holy Communion. We do that in the Episcopalian Church, too. But I didn't think I ought to do it here, with all those Catholics watching. After all, they know who we are here in East Hampton. My father didn't give a damn and he went up and took Communion. He takes the straightforward Annapolis line when it comes to dealing with God.

The music was a letdown. Most Holy Trinity, the local Catholic church, didn't have much of a choir. I don't know why it is, but it seems to me Protestants sing better. "Episcopalians certainly do" was my father's verdict on the matter. I don't know what God thinks, of course, but that's my view. The Admiral was especially critical. He likes a rollicking good hymn and sings along, putting in a pretty good bass, very loud. Whatever church he's in. But the supporting cast here hadn't been up to his standards.

" 'Silent Night' was fine. But if I'm going to attend Catholic mass, I want my 'Adeste Fideles' in Latin. Latin sounds better, has a weight and grandeur the translation lacks. And I enjoy a good, rousing chorus of 'Good King Wenceslas,' not a tinny little rendition."

We went to the Maidstone Arms for brunch. Eggs Benedict and steaming pots of coffee, lots of hot breads. The Admiral was cheerier now. Matt Lauer and his wife were there, attractive people. Everyone said hello. Calling out "Merry Christmas." The waitresses were more focused than usual. You actually got most of what you ordered. When we got back to the house, Fed Ex had come by, a supplementary fee having guaranteed delivery on the holiday, leaving two packages, both of them for Emma Driver. "Wow!" was all she said, picking them up and hugging the boxes to herself. From her parents? Had Odets and the Infanta finally done something constructive, supplying her address? No one dared ask.

Jesse Maine was also there, lounging by his pickup, and calling out "Noels" and "Season's Greetings" and getting kissed by the ladies.

"Okay, miss?" he asked Emma. "Our schemes and such all set?"

"I think so, Jesse. I'm not terribly good at wrapping but I used lots of scarlet ribbon. I think it'll be okay."

She and Jesse had their plots, so we all stepped back to let them play out. Alix gave me a kiss out there in the driveway, better than either hot breads or eggs Benedict. We'd agreed to exchange gifts here on Further Lane after Emma got back. But it was over my father's objections.

"I like to open the presents early. Damned foolishness waiting till afternoon. Show me a child doesn't want to go downstairs early Christmas morning and see what's under the tree, I'll show you a Prozac-popping adult in the making. It's unnatural not to get at the gifts early." He was like that: Lionel trains for girls, opening presents at dawn.

"I'd cut Emma a little slack on that, father. When did this kid ever have a normal Christmas morning?"

"Well, yes, yes. I see the point. Of course." He barked at me for a bit more and then calmed down, looking slightly abashed. He knew he'd been unfair to Emma, and his anger was directed at himself. Alix, as she was so good at doing, soothed him with a non sequitur.

"My old pa, the earl, once cut a chap dead for passing port to the left. Never spoke to him again. Not even in the lobbies of the House of Lords. Or at the club, both being members of Brats. Fought side by side with Templer's chaps in Malaya. I dare say you know some of those fellows, Admiral."

"Indeed I do. Hard campaigning, that. You respect a man who fought with Templer."

"Right-o!" Alix said. "Meant that much. Pa was quite eloquent on the matter. Surprised all of us, he's usually so taciturn. But not this time.

" 'They've gone too far, now,' he said. 'Socialized medicine, losing India, now, the Channel Tunnel and passing port to the left. Don't chaps realize why we fought two World Wars? Why Kitchener went up the Nile? Why Drake walked away from his game of bowls to go out and sink the Armada? Bloody Spaniards! You expect those fellows to pass port to the left, Napoleon, Hitler, Mao Tse-tung. But not Englishmen! Not decent chaps!' "

"Gosh," I said, having lived in London and understanding how strongly they felt about some things.

My father gathered Alix into his arms, comforting her, attempting to convey his respect for her father the earl. A less subtle personage, but a man much like himself.

Emma and Jesse Maine were back at the house on Further Lane by about two on a cold, sunny Christmas afternoon. "She is something," Jesse told me, shaking his head and marveling. "A small toy, a good wool sweater for each of a dozen kids I told her about. I told her how old they were, about what size. And in each gift package, her idea, not mine, a twenty-dollar bill. And a corny Christmas card. There'll be some happy little Shinnecocks this Christmas."

"A corny card." She got that from Jake Marley. The rest? Well, there's "rich" and there's "rich." Emma had the dough, but what she really had came from inside, didn't it? From the marrow. Or maybe from Mother Superior at her convent, since Emma was forever quoting that good woman: "To whom much is given, girls, much is asked."

And amen to that, say I.

We went into the Admiral's den to exchange gifts. Emma had bought leather belts for everyone.

"At the Coach factory outlet on Main Street. As their advertisement reads: 'Excellent value at fair prices.' Everyone needs a good belt. I hope they fit. I guessed at sizes. But the leather's first-rate. I know it is. There are Italian girls from Milano at the convent. They know good leather."

Well, my belt fit. Barely. My father's didn't. Inga, I don't know. Alix said hers was perfect. But you know how she lies. Jesse? He didn't share his confidences.

Emma opened the Fed Ex presents first, wanting us to know her parents hadn't forgotten. "Look, look," she enthused, holding up her gifts.

Dick had sent a sterling-silver frame from Tiffany with a photo of himself; Nicole a very pretty party dress from Bonne Nuit that didn't quite fit.

"Well, she hasn't measured me in some time," Emma explained away her mother's gaffe.

But she loved her Lionel trains from the Admiral.

"See, I told you!" he said in justifiable triumph. "Girls are just as good as boys. Better, even."

It was nice to see him on the floor of the den with Emma, setting up the tracks so they ran around and under cocktail tables, armchairs, and past the fireplace; wiring up the transformer; adjusting the crossing gate to go up and down properly. And only shocking himself once, and then not seriously, by touching a live third rail. Blame that awkwardness on his damaged fingers.

Christmas is really nice when you're with people you love.

Alix thought so, too. "I do love you, Beecher Stowe."

We exchanged gifts, too. But that's sort of private, what we gave each other. If you don't mind.

Inga's turkey was an enormous success (she broke her own rule and joined us at table), and the Admiral, notably, dove into the creamed onions with a considerable gusto while I ladled out the giblet gravy and kept uncorking bottles of a particularly nuanced Château Haut-Brion.

Christmas permits the minor bending of rules. So Alix convinced us to permit Emma a mere soupçon of a taste, dipping the tip of her tongue into Her Ladyship's glass.

"Mmm," said Emma, licking her lips, "very nice. You always recognize a Grand Cru, don't you? Even when, as in this case, it's perhaps a trifle corky."

It would have spoiled the moment to wonder aloud why her parents, knowing where to send gifts, hadn't bothered to come by.

Chapter Twenty-four

"The count kept ordering wine. My mom had to speak sternly."

The sleek stretch limo in gleaming white rolled silently down Further Lane to enter our driveway just before nine next morning, Boxing Day, December 26.

"Beecher, Beecher! Alix! Admiral, come see! Inga, I told you they wouldn't forget me over Christmas! I told you! I guaranteed it, didn't I?"

"By God!" the Admiral said, appalled but yet impressed by the sheer length of the limo. "A day late but hardly a dollar short, eh?"

Alix and Inga got Emma dressed in white kneesocks and Mary Janes and the navy blue velvet dress Her Ladyship had gotten her at Punch on Newtown Lane. By 9:30 she was ready, the liveried chauffeur bowing and scraping in the best tradition, referring to a written schedule of some sort, and, supposedly, assuring us:

"The young lady's to be back here by four, sir."

"Fine."

There was of course no one else in the car. Had we really expected there might be?

My father, the professional, consulted with Emma, then with the chauffeur, on Dick Driver's unlisted phone number and several other identification cross-references. Emma and he agreed that all checked out. So off she went. For a belated Christmas with her parents. As we all sent up a small but genuine huzzah!

Happy for her.

I guess we all, maybe even Emma, understood the significance of the hired limo. If either Dick or Nicole showed up with his or her own wheels, it would be a point scored against the other. That's how it was in these long-running legal and emotional scrimmages. A rented car, on the other hand, was neutral turf. The demilitarized zone. That night, over dinner, and still red-cheeked and breathless from her adventures, Emma gave us her account of a delicious day spent with her mother and father.

"It was a really neat limo, first of all, *première classe sans doute,* Admiral. With a TV in back and bottles of Evian and an ice bucket and fresh flowers in a vase. Cashew nuts, too. I love cashew nuts; Mother Superior lets us have them on feast days. And an intercom so the driver and I could talk. And room to lie down even. Stretched out, Alix. You would have loved it, even more room than your Hummer. And a sun roof. I stood on one of the seats and rode along for a while with my head out. Like the Queen in London, reviewing the troops. But it was too cold to stay out there long."

"The Trooping of the Colour," Her Ladyship said, "one of those hoary old traditions people make sport of, but which I suspect they'd miss terribly if they were done away with. You know, rather like foxhunting and Guy Fawkes Day."

Emma resumed her report: "My father had me first. And (this triumphantly) he was all alone! No cover girls. Not even one! He even left Miss Lithuania home. I mean, I've nothing against cover girls but, you know, we had a chance to talk. He might run for President, he said. Millions of voters want him to. And we drove someplace for lunch. The best tunafish sandwiches ever—lots of mayonnaise, and nice soft white bread. Not like European bread at all. He said that new photo he'd sent me was a portrait by Bachrach, is that the name? They only do pictures of famous people."

"Yes, very fine photographers," the Admiral said.

"And we drove around for a while past lots of big houses and estates and stuff and my father said if I really, *really* liked the Hamptons, he might buy a place out here one of these days. A big place, not like the house we rented here one summer. He's got a new Ferrari, too. But he thought the limo was better for driving around with me, so I didn't actually get to ride in the Ferrari. It's bright red.

"He used the cell phone a lot. Even the day after Christmas, big business is big business. That's what he said. 'If they publish the *Wall Street Journal* that day, it's a workday.' He let me call a girl I know from the convent. She lives in San Francisco. I had her number, but the maid said she wasn't there. And we toured a very posh country club he said he was thinking of joining.

"But it was mostly closed. For winter, I guess. The grass was all brown. I did tell you about lunch, didn't I? Tunafish with lots of mayo?"

Once she'd been kissed good-bye by her father ("He had to get back to Manhattan—a chopper was coming for him"), the limo whisked Emma off to Nicole and the Impaler.

"I was hoping maybe he stayed behind in Transylvania, but I guess they wanted to be together for Christmas."

"You don't like him?" Alix asked.

"He's okay. Sort of dopey. But real handsome. I think he's younger than Mommie. But don't tell anyone I said that, okay? I call him Count all the time and he likes that. He likes to be called Count and not Vlad."

"Or the Impaler?" I asked, not able to resist.

Emma looked solemn and shook her head. "*Pas du tout*, Beecher. I'd never do that. Wouldn't be polite making fun. Transylvanian people are sensitive, you know. Especially about Dracula and all those scary movies. Wolfbane and not looking into mirrors, and people with long canine teeth, and sprigs of garlic and stuff."

Her mother also took her to lunch. Not tunafish this time. "Mostly like finger food. Salads. Greens. Shrimp and chilled lobster. I don't know the name of the place, but it was pretty nice. I had a bacon, lettuce, and tomato sandwich. With lots of chips.

And low-fat milk, though I don't know why. I'm skinny enough as it is. The count kept ordering wine. My mom had to speak sternly."

"She do that a lot?" the Admiral asked.

"Well, she makes her point of view known. I think that was one of the problems with her and Daddy when I was little."

They drove around, too, as Dick Driver had done. Visited Shelter Island on the car ferry. Emma was a bit vague as to the geography. "But we saw some deer grazing on trees."

"Browsing," my father put in. "Deer graze on grass but browse on trees and bushes. Especially the lower limbs."

"*Merci bien, mynheer.* I'll straighten out the girls on that back at the convent. A middle former always enjoys scoring a point of grammar or vocabulary with the upper form."

Then, in her enthusiasm, Emma told us about visiting the aquarium. Sharks, octopi, sardines, a porpoise, jellyfish, and some frisky seals.

"Well," Alix said when Emma finished and went upstairs to change out of her party clothes, "at least in the end her parents did the correct thing. She really did seem to have had a grand day, didn't she?"

"Tunafish sandwiches. A Ferrari she saw but didn't get to ride in? A country club that was closed? A ride on the Shelter Island ferry? Short rations, those, don't you think?" The Admiral wasn't cutting Mr. and Mrs. Driver much Christmas slack. Not when measured against a set of electric trains.

"What do you think, Beecher?" my father asked.

"Oh, sure. The kid seemed happy, didn't she?"

"Well, yes. I grant you that."

"Yeah," I said. Letting it go at that.

Alix sensed I was going to say more. "And . . . ?" she asked.

"Well," I said, "only there's no aquarium in the Hamptons."

Chapter Twenty-five

*"Not a child's fault, of course.
Your choice of parents."*

So we'd caught the kid in a lie. So what? Alix figured it all out pretty well. At least I thought so. Alix knew about lies (or, as she put it, "the versions, so to speak, of the same truth"), part of her stock in trade, always had been:

"Emma doesn't want to be a victim. To be pitied. She'd guaranteed her parents wouldn't let Christmas pass without seeing their daughter. Promised us they'd be here. So in the end she had to arrange her own outing, her own idyllic day with the loving parents, and ordered up a stretch limo with her credit cards. Invented the whole day . . ."

"But why the deuce would a child—?" the Admiral protested.

"Don't you see, sir," Alix said quietly, "she had to protect her own parents' image. Couldn't permit the world to see them as the self-absorbed and thoughtless people they apparently are. She was protecting Nicole and Dick.

"And, at the same time, she didn't want you and me and Beecher to pity her and be sad. She didn't want to spoil *our* Christmas with *her* disappointments."

"But as adults we can't encourage this sort of, well, mythmaking, can we?" the Admiral objected.

"We can if the myth is crafted not of malice but out of love," Alix said quite firmly.

"Should I speak to her?" my father asked.

Alix's response rather keenly indicated what she thought of that particular notion.

"Only if to agree the local aquarium does indeed sound a super place."

Then we had a fright, uncomfortably close to a kidnap. Thanks to Jesse Maine, it was short-circuited. And though it turned out to be more opera buffa than genuine, it put all of us, especially the Admiral, on the alert.

"That Odets," Jesse reported. "He's telling me her daddy wanted young Emma to visit him in Manhattan for a few hours today. Except that it's got to be hush-hush. Don't want the wife to know about it. Or you and your daddy, Beecher."

"But that's absurd," I protested. "Driver's her father. If he wants to see his daughter over Christmas, that's grand. It's what we've been hoping for. Let him send a car or fly out here and pick her up. So long as Emma doesn't object, why would we?"

"Beats me. But Odets says he'd like to sort of spirit her away, get her to New York and back, all in the same day with no one the wiser. I told him I was sure we could handle that for him."

"Jesse, you can't do that."

"I know I can't. And I ain't. Have a little faith, Beecher. I'm playing this boy like a big bass on light tackle."

The reason Driver wanted his daughter in Manhattan turned out to be a photo op. The *Regis and Kathie Lee Show* (she was still there) was doing a holiday special during the Christmas school break at the Rockefeller Center ice rink and at FAO Schwarz. They wanted some celebrity parents and their kids and had asked Driver (Madonna's and Trump's and the Giulianis' kids were also on the producer's wish list).

Jesse went on, "Lefty says the kids'll get free teddy bears and such. I told him, 'Teddy bears? The kid smokes.' Says Lefty, 'Don't matter. Driver says a Christmas video of him with the daughter is just what them judges need to see over there in that World Court in Belgium.'"

"Holland," I said.

"Teddy bears," said Alix. "Regardless of motive, it's a charming idea. Very old-world. Y'know, Beecher, I still have a favorite teddy bear myself."

"I've met him. Name of Nubar," I said.

"Precisely. Named for that delightful chap Nubar Gulbenkian who used to sue Fleet Street regularly for one shilling in damages. Enjoyed court proceedings. Had Fortnum & Mason send in lunch in hampers during the trial. Chilled champagne, potted shrimp and pheasant."

"A photo op indeed!" my father thundered. "I'll be damned if we'll play cat's-paw in a custody fight."

"Shouldn't we ask Emma? Maybe she'd enjoy a day in town with her father."

"Then let him contact us directly," the Admiral riposted, "and not send around snoopers!"

I don't know why Jesse was grinning so broadly. "Well, you can stop arguing. About five A.M. this morning me and Odets met down by the Reutersham parking lot and I told him the deal's off. Security's so tight along Further Lane, with all them rich Protestants, no one's borrowing Miss Emma for the day. Not even me with all my Native American wiles. But as disappointed as his boss is going to be, Admiral, might not be a bad idea to keep a close lookout in case they try again."

My father thanked Jesse and told him we'd "secure our flanks with all hands on deck."

Jesse admitted he had toyed with the idea of sending a ringer into Manhattan in Odets' limo just to embarrass Lefty and annoy Mr. Driver.

"Where do you find a ringer for a ten-year old girl?" I asked.

"I was going to tog out Phil Swift Rabbit in a stocking cap and woman's coat and send him. He ain't got nothing better to do and enjoys a nice ride."

"Phil Swift Rabbit's forty and he's got one eye," I protested.

"I know. But he's small and skinny and there ain't much light at five A.M."

"Jesus, Jesse" was all my father could say, and we all agreed not to tell Emma. Though Alix argued it was the kind of devious plot the kid would love.

Jacob Marley's home, the big house vaguely recalled by young Emma Driver, had been sold when they settled the estate. The unmarried Sis had never lived there in any case, only filling in on occasion to play hostess for her brother. She had her own place, a house on the east bank of Three Mile Harbor, overlooking a small marina she owned and, as something of a hobby, managed.

"I like boats, the smell of salt," she told the curious, "I like boat people. And from this house I look out on a pleasant body of salt water, into which the sun sinks each evening at dusk. If your tastes are anything like mine, what better place to live? Anywhere?" To intimates she admitted there was another, tongue-in-cheek motive:

"And I may be the only 'marina operator' listed by the Vassar Alumnae bulletin."

The Admiral drove us over in his car. There was plenty of parking. Few people went boating at Three Mile Harbor in the cold December. A weathered old man scratching himself manned the naval stores and bait shop at the head of the marina property. Glancing out through a streaked and frosted window at us, and calculating shrewdly that we weren't going to buy bait or shop for tarred line and turnbuckles, he ignored us. Alix and I returned to the car while my father and Emma walked up the path to Sis's house.

"This isn't it," Emma said flatly, "this isn't the house I remember."

"No," said my father gently, "you're right, that was another house, Jake's place. That's been sold."

The Admiral called out, alerting Sis to their arrival, not wanting to startle her. After a moment or two, a tall, physically impressive woman came out onto the broad veranda hung with its faux gas-lamps, unlit now of course in the gray but bright winter morning. My father hadn't seen Sis for a time, but she was a familiar figure in her gum boots, wide-wale corduroy pants, and an oversized man's denim shirt, with red workmen's suspenders, a cigarette in her crimsoned mouth, and a man's felt hat cocked jauntily over one eye, topping off the ensemble. There was a lean, rangy elegance about her despite the odd getup. Even the snapbrim gray fedora looked right. The look was Roz Russell out of Kate Hepburn, with overtones in the husky voice of Jean Arthur, of the *Mr. Deeds* days, the era of Jefferson Smith.

As my father made the introductions, pleased to see Emma curtsey nicely and extend a firm hand to her hostess, he stared into Sis's face, looking for any indication her hostility to Driver was carrying over to his daughter.

"If there had been," he told me when he got back, "I wouldn't have left Emma there alone with Sis. I would have found some excuse to stay, discuss the weather, hint I could use a cup of coffee against the chill. But there wasn't. So I issued 'good day to all here' and left."

"And Emma didn't seem intimidated?"

The admiral gave me a look.

"Not our Emma. She said, '*va bene*,' and went off with Sis, like a couple of sorority sisters."

I was less confident about Sis, the keeper of her brother's flame. As heiress and executrix, she knew what her brother had done to secure the happiness and well-being of the child of his worst enemy. You could have written novels about it; stage plays; Proust crossed with Faulkner by way of Ibsen. Old Marley, betrayed by his protégé Driver, still the benefactor of the rogue's only child. Sis could have been forgiven a natural resentment.

Here's what Emma herself, and later Sis, told us of their meeting.

Sis, who never had a child, never even came close, wasn't famous for tact:

"Not a child's fault, of course, your choice of parents."

"Mo, ma'am," the girl said, having been thoroughly coached by the Admiral to try being agreeable.

"Come sit by me, dear." They were in a wonderfully cluttered living room with overstuffed furniture, ship models, highly polished brass sextants, compasses, and ships' bells, with oil paintings of ancient sea battles, British and French men o' war mostly, firing broadsides. It was a glorious room such as children love, and Emma stared at the paintings and ached to get up and touch the ship models. Beyond vast picture windows, boats' masts and rigging stood out against an expanse of water.

"*Merci bien*, dear lady."

"Chocolates?"

"*Danke.*"

"What the devil language do you speak?"

"Several tongues. Our school in Switzerland is known, humorously, as the Tower of Babel."

When the kid was seated and munching, Sis started up, her language to the point, clipped and salty, but not vulgar:

"Your father, I need not inform you, killed my brother Jake."

"I understood Mr. Marley took a pleurisy, lingered for a time, and passed away peacefully though coughing."

"Stuff and nonsense. It was murder. Murder two, manslaughter at the very least."

"If that's a fact, *Fraulein* Marley, they kept it from me, I assure you, *chère Mademoiselle*."

"Don't wonder. Dick Driver killed him surer than hell, as if he'd pulled the trigger. Devoured the man's company, stole his good name, accepted credit for great projects and enormous monuments he hadn't built. Did this to a man who took your father in as a novice draftsman and taught him the ropes, promoted him to junior partner. And did Dick Driver thank his benefactor, express his gratitude, demonstrate loyalty? The hell!"

Emma thought it was time to say something.

"My father always spoke highly of Mr. Marley in my presence."

Sis bounced nimbly to her feet, very much still the sailor and a quick mover despite age.

"A hypocrite as well. Murder and hypocrisy both, which is the greater sin, eh? Have another chocolate."

Emma tried to recall which were the seven capital sins (gluttony, envy, sloth, and covetousness being among them) the nuns at La Tour were forever drilling into them, but couldn't recall hypocrisy being among them nor its relative rank. "I have no idea, Signorina."

"The square ones are especially fine. Coconut meat insides."

"I do like coconut insides. *Muchas gracias.*"

"Well, then, on the assumption you can walk and chew chocolates at the same time, girl," Sis wisecracked, grinning widely at her own stab at humor, "get yourself off that couch and I'll show you around the place. Those ship models are something, aren't they?"

Marley's marina was a pocket-size but professionally rigged operation on the eastern shore of Three Mile Harbor, directly across the water from Tony Duke's Boys' Harbor. "Tony puts on a dandy fireworks show every Bastille Day," Sis said enthusiastically. "Gets George Plimpton to set them off. About ten years ago some rockets went screwy and landed among the picnickers and boaters, damned near killed people. You could hear the cursing and cries for help all the way over here on the other shore. That was a night to remember, by God! You would have loved it, girlie."

"*Ach du lieber,* I'm sure, *Fraulein.*"

The marina tour was brief but included an onboard inspection of Sis Marley's own personal pleasure craft, a sleek cigarette boat she piloted herself. "It ought to be pulled by now and cocooned in plastic for the winter. But so long as the harbor hasn't yet frozen solid, I keep it in the water and take her out codfishing of a clear morning if the wind is down. Down in Miami, if you ever get there, this is the sort of boat they run drugs in through Biscayne Bay from the Bahamas. Gun battles night after night, you'd think we were back in Prohibition with Al Capone and the Untouchables fighting it out with machine guns. Get them to teach you girls about those days at your school. Part of history, and don't you forget it."

"My word," said Emma (now sailing under her own name), delighted to get off the subject of her father's penchant for murder (or manslaughter) and hypocrisy. And onto violence and mayhem blamed on others.

They were getting on so well by now, Sis and Emma (*not* Sis and the rest of the Drivers) that the old woman said, "Can you swim?"

"Yes, though the water must be pretty cold, don't you think?"

"Cold as a well-digger's ass, girlie. But we're not going swimming. It's only when I take someone out in a boat, I like to know about their survival skills, see? That makes sense, doesn't it?"

"Yes ma'am. And are you taking me out? *Che bella cosa!*"

Sis bundled Emma into a huge yellow life vest, a personal-flotation device that fastened over her Bogner skiing anorak, and they sped out of Three Mile Harbor to bounce around Gardiners Bay for an hour or two, the big cigarette boat easily exceeding whatever speed limits they had in summer, but which were conveniently ignored in winter.

"How's that, kiddo?" Sis shouted, spitting to leeward and watching Emma, who was briefly permitted to handle the wheel. "Isn't she a corker?"

Emma assumed Sis meant the speedboat and responded with enthusiasm:

"*Formidable! Wunderbar!* and *Olé!* as well!"

Sis tucked a fresh cigarette into a corner of her mouth and grinned broadly when the Zippo lighter set it aflame. Having a kid around was fun.

Even one that was Dick Driver's whelp.

Then Emma asked the question she'd been waiting to ask, swallowing hard first:

"Why is it the fishermen keep stealing Mr. Marley's bones?

"What are you talking about? What fishermen?"

"A gentleman named Bob White told us about it at the Candy Kitchen over thick shakes."

"First of all, Miss Smartyboots, they're not fishermen. They're Baymen, a hard but highly honorable profession. And a true profession, not just buying a subscription to *Field & Stream* and getting togged out in Ralph Lauren hipboots and little hats with flies stuck on, and playing at fishing. Releasing-live and that crap. Baymen keep their catch. Sell it at market price, or clean, cook, and eat it at home. Read Peter Matthiessen. He did a book about them, *Men's Lives*. Hell of a book. Eloquent and a heartbreaker."

"I'm sure," Emma said, wanting to appear agreeable.

"Yeah, but you don't appreciate what that title means."

"No, ma'am."

"Matthiessen quoted somebody from long ago saying that when people went to the market and bought fish, 'It isn't fish you're buying, it's men's lives.'"

Emma nodded, solemn, as Sis continued.

"And they don't really steal Jake's bones, y'know; they sort of borrow them."

"Oh, then that makes a difference."

"Sure does. They're making a point of sorts. An illegal point is my contention. That even if I bought the graveyard fair and square, pursuant to brother Jake's last will and so on, they think they've still got squatters' rights."

"What are those?"

"Legal easements and such, stuff only a damned lawyer understands, that boil down to they have a right, under usage and the seventeenth- and eighteenth-Century royal patents, to be buried in the Old Churchyard, in land owned by parties of another part, meaning me and Jake's estate. I say they haven't. They say they have. I retained a lawyer, they got one. SOBs, both of them. End of this month we'll know for sure, when the Old Churchyard trustees hand down their final say-so on the matter. Some of the Baymen are highly offended that I'm standing up for my rights. And for Jake's wishes from beyond the grave."

"So they steal his bones."

"Borrow."

"Borrow," the girl agreed. Which inspired one final sortie from Sis:

"And in any event, it wasn't Baymen my brother wanted kept out of those graves. Not my responsibility to explain things to them if they can't figure that out for themselves.

"It was the late arrivals and the newly rich Jake resented. I can hear him now, ranting and ripping at a great rate: 'I don't need Calvin Klein or that pipsqueak Dick Cavett planted next to me over the centuries. Or Donna Karan. A man dies, he ought to get some rest. Peace at last, peace at last, God Almighty, peace at last. Which doesn't mean Wall Streeters or Betty Friedan. I wouldn't mind Billy Joel or Carl Yastremski or Ben Bradlee. But not that wife of his! I don't need Sally Quinn and the earthworms both, nattering at me for all eternity, no sir!' "

Sis Marley nodded vigorously at young Emma.

"That was Jake. Never a word against the Baymen. Just the out-siders and rock stars and damned phonies. And your daddy."

Emma sort of snuffled then, tugging a dainty handkerchief from her sleeve.

"You didn't take a chill out there in the boat, did you?" Sis Marley shouted angrily, frightened she might have gone too far. "Admiral Stowe'll be giving me hell if you did."

"No, ma'am."

"Come here, let me feel your forehead, see if you're burning up."

She placed a solicitous hand on the child's forehead. "Cool. That's good."

Emma snuffled or sniffled again.

"What in hell . . . ?"

"Je suis triste, madame. C'est tout."

"Give me that in English, kiddo."

"I said I'm sad, that's all."

"Oh, hell, not to worry. They always bring Jake back."

"Which is wonderful. And reassuring. But I meant I was sad that when Mr. Hucko washes up, he can't be 'planted' in the Old

Churchyard, where a Bayman belongs. That's what Bob White said. That you'll turn Reds Hucko away and won't let him in there with Mr. Marley and Jackson Pollock and the rest."

Sis just shook her head but made no response. It was too damned complicated for a child and, besides that, in litigation. She didn't have to justify herself to anyone, didn't choose to debate the issue or get her young guest's nose running again. So to mollify the kid, she called the Admiral for his approval of Emma's staying for dinner. So that, as dusk closed in, Sis was hard at it, preparing the meal, letting Emma shell peas in the big old country kitchen. During which time, Sis Marley changed the subject away from her and her dead brother and back to where Dick Driver was the villain.

"You listen up, now, girlie, to a version of what happened that you surely never heard out of your daddy's mouth."

She recounted her brother's earlier tragedies, then his decline into bitterness and eventually into hate, much of it occasioned by ill-treatment at the hands of Emma's father.

"And where's that bastard now?"

"I'm sure I don't know," Emma said, technically correct, and sensing it wouldn't be wise to reveal Dick Driver was actually supposed to have been here in the Hamptons, in recent days taking her for limo rides. "He travels a lot. I don't have to tell you, construction men go wherever there's a building to be put up or a bridge to be built. He used to send postcards to the convent from the most exotic places. I wrote back care of his bankers. Now that there's E-mail, communication is faster. But I do miss the postcards. I kept a collection. Even the nuns enjoyed seeing them."

All during the day and into the evening and through a rather glorious dinner, Sis had expressed no interest in or curiosity about Emma's mother.

Chapter Twenty-six

Like one of those old movies about Welsh coal miners. With Donald Crisp leading . . .

In the cheerful seasonal chaos leading up to Christmas, it was understandable that the controversy over the Old Churchyard and sale of plots to the Marley estate had cooled.

With trees to be trimmed and shopping to be done, not even the most ferocious of Baymen was even marginally interested in graveyards. It took Peanuts Murphy to remind local people of what was at stake. And even he waited until the morning after Christmas, December 26, to relight the dampened fires of protest.

"We got six damned days!" Peanuts announced, "and that's it! Six days. If the cemetery trustees don't reverse theirselves by the end of the year and cancel the sale of plots to the Marleys, it's over. Once December 31 is come and gone, we've lost and Mean Jake's won! He's dead and we ain't but he's gonna beat us."

He placed phone calls, buttonholed men in the street, dropped by their homes, pounding on doors and shouting at windows, roamed the Montauk docks searching for men mending nets and looking into bilges. He stuck his head into Wolfie's Tavern before eleven, when only the serious morning beer-and-a-shot drinkers would be there, and generally made a nuisance of himself. Which didn't discourage Peanuts one bit. In the words of the Marine Corps recruiting commercials, he reckoned he needed "only a few good men" to convince the trustees of error and get them to reverse their approval of the Marley estate's purchase of 109 gravesites in the Old Churchyard.

But how to convince them when he was having trouble even finding them? The trustees were a nicely balanced demographic mix of blue-collar and moneyed locals. One trustee was in the hospital UpIsland having a hernia operation. Another was skiing at Stowe, Vermont, with the grandchildren. A third was visiting relatives in Pittsburgh over Christmas. And no trustee meeting was scheduled before January 15. By mid-afternoon of the day after Christmas, Murphy was licked. And knew it. How could he whip together a convincingly hostile crowd to pressure the trustees into action when the trustees wouldn't cooperate by staying in town where he could find them and change their minds, wheedling and threatening if need be?

Then it came to Peanuts! If he couldn't sway the town, why not scare hell out of the Marley estate? Namely, Sis. Here was something which might be done. They knew where she lived, she never went anywhere, and she had it within herself to come to a decision without a quorum or any of that other crap and red tape. Now all Peanuts had to do was rally a few dozen or half a hundred Baymen.

Which, even as stubborn as she was, might just be sufficient to impress the old lady. If only he could get the boys to turn out in the cold with snow threatening.

My father took the call. When he hung up, he looked at Alix and me.

"Jesse Maine. He says there's trouble brewing over at Sis Marley's."

"What is it?"

"Peanuts Murphy got some Baymen and other locals whipped up about the cemetery. The Bonac Boys're planning a march on her house. With the trustees' sale deadline New Year's Eve at midnight, they're out to get Sis to renege."

"Oh, Beecher. Emma!"

150

"That's what I'm thinking. We'd better get over there. I don't like having Emma alone with the old lady if there's trouble."

Alix wanted to go with us, but the Admiral ordered her to stay here manning the command post and taking messages. "Call Jesse back and tell him we're on our way to Three Mile Harbor. If he can meet us there, fine."

I'm not sure Alix bought it, but she stayed.

"You bring Emma back here, whatever happens," she told me.

"Don't worry. She'll be fine."

We drove up in my Blazer to Three Mile Harbor and pulled onto the shoulder just short of where the Marley property began. No mob scene yet, not that we could see. A couple of Baymen lounged about the bait shop, shuffling their feet and trying to stay warm. It wasn't a barricade that they were manning as much as it was informational picketing. Beyond them, beyond the gate, down the flagstoned path, Sis Marley's big old house sat there peaceful enough, a warm, well-lighted place, the faux gas lamps of the porch and verandah throwing a soft light. Above us, the sky was dark. No moon, the stars masked over by cloud. It really did feel as if snow was coming—you know that cold, damp feel. I killed the motor, started to get out. But the Admiral stopped me.

"To hear Jesse talk, I thought we'd have Baymen scaling the walls and having a go at the front door with battering rams. Let's sit here a bit and see what happens. We shouldn't be the ones to start something."

When it came to small-unit tactics, I took my lead from my father. He was the Annapolis graduate, the professional; I wasn't. I'd attended a few wars as an onlooker, writing about them. We didn't have long to wait.

You could see the Baymen coming a quarter mile away from the torchlights they carried, could hear the singing. It was like one of those old Hollywood movies with the Welsh coal miners marching through the village to confront the mine owner, who was always Donald Crisp or someone. Or maybe Donald Crisp was the head miner, their union shop steward . . .

Only in this case they weren't heading to a coal mine but to the Old Churchyard, via the Marley place. And of a mind to take Sister with them. By force, if necessary. If the trustees wouldn't reverse themselves, Sis Marley would have to.

"Okay, Beecher," my father said. "They've started it. Let's go up there to the house so we can stand by Sis and face them down if necessary."

"Okay."

I knew one of the three Baymen at the gate, the biggest, most menacing of the three. "Hi, Beecher. Cold night."

"Sure is, Henny," I said, without breaking stride.

We were past them by then and through the gate. One of the others seemed about to start something but saw the Admiral's hard face, his scarred hands, and didn't. My father rapped on the door, then tugged on the cord dangling from a big ship's bell.

"It's Beecher Stowe, Sis, and my son. Open up. Cold out here."

The door swung open and there, standing in the light, was Sis Marley with, by her side, young Emma Driver.

"Hi, Admiral," Emma said cheerfully. "This is a real nice house. Did you know Auntie Sis has a whole fleet of boats out back? We took one for a ride. She let me drive, too. Hundreds of boats, all sizes. Like the Spanish Armada they taught us about last term at the convent."

"I do, Emma. A fine fleet. And no Drake to confront them." Annapolis men are precise about such matters.

Now Sis Marley spoke up, a bit sour about it, I thought.

"Well, come in, come in if you must. We're just about finished dinner. Don't let all the warmth leak out into the night."

"Thank you, Sis," my father said. He had the old courtier's gallantry, whatever his inner reservations, and understood that with a harridan like Sis, charm might take you a long way. She had, after all, graduated from Vassar. I didn't know whether to smile amiably or look solemn, in keeping with a crisis atmosphere. The Bonackers were still a few hundred yards down the road, but I knew they were coming, could see their lights, dancing, flickering in the wind. I wasn't yet sure if Sis knew they were coming. And why.

Sis Marley planted her big hands on her corduroyed haunches,

Emma small but standing straight, very much at her side, one hand raised sufficiently high to touch one of Sis's big paws. Sensing her gesture, Sis relaxed and opened that hand so that the child could slip her own small, slender hand into that of Sis Marley. So we stepped inside and I closed the door behind us, wondering if I ought to turn the latch and lock it against the approaching Baymen.

"Pull up to that fire, Beecher," Sis said, addressing my father. "There's snow coming if I'm not mistaken, and I've got coffee on the stove. With fresh cinnamon sticks to flavor it."

"Fine, Sis." Let things develop at her pace.

The windows in the front of the old house brightened, as the torchlights neared, and now you could hear the men, not individual voices but a kind of low, communal rumbling. I looked down at Emma, wanting to know if she were scared. And how badly.

Sis fetched the coffee and then she said, quite offhandedly, "So Peanuts Murphy and his cronies are about to make a house call." So she *did* know, knew just what was happening, but didn't seem shaken by it.

"Looks like it, Sis," my father said.

Emma, sensing something but not knowing what, said, "Hi, Beecher! Where's Alix?"

She wasn't scared. Not much, anyway.

"At the command post, Emma. In charge of telephone calls and messages from on high. You know."

Over the coffee Sis Marley and the Admiral talked. Not wanting to alarm a child, they used understated terms. Emma caught on anyway.

"I thought you might have Chief Maine along," she suggested. "He's the sort of fellow for nights like this. All those battles with the Pequots."

The Admiral looked down at her, disapprovingly. "You forget, young lady, this is Sis Marley's house and property. She's in charge here, and not some fellows out there singing songs and waving torches. As for me, this is the work I do. Have done for years. And you may not know it because my boy doesn't brag on himself, but

Beecher faced down that mob in Algiers and saved the princess a couple of years back. Getting shot in the doing, as well. You've got professionals here, Emma. We're equipped to handle this."

Emma's mouth fell open and she looked up at me, eyes widened in admiration.

"You never told me about that, Beecher. Wow! Algiers! Was it the Casbah? How big a mob was it? Where did you get shot? What princess did you save? Tell me it was Diana, or Caroline of Monaco, or someone like that? Please, please, please!"

"Have another cookie," Sis told her, handing around a tray with a big kettle steaming away. The cinnamon sticks smelled wonderful. "I'd like to hear that story m'self, Beecher."

"Yes, ma'am," I said.

Now came a chant from outside, loud and growing louder.

"Hucko, Hucko! Bury Reds!/ Hucko, Hucko! Bury Reds!/ Hucko, Hucko! Bury Reds . . ."

Chapter Twenty-seven

Damned Marleys shut us out. Them and their Hollywood friends . . .

"Damn fools," Sis said in the slightly smug tones of a Vassar graduate, "how do you bury a fellow lost at sea?"

The Admiral nodded.

"They don't think these things through, Sis. Let's get Murphy in here out of the cold. Talk to him quietly. Make him see sense over a cup of your coffee with cinnamon."

"I won't have trailer-park trash in my house, Beecher. Hell with them!"

"They're Baymen, Sis, good men," my father said quietly, "not trash. You of all people know better than that."

She nodded, accepting the scolding. Hadn't she earlier defended the Baymen to Emma Driver?

"I do. You're right. It was anger talking. All that breaking into Jake's mausoleum and stealing his bones. Damn-fool thing to do. I don't take such matters lightly."

"Nor should you," the Admiral agreed.

Outside, the light of torches was closer still and the chant deep-throated, louder. They didn't sing as well as the Welsh miners, but when it came to loud, they needn't apologize to anyone.

155

Menacing. It was that, too. Even if it came from men we all knew. Had known always. I glanced down again at Emma, who didn't know these men and was only a kid, tugging Sis's hand. Not scared, just bonding or something like that. She didn't scare easily, give her that.

Somewhere in the house, a phone rang. In ways, Emma reminded me of . . .

"A Lady Dunraven calling, Beecher," Sis said. When my father reached for the phone, the old lady pulled it back. "No, your son."

"Yes?" I said.

"Alix, Beecher. Jesse Maine's en route. I told him you and the Admiral were over there."

"Good, we might need reinforcements."

"How's Emma?"

"Cool, just fine. Emma is a Junior League 'Alix.' "

"What does that mean, 'Junior League'?"

"It means 'of good family.' The right schools, the right stuff, and all that."

"Oh, good."

"Alix, we may have a small riot here. Stay by the phone. I'll call you back."

By now, my father was calling signals.

"Stay here with the women," he told me. "I'm going out to talk to Murphy if he's the one in charge and won't come in."

He opened the door and stepped out into the flickering illumination of the torches. I didn't wait but went with him, ignoring his directions and brushing past Sis.

"Murphy!"

"I'm here, Admiral. Right up front where you can see me."

"You make a habit of this, Murphy? Leading a mob of men by night up to the front door of a single woman alone?"

"You know I ain't, Admiral."

"Well, then, why are you—"

"You know damn well why. The Old Churchyard. The damned Marleys shut us out. Their rich friends, their Hollywood pals get planted. But when Reds Hucko washes up—"

"The trustees sold those gravesites, Murphy. The Marleys bought them. Fair and square. Blame the trustees. Maybe you and I think they shouldn't have put them up for sale. But they did. And . . ."

"To hell with you, Admiral!" a man yelled from behind Peanuts Murphy. And then someone threw something, I don't know what, but it hit the house with a thud. The front line of the crowd seemed to be surging toward us. Not fast, but moving. There were forty or fifty of them, two of us.

"Can't you control a few men, Murphy?" my father asked quietly, disdain in his voice, very near a cool contempt. "I thought you were their leader."

"Why, you son of a—"

"Peanuts!" I said, "don't say things you'll want to take back."

"Oh, yeah."

The first rank of Bonac Boys was at the porch steps now, coming on.

It was then the door opened behind us and Sis Marley came out. Emma Driver hanging on to her.

Seeing them standing there in the porch light, the old woman and the kid, seemed to give pause to the leading ranks of Baymen and Bonac Boys.

Mean Jake's sister and heir grasped the moment. Forty years earlier she'd graduated from Vassar and had spent all that time living it down, shaking off the good breeding. Now was her chance fully and finally to put Vassar to rest.

"Listen to me, you fellows," said Sis, tossing aside a cigarette to make room for talk, her voice carrying easily in the suddenly still night, "If you had the brains of a piss clam, you'd know there never was a problem with burying Reds. Or any genuine Bayman. Instead, you've been listening to a lot of crap, sorry to talk so, girl . . ."

"It's okay, Auntie Sis."

". . . stuff that troublemakers were peddling cheap. And you bought high. Don't you know there isn't a man in East Hampton Jacob Marley would rather rest alongside than Hucko. I could name people, lots of 'em, he wouldn't be comfortable with, but a Bayman like Reds, a fisherman, wouldn't be among them.

"But just in case you're still confused, any of you, listen up to what I'm telling you."

There was a real hush now, forty or fifty men standing still in the cold night, listening. Maybe they weren't going to buy what she told them, but they were willing to hear it. In the back ranks, taller than most, I could just see Jesse Maine. Jesse and a half dozen of the Shinnecocks, including that new shaman, the one who looked into men's eyes. Having Jesse there made me feel better. And then Sis Marley began and made everyone feel better:

"Until December 31 when the trustees' sale is final, I didn't want to go public, make any announcments. Then this innocent young child here, brought up strictly over there in Switzerland by the holy Sisters, asked me to explain things so she'd understand. She pinned me down, so to speak, about just what was at issue here. So in response to *her* questions, and any confusion there might be among still be among *you*, let me say this:

"Since men first went down to the sea in ships here on the East End, their dead have been buried in the Old Churchyard, if found. And if they never were found, a stone was set up there in their name. Jake Marley didn't leave behind instructions to buy up cemetery space to keep Baymen out; he wanted the Old Churchyard kept local, so there'd always be room there for men like Reds Hucko. And for others who lived and worked out here, artists like Pollack, a good man like Alan Pakula, a gentleman like Tony Duke when it's his time. Jake didn't want the last hundred plots taken over by movie stars and CEOs and rich outsiders buying up graves, the way they buy acreage on Further Lane or down by Georgica Pond.

"No one's banishing Reds Hucko or any other decent East Hampton Bayman from a plot near my brother. Jacob Marley knew the value of good land and could afford what it cost, saving the Churchyard *for* you. Not in spite of you."

Peanuts, up front, rubbed a big hand over his face, not knowing quite what to say, what to believe. The rest of them murmured, going from one foot to another, in an uncomfortable silence. Which Sis Marley now broke.

"There's snow coming, maybe a big one. So I think you and the Stowes and the Shinnecocks and everyone should just go home now nice and quiet. But talk it over among you. And if you want, come by the Old Churchyard Tuesday or Wednesday morning after the storm, say by about ten, we'll have a little service for Reds Hucko. Fetch a preacher, one Reds would feel comfortable about, not some Holy Joe, and make the arrangements. Or whistle up that tame nun of yours, the Sister Infanta they're all talking about. If she's busy, praying down there by the high water mark, I'll read the damned lesson m'self. No charge. Not for Reds. And we'll set up a stone. Let Peanuts decide the words to chisel into it. And we'll have ourselves a service. Courtesy of the late Jake Marley. For Reds Hucko. And ditto for any Bonacker goes back a generation or several. So long as there's gravesites there, the men of East Hampton waters will be welcomed. Whether the body's washed up or not.

"And now, Amen! And God bless all here. Good night."

The men broke up now, a bit shamed, some dousing their torches, a few keeping them for illumination down Three Mile Harbor Road to where they left their trucks. In the light you could see the first flakes of snow falling. Real snow, this time, not that teasing you get before Christmas.

We bundled a sleepy Emma Driver into one of Sis Marley's big old down comforters and carried her back down the lane to where the Blazer waited. Jesse walked with us the length of the lane, just to be sure nothing happened. Not that it would; not after what Sis told the Baymen.

But Tuesday at ten wouldn't work out. Not because of the Bonac Boys or second thoughts by Sis. But because of last winter's first big snow . . .

Chapter Twenty-eight

I love Alix's feet but prefer them toasty warm,
if you know what I mean . . .

I suggest that if you've seen one blizzard, you've seen them all, but this snow did have its moments. Not that a self-respecting Great Plains blizzard lashing the Dakotas or a six-footer closing Snowqualmie Pass, would have taken notice, but for East Hampton it was pretty fair. And would end up being memorable. Mainly because at the height of the storm, at its worst, Emma got us all, even the Admiral, down with a serious bout of the guilts.

"Mother Superior always asks, shouldn't we be helping out in some way, girls? And not just letting people freeze to death or go hungry? You know, the way she had us tithing for the Manila streetwalkers last year?" Alix Dunraven was not only willing to go along with Emma and Mother Superior in "helping out," she was desperate to try out what the car dealers told her the Hummer was capable of in a pinch. Or a deep snow.

The night before, driving home from "rescuing" Sis Marley (who really didn't need much rescuing), the snow was already falling. By the time I fell asleep about one A.M., getting up one last time to be sure to tuck in the big old L.L. Bean down comforter around Alix's feet (I love her feet anyway but prefer them toasty warm, if you know what I mean), it was really coming down heavy. You could see that from my bedroom window in the yellow headlights of the occasional car driving along Further Lane. At seven, when I first stirred, I knew it was a big one, with cornices already building in a serious way on the roof of the garage, and shrubs and even the tall privet hedges bending low under the weight of snow. I love big storms of any sort—wind, rain, snow, ice. Always have. If there's an AP dispatch about a typhoon in Bangladesh or an avalanche on Mont Blanc, I digest it line for line, avid for details. Such events bring out the boy in me, and because I'm forever suspecting Alix is more like I am than she really thinks she is, it made me want to share the excitement, and my enthusiasm, with Her Ladyship.

"Alix, wake up, wake up! Look at the snow!"

"Super, darling," she murmured sleepily, a cosmopolitan who'd skied Val d'Isère and surely had seen snow previously, lifting both arms to draw me back to bed.

Yes, well, you know how I am, how I went back. Malleable, isn't that the operative word?

A bit later she got around to looking out the window and she, too, jumped up and ran about the bedroom, clapping her hands. Seeing a naked Alix run about and clap her hands is always pleasant, and once she slowed I caught up and kissed her here and there and kind of stroked various parts of her, as one does on a cold morning. Enjoying all the snow at the same time.

If you know what I mean.

Over breakfast she said, "What a marvelous opportunity to try out the Hummer, darling. See if it's what the brochures claim."

Emma joined us before we were finished.

"Gosh, did you see all the snow? And it's still coming down. The Admiral says if the temperature's below twenty Farenheit and the wind is blowing over a certain speed, this might qualify as an official 'blizzard.' Do you think it will, Beecher?"

I told her I did, yes.

"The Admiral and I had sausage and eggs. Inga made them. She lets me have lots of ketchup, too. The Brides of Christ, unfortunately, don't allow ketchup at table. A light vinaigrette but no ketchup. The French influence, don't you think, Alix?"

"I'm sure you're right. Though we English are hardly the ones to ask about cuisine, haute or otherwise."

"The Admiral said he'd make us grits one morning. What *are* grits, Beecher, do you know?"

"A southern dish. Some grainy kind of thing. I don't like it much."

"Nor does the Admiral," Emma said. "But he says they served it at the Naval Academy and so it reminds him of when he was twenty and that always cheers him up."

She hadn't yet been afflicted by the guilts; nor had she started working her ways on us, but was still regarding the blizzard as an entertainment we'd put on for her delectation.

"*Vive la neige!*" she called out, "hooray for snow!"

And when Alix told her we were taking out the Hummer, Emma volunteered instantly to brush the car free of snow. "Have you a good broom, Beecher?" she inquired. "That's what's needed with snow this dry and soft."

And that's what you want around in a snowstorm, a Hummer idling at the curb and a kid who lives in Switzerland and knows all about clearing off the snow.

"One broom coming up."

According to the Weather Channel, one of my father's favorite listening posts during foul weather, the snow might continue for another eight or ten hours on the East End of Long Island and could total twenty inches before ending. The temperature was twenty-one, the wind was gusting to twenty-five miles per hour.

"Not yet blizzard conditions," a slightly disappointed Admiral informed us. Clearly, my own passion for storms was inherited.

Togged out in mittens, boots, and her familiar anorak by Willy Bogner, her red nose and cheeks courtesy of East Hampton, Emma had done a workmanlike job of getting the snow off Alix's Hummer.

"Can I drive, Alix?"

"You're underage," I said flatly. Emma ignored me.

"If my feet reach the pedals I should be able to handle it, Alix. You could sit next to me and take over if I lose control."

"You've got to be seventeen," I said, "or sixteen if you're in driver's ed."

"When the snow's cleared, Emma," the Admiral said, neatly undercutting my principled stance, "I'll roll out the Packard and give you a lesson in the driveway. So long as we don't venture onto the village roads, you'll be all right."

The kid gave me a look.

"A smashing notion, Admiral," Alix enthused, "Beecher's caution does him credit. But in life, one takes one's chances, doesn't one?"

"Come on," I said, "let's get rolling or Emma'll have to sweep the Hummer again."

The plows had already come past once, clearing Further Lane, but blocking our gravel drive with a foot and a half of plowed snow. Alix didn't hesitate but shifted into four-wheel drive and low gear, bucking the Hummer right through, tossing up fluffy snow to right and left.

"Jolly good!" she said. "Power to spare, I'd warrant."

"Can I at least steer?"

"Perhaps later, Emma. Let me get the feel of it on snow."

Va va vroooom!

At Egypt Lane we turned south to roll down between the parallel fairways of the golf course to Old Beach to see the ocean.

"Golly, look at those waves," Alix said. "Remember when we swam out there with Prince Fatoosh?"

"I do. We raced and you won."

"Well, you came second, Beecher. Don't be modest, now."

"Who's Prince Fatoosh?" Emma wanted to know.

"Arab friend of ours," I said. "He and I were at Harvard together, Dunster House, Dunster funsters, both."

"We had an Arab girl at the convent. But she didn't get on. Kept kneeling down to face Mecca at the most awkward times. Such as when Sister was saying the rosary. Or during math class. It didn't go over at all well. But she was allowed to drive cars when she was only six. She said her father the sheikh had blocks fastened to the pedals so her feet could reach."

"Can we walk on the beach?" Alix asked.

There was already a foot of snow down and drifting much deeper in places and the wind was getting up. I wasn't much for walking on beaches in blizzards.

As we retraced our tire tracks up Old Beach Lane, Richard Ryan's red pickup pulled up alongside, another East Hamptoner enjoying the snow. "Wind's out of the northeast now," Richard Ryan shouted through a rolled-down window. "Lazy Point's cut off and they'll be getting green water from Gardiners Bay across Gerard Drive at high tide." Richard looked happy about all these promising developments. It was clear the Admiral and I weren't the only ones to enjoy a good storm. Why that book about a "perfect" storm sold so well. I felt pretty good about things and waved Richard off with a "Happy New Year!" Richard shouted and waved back.

"Let's drive into town and look around," I suggested. "With the Christmas trees still lighted along Main Street and Newtown Lane, it ought to be lovely."

At Pantigo Lane, across from Gay Lane and in front of the Methodist church, we ran into Reverend Parker, shoveling the church sidewalk.

"Hi, Beecher. Enjoying the storm?"

"Yes, we are." I got down from the Hummer and reintroduced him to Alix, who'd met him last year, and to Emma.

"Here, Rev, take a breather. Give me that shovel," I said.

He was winded and handed it over without an argument. I worked for a time while he chatted with the ladies. "Today everyone'll just stay home. But I worry about tomorrow. Some of the old folks, they don't buy provisions more than a day ahead. They'll be getting pretty hungry by tomorrow night. And I ought to get around and see if they've got food. And enough heat."

"Won't the village or the town do that?"

"Oh, sure. They're pretty good. It's just some of the old folks won't answer the door unless it's someone they know."

Reverend Parker was looking at the Hummer. Much in the longing way a teenage boy looks at a classmate's brand-new, secondhand convertible, an eager, pleasant hunger on his face.

Which was when Emma Driver got the guilts and spoke up.

"Just suppose . . ." she began in that wheedling way of hers, as she had on that first night at the Admiral's house when he had let her stay over.

But her idea wasn't a bad one. Not bad at all. Make ourselves useful in the storm, get some good out of the Hummer. Pry a list out of Rev. Parker of the old folks he thought might be the worst off, then stock up some provisions and maybe firewood and candles, in case the electricity went out in the storm, and drive the Rev. and a few of his helpers around town in the Hummer through the drifts.

"Why, that's a smashing notion," Alix announced. And of course the Rev. didn't see anything wrong with it. Even when Emma, as she usually did, went a bit too far:

"At our convent, Mother Superior stresses direct action. 'There's the difference between Roman Catholics and other Christians,' she always says. 'Protestants give you a good hymn and wring their hands over stuff, but we go out and do something about it.' Mother Superior always says—"

"Emma," I interrupted, "why don't you start taking notes of groceries and other stuff the Rev. thinks people might need?"

Soon we'd emptied a few shelves at the IGA grocery store on North Main Street and loaded up the Hummer with the necessities.

"I don't know how to thank you, Beecher," the Rev. began . . .

"It's nothing. Thank Emma for the idea. I'm just salving my conscience."

Full dark comes early in East Hampton the last week of the year, and with the snow falling heavier than ever, we were working with full headlights from about three o'clock on. Rev. Parker had assigned two sturdy young women to us, and it was they who got the old folks to open their doors while Alix and I, with Emma's assistance, carried in the supplies. The old people were pretty nice, coming out into the storm to wave their thanks and call out a New Year's greeting. By seven, we'd stopped at every house on the list, been greeted, thanked, even kissed.

When we got back to Further Lane, the Admiral saw our lights and came up to the gate house.

"Well, you've had yourselves a day. Come in, come in, get out of the cold."

"We did," I said. "Though I meant to get out the toboggan and never quite got around to it."

When he looked down at Emma, he saw a tired little girl. But not yet that tired . . .

"Tomorrow, Admiral, I thought we might get a list of Catholics and Jewish pensioners. Load up again and go out."

He nodded.

"Not a bad idea. I happen to know the Catholic pastor here, Father Desmond. I'll give him a call tonight. He probably knows the rabbi as well."

My father is a wonderful man. But I'd never before known him to display interest in any local clergy not his own or to demonstrate much philanthropic industry. Emma Driver, it seemed, was contagious. Not even Scrooge had suddenly gotten so virtuous.

Inga produced a hearty winter's-night dinner, and we were invited to share my father's table so as not to have to scrounge on our own after a day of running errands in the storm. Before dessert and coffee had been served, Emma was asleep. I caried her upstairs and Inga took over then. "I'll get her to bed," she said. "A fine girl, this one. Fine."

"Yes. She is fine."

My father had some good brandy, and Alix and I joined him before the fire in his den.

"Your Hummer live up to the press notices, Alix?" he asked, lifting his snifter to us.

"Very much so, Admiral. As did young Emma. And your son and heir. Top marks all 'round."

It was my turn now, and I toasted her. "We had a good driver, father. King Richard Petty couldn't have done better. Or A. J. Foyt. No one could have."

"Well, now," Alix said, "don't overlook Ascari and John Surtees and those chaps," pleased but blushing, "and let's not talk rot, shall we?" At the tall french doors she pulled back draperies to look out onto the Admiral's snow-covered lawns into the darkness, pleased but embarrassed by compliments.

It was still snowing when we undressed and got into bed, moving fast against the chill and tugging the down comforter over and around us.

"Oh, Beecher," Alix said, "East Hampton out of season is super. How could you possibly think I'd be bored?"

"Underestimated both you and East Hampton," I said, pulling her closer, determined not to be boring, either.

In the morning the snow was nearly two feet deep but except for a few last vagrant flakes, the storm had ended. A thin sun struggled to brighten the gray sky and welcome a glistening, sparkling new world, and as I looked out at it, there along Further Lane came the day's first cross-country skier, making the first lovely tracks in the season's first lovely snow. And then, as I savored the stillness and calm, there came bursting from my father's front door a small whirlwind in the shape of a little girl in a Willy Bogner anorak and red mittens, who braked abruptly to a stop, looked all about, until, with a gleeful shout and a huge grin, she threw herself backward through the air to land fluffily in the fresh, new, untracked East Hampton snow.

Where, flat on her back, Emma Driver then proceeded to flail arms and legs this way and that, joyously crafting angels in the snow.

Chapter Twenty-nine

Then Peanuts and the lads raised their voices
a cappella with the Marines' Hymn . . .

Well, it was some funeral. Maybe the best ever out here, though a few archivists held out for 1919, when Captain Chelm came home from France and the Great War and shot his wife's cousin, Ruggles, for cuckolding the captain while he was off fighting the Germans. There was a tremendous turnout back then, the entire Maidstone Club en masse, Ruggles being both popular and a scratch golfer.

But they at least had a body; Reds Hucko's funeral was on its own, so to speak.

By ten on Wednesday morning they were still shoveling out a footpath into the Old Churchyard and plowing Abrahams Path and Old Stone Highway and the roads that got you there. So the plows came first, almost in echelon, clearing the way. Then the fire engines of three companies—Springs, East Hampton, and Amagansett. Reds had done time in all three fire companies, and each had its proud claim on him.

Then the fleet of Schwenk oil-delivery trucks, the Hampton Jitneys, the cop cars, Doc Whitmore's tree-nursery trucks, and the Tortorella Pool people for whom George Plimpton did commercials.

Plus every pickup in town. They were double-parked for half a mile down Old Stone Highway to the wrought-iron gate of the Churchyard. Even the preacher, fetched by a Suffolk Country police cruiser, had to drive the last five hundred yards along the shoulder to get there at all. Sister Infanta de Castille was on hand, loudly (some felt, "showily") telling her beads, and in full regalia, having been trucked in from Sag Harbor by pickup.

The troubled Old Churchyard itself, buried silent and tranquil under a white shroud, was no longer a municipal battlefield. Peace on earth, good will toward men.

Once we were through the gate and inside the white board fence (some of the spillover crowded just outside), along came a Marine Corps color guard (Reds had served, and gallantly, several wars ago) and a sort of receiving line, where Wyseman Clagett, who despised Hucko, mysteriously presided and thanked people for coming. The preacher was asked to be brief, making no mention of rap sheets or money owed. And there was but one true hymn, and Emma Driver was asked to sing it, which she did in a thin, high voice and in Latin, "*Tantum Ergo*." Neither Reds nor the Marleys, and certainly not the Unitarian preacher, were Roman Catholics, but that was okay. It was the only genuine church hymn Emma knew by heart and she sang it pretty well. "For a girl without a voice," as she herself admitted. And after the preacher preached and got Reds' name wrong, calling him Red, Sis Marley read, fleshing out scripture with allegorical references to "shipmates" and bringing in "a good catch," much as Father Mapple did in the opening pages of *Moby-Dick*. Toward the end, Peanuts and some of the lads raised their voices *a cappella*, in a chorus of the Marines' Hymn. Then, when Reds was properly planted in absentia, Bonackers and everyone slogged along in the drifted snow to form a straggling line of mourners, men and women both, tossing their flowers atop the snow covering Reds' grave. Or what would be his grave, if and when. I noticed that a lot of them, maybe most, then went over past Jake Marley's mausoleum to give the chill, polished marble a touch for luck, a rub of the relic, so to speak. Or maybe just signaling regrets for having stolen his bones.

They were still shuffling past and headed out toward their pick-ups when yet one more police cruiser came speeding up, siren wailing, lights spinning madly atop the roof, brakes pumping, tires skidding across the lane and the car itself nearly sideways. Before it was fully stopped, the passenger side door was thrown open. What was this? Didn't the cops recognize the solemnity of the moment?

Out stepped a hulking, red-headed fellow with a bowl haircut, wearing traditional Bayman's sea boots, overalls, and an incongruously luxuriant full-length sable fur coat that might have seen better days under a previous owner.

"Well, boys," called out Reds Hucko, tugging a liter bottle of Stolichnaya from the fur coat's pocket and leaping nimbly a foot or so off the frozen ground to click his heels together before descending to announce: "Ain't the first funeral I ever missed and won't be the last. But here I am back in Springs, too late for Christmas but just in time for a helluva New Year's."

Chapter Thirty

"Small blue sharks and dogfish was biting chunks out of me."

Well, of course Reds hadn't drowned at all. Not that it wasn't a near thing.

In deference to the cold and a lowering gray sky, and because the pickup trucks were obstructing local traffic, the cops moved the mourners, all of us, by motorcade down Old Stone Highway to Springs-Fireplace Road. We parked our vehicles at Ashawag Hall to hear Reds's story and to welcome him back from the dead. Even Sis Marley went along, too curious not to. When we were all jammed into the hall, dozens standing out in the corridor looking in and listening through doors ajar, or standing atop snowdrifts outside the opened windows, Reds lit a stinking yellow cigarette I suspect was Russian, and spoke his piece.

"I don't know just how I went overboard, but I did," Reds began, "standing the midnight-to-four A.M. watch and hugging close a pint of rye, to stave off the cold and raise my spirits, and next thing you knew I was over the rail and under; green water atop of me and all around and six hundred fathoms below, and the good trawler *Wendy Engel* vanishing fast. I must of slipped on an icy deck because I was drunk but not that drunk. Which, I told myself at the time and bitterly, was a damned shame because I wasn't going to last very long out there in the north Atlantic in November, and it might be a considerable relief, in a situation like that, to be thoroughly stewed."

He was wearing cold-weather survival gear, which was a rule on the *Wendy*, and that helped. But even a survival suit can keep you alive only so long in a November ocean. It was the survival suit's electric light that saved him, switching on automatically on immersion, blinking on and off, on and off, drawing a Russian eye when they were close enough to . . .

"It was blowing a half gale and I was almost out of it, shivering hard and swallowing seawater, trying to stay awake. They say if you just fall asleep, that's the easy part of freezing to death. Don't feel a thing. But when did I ever take the easy way on anything, even dying? So I kept cursing and swearing, clenching and unclenching my fists and kicking my feet underwater, not willing yet to die and trying not to freeze. And this Russian trawler's lookout, and a good man he is, I can tell you for sure, must of seen the survival light blinking just about the same time I was snagged by their net and damned near jerked out of the water, the speed they was moving along, and a good break, too. Because next thing I knew I was in no danger whatever of falling asleep, but wide-awake in a damned dragger's net half-drowned along with maybe ten tons of halibut and cod and big squids, and if the lookout hadn't seen me in there amongst the fish, I would of either drowned or been bitten to death, the way those bastards were working on me out there in the north Atlantic, being towed along at eight knots with cod and halibuts and the occasional small blue shark and dogfish biting chunks out of me, out of sheer cussedness, or maybe seizing the chance to get back at a Bayman."

Reds paused.

"I wouldn't choose to do it again if I had my druthers, but riding a fast dragger's net through the ocean amid a load of fish, do give you an appreciation of how your average cod feels. Or a poor, damned halibut."

By the time the Russians got Reds aboard, and not too happy about being saddled with him either, maritime rules being what they were, the law of the sea and all that, the captain was swearing and cussing, resentful of being distracted by rescuing *Amerikanskis* when all he wanted was to fill his holds with fish. But they got Reds Hucko thawed out, sitting up and taking borscht, and until the morning three weeks later they nosed up to the wharf at Murmansk, to hear Reds tell about it, you had a regular *Two Years before the Mast* brought up-to-date. Though not so up-to-date that anyone, including Reds, thought maybe someone ought to send a radiogram to Montauk to inform friends and fellow barflies that their pal Reds wasn't dead after all, and maybe it wasn't really necessary to steal Jake Marley's bones yet again in protest.

Asked about that, Reds shrugged. "Well, I got no family. And I owe a little money to several around here. Being a month at sea ain't no novelty and the Russkis was feeding me steady, sharing the Stoli and not working me too hard. One of their boys broke his shoulder the week before, and they was shorthanded and I was healthy and knew the work. The skipper had no reason to put in at any port just to accommodate me, and I saw his point of view, so I shipped on as a member of the crew. Plus, they had three women on board, a nurse, the cook, and the radioman, none of them Cindy Crawford, but one that spoke American. And two that washed regular. So I got along pretty well." He pulled at the Stoli to clear his throat and continued. "You know, boys, I never before considered a woman at sea worth a damn, but out there with them Russkis, I began having second thoughts."

When they paid off the crew, Reds got a half-share, which he accepted as fair, and bought this secondhand sable coat and some vodka, and took passage aboard Moskva Air to Iceland, where he picked up an Icelandic Airlines flight to JFK after a short delay. "I lost two days at Reykjavík in the company of a frisky forty-year-old blonde widow woman named Hjalmarsdottir." The East Coast blizzard diverted his flight to Atlanta, then Boston, and for the past eighteen hours he'd been on trains getting back to Long Island.

He shook his head as if in amazement at the odd ways in which the Lord worked, and he allowed that he was a grateful and fortunate man. It was then that someone, I don't know who, shouted out that they ought to give a hip-hip-hooray for Sister Infanta de Castille. Or at least move an official vote of thanks.

Not being in on the joke, Reds asked, "And who in hell might she be?"

So they told him how she led them down to the sea, looked out across the waters and prayed, and urged the Bonac Boys, "Pray without ceasing." And how they might have doubted it then, but look how it worked out. And brought Reds back alive.

"Well, I'll be damned," Reds Hucko said, impressed despite himself. And jumped up again to click his heels together.

Later on Sis Marley and some of the Bonac Boys took Reds back to the Old Churchyard and showed him his headstone and Sis reiterated her promise that Reds would always have a place there, quite near brother Jake.

Reds was not a man easily moved to tears, but at that, he rubbed a big knuckled fist into his right eye and cleared his throat aloud. Murphy, alarmed at how emotional Hucko had become, announced tersely, "I don't like that cough, Hucko," and suggested they drop by Wolfie's Tavern for a glass to cut the phlegm.

Chapter Thirty-one

*The Danube, ferocious mit cannons, und Turks!
Dose bastards!*

Considering Christmas and other distractions (Her Ladyship in residence for one; burying Reds and then welcoming him back from the dead; the blizzard; aiding and abetting Emma's schemes, including a phantom "day" spent with her missing parents at aquariums that didn't yet exist; negotiating a cease-fire between Sis and the Bonac Boys), I marvel that I got anything at all done, cutting and editing my *Parade* magazine pieces into something resembling a book.

But by waking early and slipping out of bed before Alix stirred (and stirred me!), I got in a couple of hours at the computer most mornings. Once Alix came down and started to read over my shoulder, issuing pithy commentary and offering constructive criticism based on her double first at Oxford ("Oh, Beecher, the subjunctive in that sentence? Mightn't the conditional be more appropriate?"), getting anything done was a challenge. Especially since she continued to be clothing-challenged and habitually edited naked, leaning against my back, tousling my hair and licking an ear before tiring of her copy-reading chores and going off to shower and dress. All of which left me pondering the literary advantages of a monastic life, where there are very few naked women hanging about.

I began to understand how Thomas Merton, once he became a Trappist (more precisely a Cistercian Monk of the Strict Observance), was able to write so many fine books so swiftly.

And now at last, on top of everything else, Dick and Nicole Driver actually arrived in the Hamptons. Not a "virtual" visit this time invented by their kid but a genuine one, though it took the connivance of Sis Marley, the most respected merchant banker on the Street, and two private eyes to get them here.

Nicole and Count Vlad (in deference to the seashore, even out of season, he was gotten up in a double-breasted navy blazer, with an ornate crest of sorts, and a yachting cap) arrived first, landing in a chartered executive jet at East Hampton Airport. It was here that Odets, still lurking, picked up their trail and tracked them into Sag Harbor, where they checked into a chintz-covered suite just down the hall from their private eye, Madamoiselle Javert, registered as Sister Infanta de Castille. Before they'd unpacked, Odets had reported in by cell phone to his client, Driver, in Manhattan, and Dick was soon speeding east on the Long Island Expressway, being chauffeured out in one of his limos in something of a frenzy. Could he allow Nicole and the Impaler to appear more Christmas-spirited than he, to register prior claims of doting on their daughter, while he remained in Manhattan bilking clients? Don't be absurd. Driver's secretary called ahead for rooms at the Meadow Club in Southampton.

"Are you a member, Mr. Driver?" she thought to ask her boss.

"They'll certainly know who I am. Tell the club to check with Alfred Gwynne Vanderbilt or one of the Whitneys if there's any question."

Wasn't Mr. Vanderbilt dead? And which Whitney, and were *they* members? the secretary wondered but was too intimidated to ask. Though by then, Dick was out the door and bundled into the limo with cell phone at the ready.

Meanwhile, Sister Infanta briefed the "anxious" mother and her boyfriend, telling them about us, the Admiral and me and Her Ladyship, and about the Further Lane house in which, ever since

her disappearance, Emma seemed to be staying with a quite un-
settling contentment.

"Get those people on the phone," snapped Nicole.

The Admiral took the call and was very cold. Quite nearly frigid
by the time he hung up.

"You deal with these wretched people, Beecher," he told me.
"You know when I don't like the cut of a man's jib, I can't help
showing it."

Nicole had apparently attempted to throw her weight around.
And in so doing, issuing instructions and demanding information,
never bothered to inquire after the well-being of her only child.

But of course I *did* know how my father got. In fact, it had long
mystified me that he'd been so effective a spy. Espionage was, after
all, a métier where one was forever running into people the cut of
whose jib one didn't like! So I agreed to phone Nicole Driver as
the go-between and find out what she and the Impaler were up to.
Maybe I could even shame her into some sort of maternal gesture
toward her own kid before Emma flew back to Switzerland and
the Brides of Christ.

After making the call, Alix (at the controls) and I drove up to
Sag Harbor over snowy roads for a talk with the former Mrs. Driver,
but before we could reach them, there was something of a dust-
up with Sister Infanta de Castille onto which we would shortly
stumble.

Mademoiselle Javert had spent half her life, and successfully so,
as a private investigator, though in rare moments of introspection,
she permitted the odd self-doubt to creep in. A week of enforced
inactivity here in the Hamptons, kept on a short leash by clients
she'd barely met in Paris, and she'd begun to lose patience. And
wasn't patience the policeman's greatest ally?

So that when Nicole Driver got into her hectoring mode, Mlle
Javert took it for only so long. Did she really need this? She'd been
a "nun" for only a week, but already she found the religious vocation so enriching, so emotionally satisfying, so . . . significant:
praying at the winter ocean for dead fishermen, grief-counseling

his comrades, welcoming back from the dead a man who arrived in a police car at his own funeral, all to the accompaniment of inspired tears and raucous laughter.

As Nicole railed about Dick and about her daughter's mischievousness, and these East Hampton people named Stowe that she was going to have to deal with, Sister Infanta de Castille cried "*Assez! Basta!* Enough!" Pacing dramatically up and down the oriental carpets of the American Hotel's best suite, she had her little say.

"Might I remind you, Madame Driver, that my illustrious ancestor Javert, an inspector of the police, was the very official who pursued that career criminal Jean Valjean through the stinking sewers of Paris, tirelessly, damply, never flagging or giving up, unmindful of the stench or what was happening to his best suit and good shoes. And what reward does he get? First that rabble-rouser Victor Hugo pens his pot boiler, and then Lloyd Webber, that little cretin, comes out with his absurd musical! There's a pair for you! Turning an open-and-shut case of petit larceny into a screed against the flics. A bestseller, *not* with an honest policeman as hero, but with a villainous Valjean! The crook who stole the loaf of bread in the first place. And the great Javert, a man of law and of probity, wading through *merde,* cruelly castigated and portrayed as the heavy! And his best shoes ruined!"

Alix and I had slipped quietly into the room halfway through this ferocious soliloquy and stood silently listening as the Impaler in his yachting cap, who frightened easily, fell back several paces into an overstuffed chair. That Madamoiselle Javert was fully togged out in the religious habit, leather belt, rosary beads, medals of Our Lady and the usual nun shoes rendered her fury more impressive. Even Nicole, of sterner stuff than her lover (you could see where Emma got her spunk), eyed Mademoiselle warily, edging away from her.

Alix, incapable of prolonged silence, broke the tension with vigorous applause, clapping and crying out: "Oh, I say, Sister, well done, well done indeed. So jolly to see you again. And to assure you I'd never previously thought of Inspector Javert in such a positive light. Perhaps someone ought do a revisionist *Les Miz* and put that scoundrel Valjean firmly in his place."

"Cayenne!" thundered Sister Infanta, "the prison colony. That's where the fellow belongs."

The Impaler, easily swayed, nodded his great, handsome, if empty, head. "Ja, duh Devil's Island for those bums, okay? Teach the fellow to be stealing breads!"

As for myself, it had not previously occurred to me to think of Victor Hugo as a cop-bashing Reverend Al Sharpton.

I made the introductions. Nicole, when she tried, could be charming, and as she was somewhat awed when faced with an authentic English aristocrat, she fell back on tradition. "Tea, mi-lady?"

"Gutt gutt," said Count Vlad, who presumably spoke Romanian, or Transylvanian, but no *known* language, grinned his agreement (my own Romanian, I must admit, is limited to "Magda Lupescu" and "King Carol").

When the tea had been ordered from room service, Nicole got quickly to the point.

"Of course Mr. Driver (I'm sure I speak for him at least in this) and I are most grateful to you for having taken in our mischievous daughter."

"A lovely child," Alix remarked. I kept quiet, having learned that was the best way to get people talking. Nicole didn't hesitate.

"The problem is that Mr. Driver and I are engaged in somewhat adversarial litigation over terms of the divorce, custody, child support and the like, and while my concern is purely the well-being of our daughter, that son of a bitch seeks financial and other advantage."

"Oh, dear," Alix murmured, lowering her eyes but nodding imperceptibly toward the "nun."

"Sorry, Sister," Nicole quickly riposted, though she of all people, since she had retained her, knew that Sister Infanta wasn't a nun at all but a private eye.

"Of course, no offense taken," the "nun" said demurely as Nicole resumed.

"Properly to appreciate my position, you realize that after I left the Icecapades and my darling child was born, there were all these latent, pent-up energies. Not even the authorship of best-sellers and subsequent fame was sufficient to fill my life. . . ."

I could see Alix's lovely eyes start to glaze.

". . . and I threw myself unstinting into good causes, much in the spirit of the third Mrs. Steinberg, Gayfryd. Even *U.S. News & World Report* took note when I picked up the fallen torch of our tragically lost Princess Di."

"Which was?" Alix asked, who had actually known Diana.

"Land mines."

Her Ladyship goggled.

"You don't say."

"But I do," responded Nicole. "Bianca Jagger and I are in the very forefront of the antipersonnel mine movement. Do you know how many million land mines there are?"

Nicole shook her head at the thought.

When we remained mute she half-whispered, as if only to herself and Bianca. "The risks we took . . ."

"Did you dig them up?" I asked, "the two of you?"

"No, we raise awareness and draw up petitions. The digging-up follows automatically."

She had other causes as well. The Newport Jazz Festival, Dutch Elm disease, and Esperanto. Then, swiftly getting back on point, she demanded:

"Has Dick Driver been in touch with you at all, Mr. Stowe? Or with your father, the general?"

"Admiral. Annapolis man, in fact. Class of forty-eight."

"I vuz myself in the Coastal Guards, a sous-officier," Count Vlad said proudly in the hodge-podge of lingos he seemed to feel appropriate to his audience, "Royal Romanian Coastal Guards, very elite corps. Mostly gentlemens of gutt family, classy top-society folks, you understand, plus a few ruffians."

"Mmm," said Her Ladyship, "I wasn't aware Romania had a seacoast. Isn't it rather tucked away there in the hills and forests, dotted with picturesque if somewhat gloomy castles and charming stone villages?"

"Der Block Zee, don't forgot nor overlooking der Block Zee," the Impaler urged. "Many great naval battles ober der Block Zee, I swear to Gott. Odessa and der battleship *Potemkin*, for one. Also the Danube, ferocious mit cannons, der Turks, dose bastards, many horrors and brave gentlemens, dround-ed und sinking down." He shook his head sadly at the very memory of bloody sea battles long ago.

"And despite these horrors, Count," Alix asked, "you still sail? I noted the yachting-club escutcheon on your blazer."

"Ja, mit der speeding boat. All mahogany, I swear to Gott genuine, not der plastics. Christ-Craft, a fine brand, endorsed by der Vatican for de commercial use of Gott's name."

He blessed himself quickly, in the right to left manner favored by the Eastern Church.

"Mahogany speeding boats. How fortunate you are," Alix said somewhat vaguely.

"Would anyone like a drink?" Nicole asked, the tea never actually having arrived. I certainly did but didn't want to say so, maintaining a stiff upper lip with people the cut of whose jib my father didn't like.

"Is there some champers?" Alix inquired, not permitting her prejudices to get in the way of a properly chilled Dom.

While we waited to see if the drinks trolley would eventually arrive, Nicole launched into a catalog of her former husband's sins.

"Last year when his father died, Dick's father, mind you, not mine, a decent old party totally unlike his son, I hurried to Geneva, snatched up my daughter from the convent, and flew to New York at my own expense to attend the funeral. But when I billed Dick later for airfare, hotels, limos, and the like, he refused to pay."

When neither Alix or I expressed outrage at this, Nicole drove home her point:

"It was *his* old man we were burying. And at *my* expense. Did you ever?"

The front desk called up, a clerk on Sister Infanta's payroll reporting in.

"A Mr. Odets is down here in the lobby asking questions about your visitors, Ms. Driver. Shall I issue a no comment?"

"Odets! That bastard," Nicole exploded. "Dick's paid thug. Mademoiselle Javert, can you—"

" 'Sister Infanta,' please. Let's try not to blow my cover."

"Of course."

Sister continued. "I'll nip down the back stairs and plant a false trail or two. A *bientôt*."

Count Vlad had a bottle tucked somewhere in the luggage and pulled it out now to pour himself a drink, not bothering to offer one to the rest of us. It seemed to be a vodka or gin with an indecipherable Balkan label.

"Chin-chin," he toasted us, drawing a raised eyebrow from Alix.

"I say, *are* they sending up some champers?" she asked.

Nicole was the one pacing now. "What concerns me, and what really should be the focus of our attention, is of course—"

"Your child," Her Ladyship offered.

"Yes, yes," Nicole said dismissively, "there's that. But I know Dick. He's a louse but clever. He'll have Howard Rubenstein putting out press releases any hour now, pleading his case and trashing me and the count, claiming it's my fault our daughter ran away. There's another court hearing coming up in The Hague next month, and he's out to score points."

Vlad looked up from his glass.

"He do that all times, Dick. What a bastard, mein Gott, worser than der Turks of old, worser even than the ruffians in our Coastal Guards."

"Well, he'd better act swiftly," Nicole declared, "because I'm ready with a preemptive strike. Just wait till I get Peggy Siegal on the phone. I don't want desk clerks issuing 'no comments' when I can get Peggy Siegal. If we're to have a public-relations war, let it begin with Peggy."

Even the London-based Alix knew about Peggy Siegal, New York's "flack from hell."

"I say, Beecher. They're rolling up the heavy artillery now. When you call on Peggy, these are indeed desperate hours."

When I brought the conversation back to Emma and inquired if either parent had any intention of seeing her while in the Hamptons and assuring themselves she'd get safely back to Switzerland and the convent, Nicole said vaguely that anything was possible and thanked us for our concern. By the time we left a few moments later, she was tearing and ranting over the phone to Peggy Siegal and drafting releases. "Put out that quote from the *National Enquirer*, what Dick said about the models. Yes, that's it, 'So many cover girls, so little time.' " She was still talking to Peggy as we left, without having settled with us just how or when, or even *if*, she wanted her daughter back.

Were the Stowe family plus Alix more or less acting *in loco parentis* until the convent reopened? Or would Dick Driver be more malleable and agree to take the kid back?

Chapter Thirty-two

The walk-in closet—the goddamned closet!—
needs a $6,500 carpet . . .

We left the Admiral comfortably ensconced before a roaring fire in his den, being cheated at poker by the kid, and drove over to confront Driver at the Meadow Club (Odets had spoken carelessly and Jesse Maine phoned with his whereabouts). Having failed totally with Nicole, I was anything but hopeful. Yet one had to try. Alix and I were in agreement on that; the Drivers were dreadful people. But they were Emma's parents.

As a member, not of the Meadow, but of the Maidstone, I was able to give the secret club handshake to a flunky and send up my name to Driver. He was truculent at first, which I fully understood, given that I had written a fairly critical piece for *Parade* about that megalomaniacal ninety-story high-rise he was building near my apartment in Sutton Place, which was going to cast into perpetual shadow much of the East Side (unless the FAA's preliminary injunction held up in court). And then there was the photo op manqué at FAO Schwarz. But when I introduced Her Ladyship, Dick overcame his sneering disdain for Grub Street and turned on the old smooth, inviting us to drinks in the club bar. That was where Driver, with or without help from the Whitneys or the late Alf

Vanderbilt, had set up a command center, issuing statements hourly through the Howard Rubenstein public-relations apparat, contradicting rival claims put out by Nicole's PR woman, and extolling Dick's charities and virtues of every sort.

Alix ordered a Dom and I took black coffee. When we'd settled in, I got to the point. "This girl of yours, Driver."

"Which one, Kim or Miss Israel?"

"Your daughter, remember?"

"Oh, sure. Good kid. How is she?"

So far, as bad as he was, Dick was one up on Nicole, who hadn't really asked.

When I nailed him on the question of which parent was willing to take responsibility and ensure that Emma returned safely to school in January, Dick became expansive.

"Look, Stowe, Your Ladyship, in theory of course a child ought to be with her mother. But a Dragon Lady like Nicole?" Dick pulled out several sheets of yellow legal-pad stationery. "Listen to this, her latest demands above and beyond alimony and basic child support. Next month at The Hague she'll formally petition the court. I got hold of the details through, well, let's not get into that."

I saw the fine hand of Odets here somewhere. But Dick began to read:

"For our daughter's bedroom, the bedroom alone, mind you, at Nicole and Vlad's place in Bucharest: $130,000 in furnishings and decorations, a $19,000 antique desk and chair, $6,500 to paint the ceiling, a bed for $6,500, a toy chest for $1,560. All that just for the kid's bedroom. For her bathroom there are $10,000 curtains, $4,500 in wallpaper, $7,540 in plumbing. The walk-in closet—the goddamned closet!—needs a $6,500 carpet, $2,300 in wallpaper, and $3,900 in prints. Prints? What prints do you need in the closet? The damned kid's ten years old!"

There was plenty more. When a club page came up with a cell phone, Driver excused himself to take the call. "Howard Rubenstein's office," he told us in an aside.

"Yes? Absolutely. If Peggy Siegal is sending out releases about me and Heidi Klum, issue a dignified 'no comment.' But then release some of the juicier stuff in Nicole's last sworn deposition, about the Impaler. Yes, that's the stuff. Pull it out of the transcript and call it in to Cindi Adams and Rush and Molloy in the *Daily News*. Liz Smith? No, give her something exclusive. You know how she gets."

When he hung up, Dick told us with a smirking grin about the trancript passage he especially liked:

"Someone got an audiotape of Nicole and the Count at a hotel in Venice during their lovemaking. Apparently in the urgency of passion, Nicole is heard to cry out, 'Impale me! Impale me!' "

He seemed quite pleased with himself, but even Alix blinked at that one. "I say, Mr. Driver!"

"Sorry, Your Ladyship," he said, trying to wipe away the smirk. I reminded Dick why we were here, that the Stowe family's only concern was the Drivers' daughter, not their lawsuits or press releases. But when I pressed the question, Dick said he might have to return quickly to the city and it would be inconvenient to be burdened with a child.

"*Your* child," I couldn't resist pointing out.

"Of course, of course. But so many things are moving too fast. Certain moneyed interests are said to be buying a vast tract out here in Montauk. I've got to see my people on this."

"Oh?" I smelled something here. "Is there a Native American tribe involved?"

Driver jumped up from the table. "Damn, yes! I thought we had the exclusive on the deal. Don't tell me it's common knowledge."

"Not at all," I said smoothly, "a few insiders only at this stage. Might I ask who your contact is?"

Driver looked around furtively. "Odets came up with him. A local fellow of enmormous influence and connections. The idea is to dredge a deep-water port at Montauk suitable for ocean liners, a shortcut avoiding all that New York Harbor traffic. A duty-free port and a Native American Indian casino all in one. Bullet trains into midtown Manhattan every hour on the hour. Every car a club car. With roulette wheels and slots if statutes permit. It'll be the biggest thing since the Opera House in Sydney. A local developer named Wyseman Clagett wants a piece of the deal, and I'm to do the contracting."

"Which Indians you dealing with?" I asked.

"The Shinnecocks. A chief named Maine."

"But he's . . ." Her Ladyship began.

"Alix, we've been sworn to secrecy. Chief Maine made us promise."

Driver's eyes were bigger than ever. This thing could be huge. He was counting the money already.

"Of course," Alix said, nonchalance at its best. "How thoughtless of me."

Chapter Thirty-three

A promising little firm headed by two men called Allen and Gates...

I made one more hapless stab at the subject of Dick's daughter, and we left, using Alix's phone to call Jesse from the car, telling him what Driver said.

"That's Montaukket land, not Shinnecock," I reminded Jesse. "You can't sell it because you don't own it. Besides, you've been claiming for years, on religious grounds, that you oppose casinos."

"Hell, Beecher, you know that and I know that. But there's a lot better profit margin if you can sell something you don't own. That way you don't have to put up no cash first. There's no damned initial investment. And this Driver is just gonna love them Montauketts down there taking the waters at Gurney's. They'll get along fine. Clagett's in it, too. And he's so crooked he'll lie even when truth wins the election. Or so I casually suggested to Lefty, who passed on the info to his boss."

Jesse Maine, who'd been hanging with Lefty Odets, was eloquent in his admiration for Driver's generosity. As he assured his new pal:

"You know, Lefty old compadre, your Mr. Driver could win friends for hisself here in the Hamptons and right across the country, setting up scholarships and all manner of gifts and grants for worthy applicants among the Shinnecock Indian Nation. Gestures like that do win favor with oppressed people. And might even convince us to let Mr. Driver in on opportunities undreamt of by less generous and charitable men."

Without letting Odets know about it, Jesse had at the same time affixed a bumper sticker on the rear of Lefty's rented car (and was wondering if he could also slip one onto Dick Driver's limo): AMERICA WAS BUILT ON INDIAN GRAVES.

This tended not to be a popular sentiment with many of the locals, but it cheered the Shinnecocks. And impressed innocent outlanders like Driver, who thought he was catching, quite early in the curve, a new wave of Native American indignation, which he might ride to a very profitable conclusion. When it came to the art of deal making, whom would a prudent investor back: a lousy Indian tribe or the bright young man who outsmarted his mentor and, in the end, took away Jacob Marley's own company?

Well, if you read the tabloids and tune in occasionally to *Entertainment Tonight* or the *Geraldo* show, you know about the twenty-four-hour firefight that ensued.

January was swiftly bearing down on us, a new year, a brand-new century, a fresh millennium, and more to the point, a return ticket on the Concorde to Paris and Emma's convent school beckoning beyond the Alps. If we—Alix, my father, and I—were ever to accomplish a single constructive act on behalf of our little girl lost, it was now. The problem was, both Nicole and Dick were threatening a return to Manhattan or other parts before a fresh blizzard buried eastern Long Island, closed down the airports, and cut the roads and railroads in between. Nicole and Count Vlad wanted to get out simply because they were bored; Dick Driver had the legitimate excuse of needing to appeal a Federal Aviation Administration injunction against his skyscraper. Left behind, in the "boring" and soon-to-be-snowbound Hamptons, to keep an eye on young Emma and Nosey Parkers like us, would be Mr. and Mrs. Driver's private eyes, and their respective PR counsels. Just how, if ever, were we going to get Nicole and Dick and their only child on the same damned page?

In consequence of trying to answer that question, we would have our own bloodless version of a "gunfight at the OK corral," featuring Dick versus Nicole, Sister Infanta versus Lefty Odets, Peggy Siegal versus Howard Rubenstein, and a ten-year-old girl in the middle. Before it was over, even Jesse and the Shinnecocks, merchant banker Henry Rousselot, Park Avenue lawyer Bryan Webb, as well as Peanuts Murphy and the Bonac Boys, would be involved. As Chief Maine put it, "It would of done credit to the Earps and the Clantons." Though there were a few frayed and hanging threads still to be tidied up.

My father, the Episcopalian, blamed Rome. "That Papal Nuncio they sent out here to check out Sister Infanta. He seems to be conducting a foreign policy all his own. Whatever happened to the separation of Church and State?"

The Admiral tended to exaggerate when it came to Catholic bashing. But on this, he did seem to have a point.

Even on the marginal question of whether a visiting Catholic prelate should be meeting with a minor émigré group such as Professor Wamba dia Wamba's. The two men had a cocktail at Nick & Toni's, but Wamba came away without anything like official recognition of the Congolese government in exile.

"De facto recognition, my dear Wamba," said the Nuncio, "must depend on the willingness of your People's Popular Front to guarantee freedom of action for our missionaries in the field. Shooting priests and raping nuns just isn't the way to go, old chap, I suggest to you in all sincerity."

"You have my word, Nuncio."

"Then, my good fellow, count on my conveying your assurances to the appropriate figures in Rome."

Less successful was the Papal Nuncio's brief meeting (this time the drinks were at Della Femina's on North Main Street) with Count Vlad.

"Transylvania," the count began, "can't be extending friendship hands to the Church, I swear to Gott, thanks to Romanian bastards."

"But it would be such a decent gesture on your part," the Nuncio persisted, "and go a long way toward convincing other nations to look favorably on an independent Transylvania."

The Impaler shook his handsome head.

"Us Transylvanians is, ourselves, der victims, Gott knows, Bishop. An oppressor state is Romania, everybody could tell you dat. But I swear to Gott, the minute dey put my own family on der throne of a free Transylvania, recognition of duh Vatican will be der first business. Dat first morning I put on duh crown, you got my vote. But don't hold no breath, Nuncio. Dem Romanians is ruffians. Worser den Turks. Don't give nothing up for free. Dey like owning Transylvania!"

"My God!" the Nuncio thought to himself. He was too polite to say, "These people are worse than the Congolese." But at least the Transylvanians didn't shoot, or not at priests. Too busy shooting one other. He and Count Vlad wrestled for the drinks check (the Impaler permitted the priest to get it).

Sister Maria Infanta took advantage of these distractions to resign the Nicole account and departed by hired car for Manhattan to take a meeting at Michael's restaurant on West Fifty-fifth with Binky Urban, the powerful ICM literary agent. Hucko's miraculous return, after a month in the north Atlantic, had deeply impressed Binky (who doesn't impress easily, I assure you). Perhaps the nun's prayers and a Russian trawler were pure coincidence. But America was hungry for heroics, and best-sellers had been conjured up from less, so that a book deal was in the works.

Was Sister really the heiress apparent to Mother Teresa's charitable mantle? If so, the "Bride of Christ's" thoughts, favorite prayers and hymns, and pithy sayings might well sell in a handsome trade paperback as interpreted and translated into readable, colloquial English by a marquee name writer. No one was quite sure if the idea would fly, but they were already talking TV movies and Internet Web sites. Also a very interested, though somewhat uneasy, party, George Plimpton, who'd been taking down Sister Infanta de Castille's every word for yet another of his oral histories.

"I admit," George told chums at the Maidstone, "she gets off some wonderful lines. But to segue from that to her being the next

Mother Teresa, well, it's a reach. For one thing, she's a poseur. Not even a genuine nun."

"Oh, hell, George!" one club member protested, knocking back a gin, "the woman tells a good story. What does it matter if she's taken vows? A bit racier if she hasn't, eh? Is there a former husband in the murky background somewhere? A discarded lover or two?"

There was that, Plimpton agreed.

Lefty Odets had also decamped, hardly in triumph and not at all in good odor with his client Dick Driver. But damned glad to be off the assignment. "I ain't tackling Rome," he informed colleagues. "And this woman, Sister Infanta, you don't mess with her." Odets instead was busily phoning Imus's producer Bernard McGuirk, desperate to book himself on the show and get across his version of events in the Hamptons before Driver did, only to be told:

"Bo Dietl was on last Thursday. Imus says enough cops for a while."

But it was Sis Marley who dominated the scene as New Year's Eve approached.

Summoned urgently by E-mail and cell phone, we convened at her house at the marina about ten one morning: the Admiral, Alix, the kid, Jesse Maine, both Nicole and Dick Driver (she accompanied by the Impaler, Dick alone and looking rather naked without Miss Lithuania), Peanuts Murphy and several Bonac Boys, restored to Sis's good graces, and a distinguished-looking gentleman, about my father's age, whom I'd met before. The Drivers looked especially uneasy, their departures for Manhattan abruptly canceled at the last moment.

"All right, boys," Sis began, calling the meeting to order, "this gent is Mr. Rousselot, who's the biggest banker around since David Rockefeller or Felix Rohatyn and just as smart, too. Henry Rousselot, chairman of Rousselot Frères, the finest merchant bankers this side of Threadneedle Street."

My father knew Henry Rousselot pretty well (Rousselot Frères were the Admiral's own private bankers) and nodded vigorous agreement as the banker got into it. Didn't take long, either.

Addressing Sis first, thanking her for the invitation, then Emma Driver, as his client, he got swiftly to her parents, opening his case with an indictment as chill as anything old Judge Welch ever handed down when assailing Senator Joe McCarthy on Capitol Hill and over nationwide television, back in the fifties:

"Mr. Driver, Ms. Driver, you may wish to consult your respective attorneys regarding what I'm about to say, but considering your less-than-pleasant record of recent litigation, I'd not recommend it. For more than half Miss Emma's life, you two have treated your only child as a volleyball, batting her back and forth across the net of your own egos and ambitions, and I think you ought to be ashamed of yourselves. Though, as Emma's banker, it's not my role to deliver lectures, but to handle her money."

He paused to let that sink in, then went on.

"When Miss Emma Driver was born some ten years ago, her father was still Jacob Marley's protégé, his junior partner, in some ways his surrogate son, succeeding, if never actually replacing, the boy killed on the Sag Harbor road trying to avoid a deer. Having no other close relatives, save his sister, who had resources of her own, Jake decided to create a little trust fund for Emma Driver that would provide for her education. She was an appealing child, and Jake still liked her father, was amused by her mother, and wanted to do something for the girl. And for them. But instead of putting in a few dollars, he bought stock. Funded the trust with stock, from the third or fourth week of Emma Driver's young life. He chose the stock, a curious new company he rather fancied, but left it to me to manage the shares as executive trustee. Sis Marley and Jake himself were the other trustees, along with an estates-and-trusts lawyer named Bryan Webb, a distinguished member, incidentally, of your Maidstone Club, who is here today, having braved the roads to drive out from his Park Avenue offices.

"Mr. Bryan Webb."

Webb—who had gone to Williams College, affected bow ties, and did a very good impersonation of Charles Osgood—smiled warmly at Emma, thinly at her parents, nodded to the rest of us, and sat down again without wasting a word.

I could see Nicole nattering at the Impaler under her breath and Dick fidgeting impatiently. He had a full schedule; what was all this about? When would this dry-as-dust banker get to the damned point?

Emma was the one Driver who seemed interested. But then, it was her money, wasn't it?

Rousselot now resumed, got to "the damned point." Which the banker's "dry-as-dust" accounting made even more impressive.

"The stock Mr. Marley purchased ten years ago in trust for Emma Driver was issued by a promising little Seattle firm headed by two young men named Allen and Gates. Their company was called Microsoft, and very few Americans had ever heard of it and even fewer knew just what it did or expected to do. A year later, on young Emma's first birthday, Jacob Marley bought more Microsoft. The market was down that year and he bought cheap. Picking up more shares because the price was lower but investing about the same amount of actual money. Over the next five or six years, depending on the Dow and on his own mood, Jake continued to buy Microsoft and to place the shares in trust for Emma Driver. The stock split. Split again. Split once more. And Emma Driver got richer. On paper, of course.

"Even though, sadly, Jake Marley and his protégé, Emma's father, Richard Driver, had by now become estranged."

When he dropped his voice and paused after that, you didn't hear a sound in Sis Marley's living room. Rousselot resumed:

"After his death, as per his wishes, Sis continued the annual contribution of Microsoft stock. The birthday cards, the little notes from Mr. Marley, stopped coming. Emma, as we now learn, eventually realized something must have happened. It was the notes she missed, the birthday cards (Jake having a weakness for gaudy, rather corny greeting cards), and not the stock certificates. She was, after all, still a child. Not yet infected with greed.

"Maybe she'll never be infected with greed. Let's hope so. And now, I'll ask Mr. Webb to touch on a point of law. Bryan?"

Webb got up again. "Mr. and Mrs. Driver will surely want to consult counsel on this. But Henry asked me to remind them that precedents exist. There are cases in which a minor divorces his or her own parents."

He started to sit down, thought better of it, and added, "I can supply the appropriate citations, of course."

Then he sat.

Wow! You should have seen Dick and Nicole. But before they could say a word, Rousselot again took the floor.

"If Emma's parents have a scintilla of good sense, they will stop this endless bickering and costly litigation and work out a simple custody-sharing agreement. One month each summer with each, a third month visiting here with Sis Marley, learning to sail and catch fish, the rest of Emma's year to be spent at the convent in Geneva, with Mother Superior acting in loco parentis. Meanwhile, Ms. Marley, Mr. Webb, and myself will continue as trustees."

I don't believe I should here reveal what Mr. Rousselot told us about Emma Driver's precise worth or the number of shares she holds through the foundation, except to say that by rough calculation, Emma is now the twelfth largest shareholder in Microsoft. And by other reckoning, pending further rulings by federal judge Thomas Penfield Jackson, she is the eighty-first richest American.

Chapter Thirty-four

Jake and Brett are perfect together, always having cocktails and meeting bullfighters...

It was our last night together, and we were glad of the respite. No Dick and Nicole Driver, disputed cemeteries, Sister Infanta de Castille, Reds Hucko, Nuncio, Professor Wamba, or the rest. We were passing a quiet evening at home before the great fire in the Admiral's book-lined den.

"Beecher," said Emma.

"Yes?"

She looked up from my father's bearskin rug, where she lay on her belly, elbows propped, reading one of her bibles, *The Sun Also Rises.*

"Weren't you disappointed when Jake Barnes didn't marry Lady Ashley?"

"More properly, Emma, it's 'Lady Brett.' The title was her husband's, not hers."

She gave me a look. "To be sure, *Herr Oberst, absolument.* But getting back to why they couldn't get married, huh?"

"I dunno. There were . . . problems." Not wanting to say more, I left it at that.

"Yes, I know. His wound and all . . ." She broke off then, only to resume:

"... and you've been wounded as well. The Admiral said so. In a place where it didn't hurt all that much."

My father started to protest this line of inquiry, but Emma was at the stage of answering her own questions and beat him to it.

"I mean, Jake and Brett are really perfect together. Always having cocktails and going dancing and catching trout and meeting neat people like Count Mippipopolous and the bullfighters. I like Jake so much better than Robert Cohn or Mike Campbell. And I'm sure Brett did, too."

"Yes, as do most of us," the Admiral threw in.

"What's an undischarged bankrupt, Admiral? Does it hurt?"

"Only your credit rating," he growled.

Emma returned to me. To me and Alix, more properly. "I think of you and Alix a lot, Beecher. How you get on so well but you don't get married, either. Even though you're a newspaperman like Jake and like cocktails, too. Though I don't know about Pamplona and the bullfights."

"Well, we think about it from time to time. At least I do," I said, wondering if I were making a sap of myself being all this candid in front of an audience of those I loved.

"I as well, on occasion, think of marriage," insisted Alix, being a good sport.

"But you keep going off," Emma said. "Like Brett."

"There is that," she conceded. "Though never with bullfighters."

The kid finally relented and gave us a break and said she thought when she were older, she'd like to *be* Brett Ashley. "You know, breaking everyone's heart all the time and going dancing and not having to work or attend classes, but just sporting about and living in Paris.

We were still mulling all that when Inga came into the den. "Callers, sir," she informed the Admiral, an eloquently raised eyebrow conveying her assessment of the "callers."

Peanuts Murphy and a small delegation of Baymen.

When they were ushered into the den in their boots and pea jackets, watch caps tugged off respectfully, the Admiral, who understood the distinctions between wardroom and fo'c'sle, exchanged a few words with Murphy to put him at ease, letting the Bayman himself set the pace. Finally, Peanuts spoke.

"We're here, Admiral, for the little girl, Miss Driver. We know how she spoke up for us with Sis Marley in the matter of the Old Churchyard, planting dead Baymen and such. And want her to know it was appreciated. So we brung along a kind of New Year's gift, Christmas being well past. A souvenir of the East End and its Baymen for her to take back over there to the Alps and all."

He was handed a brown-paper shopping bag by one of the other Bonackers and Alix shoved Emma forward toward where my father and the half dozen large men stood awkwardly, boots shuffling on the thick carpets.

"It's yours, Emma. They fetched it here for you," Alix said quietly.

"Why, that's awfully nice of you, Mr. Murphy. But it was all Auntie Sis's idea to bury Mr. Hucko. I only wondered aloud from time to time. She made up her own mind on account of she likes Baymen and doesn't want her brother's bones borrowed again."

Peanuts had his own view of that, recalling that Sis Marley hadn't budged a damned inch on the question of cemetery plots until this kid showed. But in the holiday spirit, he said only, "Sure, sure, girlie. I know. But we brung this anyhows. Making you an honorary Bub. Which is what we call local people out here. And so you'll remember this here Christmas in the Hamptons, okay?"

As he held out the shopping bag to Emma, she asked eagerly, "Oh, do tell me what it is, *je vous prie, mon capitaine*, tell me, tell me!"

What it was, was a pair of hip boots and a billed cap such as Baymen wore at sea when they weren't sporting watch caps.

"Probably they ain't seen nothing like them hip boots in the Alps," Peanuts remarked with a big grin.

"I'm sure they haven't. And the cap is handsome as well. The other girls and even the Brides of Christ will be totally floored."

"Hucko would of been here, too. But he was, well, he ain't feeling so good."

"Hungover," offered one of the other Baymen pleasantly. "We closed Wolfie's last night."

"*Quel dommage*," Emma said, "probably took a chill on the Russian trawler. Or while he was in the net with halibuts and the sharks biting him."

"I'm sure, Emma," my father agreed, relieved to have gotten off the subject of Brett Ashley, and not wanting to field questions about hangovers, not from a ten-year-old.

Chapter Thirty-five

The Brides of Christ have a mail-order account at Bloomie's.

I believe we were all relieved when Dick and Nicole Driver fell again to bickering on the morning their daughter was about to depart for Europe and return to the Brides of Christ.

It would have been anticlimactic, a terrible shock to the system, if either or both of these monsters had miraculously become likable. You'd have to shift emotional gears and be pleasant. Ask them to cocktails. Actually spend time with them, hear their prattle, meet Miss Lithuania, and exchange banalities with the Impaler. And God knows how poor Emma would have reacted. After all, in the past few years she saw her mother and father only rarely, and then usually while being kidnapped.

Little chance of a dramatic rehabilitation, however. Dick was especially out of sorts, the FAA having just been upheld by the courts in its ruling against his Sutton Place high-rise on grounds it posed an aerial navigation hazard to jet traffic in and out of LaGuardia Airport. Frustrated in Sutton Place, Dick's grandiose projects had been reduced to the bullet train from Montauk and its bothersome trackbed. And financing an improved trackbed (Driver had absolutely no intention of risking his own capital) depended on formal agreements not yet signed with several different and feuding (damn the confusion!) Indian tribes.

Nicole had her own irritations: still in a snit over Mademoiselle Javert's religious conversion and having lately been blackballed by the Sag Harbor Yacht Club (The Impaler had become the club's barroom bore with his war stories about the Royal Romanian "Coastal Guards"). So in mid-spat, both Drivers announced they would depart East Hampton in his and her limos. Each then showily offered a ride into Manhattan to their daughter.

Who, by now, sensed their insincerity and instead showed her return ticket on the Long Island Railroad.

"The 11:45 A.M. will have me in the city by mid-afternoon," said Emma. "Lady Alix's taking me to Bloomingdale's. The Brides of Christ have an account. Even our chaplain, Père Henri, 'Dancing Harry,' dotes on Bloomie's. Says on Saturdays it's wall-to-wall interior decorators, especially in housewares and the bath shop. And Alix's offered me the couch in her room at the Carlyle. Bobby Short's playing the dinner show. Since we're flying morning Concordes to Europe, hers to Heathrow, mine to Charles de Gaulle, we'll have the evening together and share a cab to JFK in the morning."

"It ought to be jolly," put in Her Ladyship. "We might stop by Elaine's. I'm sure dropping Beecher's name will get us a decent table," said Her Ladyship. "Elaine being partial to hard cases."

"Your title will be more than sufficient," I assured her, once again pleased at being endorsed as a "hard case."

Nicole looked toward the Impaler before informing Alix brightly, "We prefer Bernadin, don't we, Count?"

"It's very gutt," he remarked. "Many fishes. In Bucharest we got wunderbar fishes also. Yanked bodily, even fresh, from der Danube, no?"

Nicole echoed him, "Very, *very* good."

Dick Driver, a man who might soon be running for President, wasn't going to let these two dominate the gourmet talk.

"Susannah might like the new Russian Tea Room," her father said carelessly, forgetting his daughter's actual name and using the protective pseudonym. "Samovars, gypsy violins, Cossack doormen, and the blinis with red caviar aren't half bad," he put in, delighted to have the opportunity to disagree yet again with his former wife on anything, even the Zagat ratings.

"Yes, well . . ." Her Ladyship said, not really responding.

By now the Drivers, both of them, had kissed their child and were being reverentially handed by concerned chauffeurs into their respective back seats. They'd shown us the sort of people they were.

But as cool and independent as she was, their kid was more difficult to categorize.

Children *do* love unconditionally.

And Emma was not quite ready to let go, running up to each sleek and idling car for yet another, final, parental kiss, a child hungry for love.

"See you next summer, Mommie."

"Ta, ta, dearest." And then Nicole had turned again to her Count, slipped an arm through his, and seemed ready to be off. Dick was a vast fake; Nicole didn't even pretend to be terribly interested. And now their daughter turned from her mother to Dick one last time.

"Daddy?"

"Yes, Emma." You sensed he very shortly would be shooting his cuffs, consulting his Rolex. Emma certainly saw the signs.

"I know you're in a rush to get away. But there's one thing I hoped we might do for Christmas. *One* thing. You and me and Mommie. All of us."

He glanced toward Nicole's car and said, "I'm afraid it's a bit late for . . ."

"No, not living together again. Something else."

"Oh?"

"Yes, you have money. And Mommie, from her books. And if I really do have all that money Mr. Rousselot was talking about . . ."

"Emma, you're a bit young to be worrying about such matters. Everything will be worked out. The courts, the bank, the lawyers, all of us will—"

She shook her head, angrily I thought, her hair bouncing.

"No, no!" Her big eyes widened.

Where was she going with this? Even Dick tensed.

And then Emma Driver told us, not just Dick and Nicole, but all of us:

"Can't we just give some of our money away? Yours, and Mommie's royalties, and my stock?"

"Give it away? But to whom?"

"I dunno. You're smarter than I am. But we might start with Reverend Parker's pensioners' list at the Methodist Church."

"But we're not Metho—"

She shook her head angrily. "It doesn't matter. It's only that we should do something, y'know. Like the original Jacob Marley warned Mr. Scrooge about on Christmas Eve when he came clanking up the stairs with his chains. All those keys and locks and cash boxes."

Dick Driver seemed out of his depth.

"Well," he said, "the nuns certainly have been putting ideas in your head, Emma. Much of it nonsense. You know, the taxes that we pay, your mother and I, and that you'll soon be paying, they help the poor. Welfare, Medicaid, organized charities, and such; they're not our business. It's enough for a man to understand his business and not to interfere with other people's. Before you do good, you've got to do well. We'll talk about it one day. I'll explain things. You and I."

"I guess," she said, temporarily giving up a lost cause.

"Sure," he agreed.

"Next summer, Daddy?" she said.

"Grand," Dick said, "that'll be grand. You'll be taller then. And . . ."

Emma waited, hoping for . . . something. Then, throwing herself at him, head back so she could stare up at him, and hugging her father about the middle, which was about as tall as she could yet reach, she said:

"I'll try to be pretty next time, Daddy. I promise."

For an instant I thought Driver's handsome face, his immense self-assurance, the entire smug facade, crumpled just slightly. Then the moment passed, and, custom-tailored shoulders squared, Dick pried himself gently—give Driver that!—from her grasp, to board his limo.

The kid stepped back, proud to have a beautiful, if distant, mother and such an important father, with their wonderful cars and men opening doors and saluting, but realizing her parents were anxious to be gone. A ten-year-old's subtly crafted, if childishly hopeful, scheme to get her mother and father together again, hadn't quite worked, had it?

Although, for a few hours there, even the Drivers had managed to bicker briefly about *her*, as real mothers and fathers are supposed to do. . . .

Emma dutifully waved a small hankie as the two limos, jousting for advantage, nearly collided in their haste at getting out of our driveway and onto westbound Further Lane.

"Touching, their concern," my father said contemptuously.

"Oh, yes. Touching," Alix agreed.

By now each of us fully understood why their only child had sought Christmas elsewhere. With a stranger named Martha Stewart. Or with people named Stowe. Or among Shinnecocks or at Sis Marley's marina. Whoever would take her in. And not with either of them. Or their absurd lovers, Dick's latest arm candy, Nicole's Impaler.

Emma sniffled briefly and blew her nose, just the once and possibly, even then, only for effect, before concluding she might as well again enhance the exchequer, and asked my father if he thought they had time for a final hand of poker.

"NO!"

So for all our good intentions, we hadn't done much for the kid, had we? But when I stammered out a sort of apology, Emma cut me off brusquely.

"*Mon cher* Beecher, that's simply rubbish. All I really missed was hot chocolate and cookies with Martha Stewart. Why, what other convent girl ever spent a better Christmas? Hanging out with you at the Blue Parrot and the Maidstone Club, and visiting the Shinnecock Indian Reservation with Chief Maine, and speeding about with Auntie Sis in her cigarette boat, and throwing snowballs at George Plimpton's twins, and rescuing the pensioners on Reverend Parker's poor list with Alix driving the Hummer through the blizzard, and attending Reds Hucko's funeral and then welcoming him back from the dead, and being given hip boots by the Baymen, and meeting Sister Infanta de Castille, and the Admiral teaching me about honey wagons and about being a spy? The other girls will be chartreuse with envy!"

"Green?" I suggested.

"Whatever. And Mother Superior as well."

I wondered if anyone else, even Emma, had recognized the words Dick used in rejecting her appeal for the poor: "It's enough for a man to understand his business and not to interfere with other people's." Or recalled just who spoke them so long ago in London.

Jacob Marley's *first* partner.

Chapter Thirty-six

"You're not at all a plain girl. You're a thin girl. Quelle différence . . ."

The snow hadn't yet melted in the New Year's cold snap, and with plenty of sun glinting off the drifts, you needed shades driving one last time to Old Beach at the Maidstone Club and then down Two Mile Hollow to the gay beach, where they had that party for the Clintons a year or more ago at Liz Robbins's wonderful old shingled house atop the dunes. I threw the Blazer into park and sat there with Emma, watching the surf for a few minutes, wanting to give her something to remember as she flew back to Geneva, what winter had been like out here in the Hamptons. Then, in a last benediction, we drove over to Lily Pond Lane for a final look at Martha Stewart's place. I tried to see if there remained in Emma's face a slim regret that things had turned out as they had. And not according to Martha Stewart's magazine.

No, she just looked happy. As a kid should.

The packing had principally been done the night before, but there are always a few memories to be tucked away in side pockets, passports to be relocated and positioned, currency and airline tickets secured. Or perhaps we simply invent such chores to distract us from the ache of separation?

Sis Marley came down to the railroad station as she had threatened to do. Elegantly turned out in a wolfskin parka over tapered, lean gray flannel slacks and Eskimo boots, Sis was good as her word, hugging the child to her bosom.

"That's an astonishing fur," Emma informed her, quite impressed.

Sis grinned her pleasure. "For all his poaching, Jesse Maine never trapped and skinned a fur like this one, sweetie."

"I'll say not."

Then, blowing her nose loudly into a red bandanna and climbing nimbly back into the "Deranged Rover," Sis Marley was swiftly away with considerable burning of rubber and controlled skids, narrowly avoiding George Plimpton's car. Plimpton, who'd just recently sold the backfiles and outtakes of his *Paris Review* for sixty-five million to somebody, had also dropped by the station—without his tape recorder but with his twins, Emma's only friends of her age in town.

"Hi, ho!" he called out heartily. The three schoolgirls nattered on at a great rate about significant projects and improbable reunions. Then, having been appropriately briefed by George's twins, Emma suggested, "Another thing we might do in New York, Alix . . ."

"Oh?"

"Might you take me dancing?"

Her Ladyship shot the Admiral and me a prudent glance before answering.

"Absolutely not, Emma!" she said sternly, having seen no encouragement in our faces. "Not until you're at least twelve."

"That's hard cheese, Alix," Emma responded in Her Ladyship's lifted phrase. "The Brazilian girls at the convent all say the best dance clubs north of Rio are all in downtown Manhattan. Look, I even have a list."

Jesse Maine was there as well, just missing by minutes Sis Marley's wolfskin.

"Gotta be an import," Jesse said. "There ain't been wolves out here since the original Gardiners in sixteen-ought-something.

Plenty of wolves back then and they had a bounty on 'em."

Jesse and Emma, guided by trustee and lawyer Bryan Webb, had their heads together over the possibilities of her establishing a small foundation of her own, this one dedicated to the education of Shinnecock children. If Dick and Nicole had opted out, their daughter surely hadn't. The paperwork, Counselor Webb was assuring everyone, would be completed shortly and copies dispatched to the convent for her scrutiny.

There was also a half squad of Bonac Boys, plus Tom Knowles of the Suffolk police, and Raymond, who made the doughnuts at Dreesen's and had children of his own. The miraculously restored-to-life Reds Hucko came in a pickup, happily hungover from yet another in series of welcome-home parties at Wolfie's.

"I prefer trains to limos, don't you?" Emma announced to us, "you can get up and stroll about, go to the bathroom and change seats, look out big windows and chat with interesting people from all over."

Jesse had been briefed and was painfully aware the kid's plot to reunite her parents hadn't worked. Not quite.

"Well, as I always say . . ." he began, trying to console her.

". . . 'sometimes you eat the bear. And sometime the bear eats you,'" she completed the thought, quoting and delighting Jesse. Who was less pleased with the disappointing turnout in the child's honor of his "entire Shinnecock Nation, in full and official tribal outfits and regalias," which in actuality meant Jesse and three other fellows with a few feathers and a slack drum, there to say goodbye in their new wool flannel shirts from the Polo Shop on Main Street, purchased as Christmas gifts by Jesse out of his bribe money from Lefty Odets.

"New Year's must of been too recent for most of them, wore out like they was," Jesse said apologetically of the missing Shin-necocks.

Wanting to cheer him, Emma said, "but you all do look awfully nice in your new Ralph Lauren shirts, Chief. Like an official Native American tribe and all, just as you said."

Jesse looked down at himself. "Not too shabby," he agreed.

"And, Jesse," Emma said, "Mother Superior will want to know—as she always says, 'God is in the details'—were you a shaman or a sachem of the Shinnecocks? I get mixed up."

He launched yet again into an explanation, which ended, "In peaceable seasons I may be the one thing, in times of war, if the Pequots is in the neighborhood, I may be t'other."

Alix, wanting to console Jesse for the poor turnout of Shinnecocks, also had her say, delivering a small lecture.

"New Year's is a time for hangovers everywhere, Chief. I assure you, in Scotland, they play a huge soccer match New Year's Day between Celtic and Rangers, the Papists versus the Presbyterians. There's always a riot and next morning's Glasgow papers run a frontpage box: THE DEAD INCLUDED . . ."

I didn't think it was precisely the appropriate note on which to say farewell, but my father filled in, somewhat more helpful.

"I'd be pleased to dance a final hornpipe, Emma, if you wish."

"Oh, would you, please! *Merci bien*. That would be most agreeable, *mon amiral*."

We were all trying our best to say good-bye. And do it properly. And not break up crying or anything, the way you tend to be especially at Christmas with the holidays ending and friends going off all in different directions. In the end the kid we'd taken in, took us.

Completely.

She was better than her own people, had Nicole's brass and Dick's guile, and more heart than either of them.

We all stood back to watch my father dance to the beat of the Shinnecocks' drum while Emma grinned and clapped hands, then, when he was finished and somewhat winded, she ran to him and he leaned down to be hugged.

"Now you keep working on your chess game, Emma. Fifteen seconds between moves. Be firm on that. Fifteen and not a second over!"

"Aye aye, sir. And do practice poker when you have time. You could be quite good at it, I believe. Especially at stud. Just takes a little work."

"Yes, yes," the Admiral said impatiently, turning away to stare off down the track so she couldn't see his face.

The shame was, I concluded, her mother and father didn't appreciate the pure gold they had here.

She was a child to be held close, to be loved, enjoyed, and treasured. As I myself was painfully aware that I should be holding close, enjoying, and treasuring, and not again letting go, Alix Dunraven.

"The train!" a boy down the platform shouted. And others picked it up. "The train, the train." In winter, East Hampton values its small distractions.

You could see it now coming at us out of the cold, clear winter morning from Amagansett way, the big headlight in the nose of the locomotive shining even in full daylight. You could hear the horn blowing and, just east of the station, the bells sounding as the crossing gates started down, their red lights lit and blinking, their big striped white-and-black arms descending across the roads to halt traffic. You could see the engineer high up staring straight ahead, chin up, eyes piercing, and fiercely so, until, catching sight of a couple of small boys on the platform waving up at him in the cab, he gave them a jolly return wave, sounding his whistle as he did, causing us all to jump back a few feet from the edge as the train rolled, rather fast still, into the East Hampton station, ready to pick up passengers and take them the hundred miles into Manhattan, into Penn Station, and to trains and planes and destinations beyond.

"Next year," Emma cried out. "Next year I'll be back. Taller, too, and maybe not so plain."

Alix whirled on her.

"We've got to have something of a heart-to-heart on that, my girl," said Her Ladyship. "You're not at all 'a plain girl.' You're 'a thin girl!' *Quelle différence*, I assure you! Look at me, I'm a thin girl, but Beecher and lots of chaps just dote! Don't they, darling?" she said, addressing me.

"Well, I . . ."

There was another round of hugs and kisses and good-byes, then

Alix was backing away from me toward the train, and Emma was with her, holding one hand. Then they were aboard. The trainman called, "All aboard!" and, hanging from the car steps in the old-fashioned and approved style of good railroad men everywhere, he waved an arm and the train began very, very slowly to move, its whistle sounding. Her Ladyship and her ward had by now taken seats and waved to us. My father shouted, though I don't think they could hear:

"Remember next year! The Santa Claus parade!"

The kid's grinning face, solemn just seconds earlier, appeared in the greasy, smoky window of the old train, one arm waving. So maybe she could hear him after all. Behind her, I could see Alix, a hand lifted though not waving, a kind of lorn salute, I guess.

My father waved, too. With a big, damaged hand snugged warmly into a bright red wool mitten. In a few years Emma wouldn't be a child anymore but a teenager, improper thoughts and all, but to the Admiral she was still very much a kid. Promising to come back again next Christmas, telling my father she was counting on him to care for the Lionel trains until she did.

The locomotive's big wheels slipped and skidded a few times more, loud and squeaking, before gradually gaining traction and moving into a smooth, powerful roll, leaving behind the painted wooden signs that proudly announced, EAST HAMPTON, and pulling the train quickly away from the little old rural station along the one-track, snowy right-of-way toward the great city.

Toward tomorrow and all the tomorrows and a world beyond.